Threat of Autumn

Robin Timmerman

Order this book online at www.trafford.com
or email orders@trafford.com

Most Trafford titles are also available at major online book retailers.

Print information available on the last page.

ISBN: 978-1-4907-7426-8 (sc)
ISBN: 978-1-4907-7428-2 (hc)
ISBN: 978-1-4907-7427-5 (e)

Library of Congress Control Number: 2016909042

Trafford rev.   06/21/2016

www.trafford.com

North America & international
toll-free: 1 888 232 4444 (USA & Canada)
fax: 812 355 4082

For Alec and Dave

PROLOGUE

The female falcon (genus peregrine, the wanderer) swung her sleek, fearsome head, surveying her domain. A small camera attached to the roof overhang, recorded her movements. The camera had been there all summer, but it meant nothing to her that people across the city watched her raise a family, while they ate their morning toast.

The valleys and river ravines where her forebears hunted had become a forest of high concrete buildings. Her task though, was essentially unchanged. The prime directive was always: Feed the young. This she and her mate had done, and now the chicks had fledged and flown away.

She still hunted though, for her own meal. She watched with keen interest the movements of two pigeons on a neighbouring balcony railing, several stories below. Their cooing echoed softly in the moist, morning air.

She left the ledge in one smooth movement, to drop with amazing speed towards her prey. Till the last second, the fat pigeon strutted trustingly on the apartment balcony railing. The kill was quick. He never knew what hit him.

The falcon rose more slowly upwards, hauling her heavy load. She had no interest in looking in the window of the building where a broken human sprawled on a staircase.

No bird would put spend any idle time watching a webcam set up to view the activities of humans.

No bird had any idle time.

1

The phone rang, shattering the quiet of the night.

Pete had grabbed at the unit, so as not to wake their three year old daughter Nevra, sleeping across the hall. Ali sat up groggily, reaching for her robe, heart in her mouth. She and Pete had been living on Middle Island for four years now and many of the residents were personal friends. A call in the night was always a worry.

As a police officer with the Middle Island station, smallest police detachment in Ontario, Pete had answered desperate calls before.

But never a call as unexpected as this.

Now Pete looked at the pale, bruised face on the starched pillow case, stamped City of Ottawa General Hospital. His first glimpse of the Old Man in six years. Walter Jakes, father of Pete. Walter Jakes, stranger.

"Dad," he said awkwardly, the word foreign on his tongue.

But the pale man was silent, not even a groan.

"What do the doctors say?" Ali asked, wrapping her arms more tightly around her chest. The room wasn't particularly cold but the experience was chilling. She and Pete both wore jeans and hoodies and had the dishevelled look of people who had dressed hastily and groggily, then set out on a three hour drive in the near dark.

'He took a terrific fall," Pete said. "Down a whole flight of stairs."

The facial bruising was dramatic but not as serious as the broken ribs and fractured hip. Walter had also suffered concussion.

Ali frowned. "What was he doing out there? The building has an elevator."

Pete shook his head, he seemed still in shock. He ran his hand almost dazedly through his short blond hair.

"I don't know," he said. "Putting out the recycling maybe. The doctor thinks he might have had a minor stroke and then lost his balance. If he hadn't been standing at the top of the stairs, it wouldn't have been so bad."

Ali's warm brown eyes brimmed with concern. Her handsome, competent, police officer husband, looked utterly lost. Her heart went out to him.

"I didn't even know he had my address," Pete marvelled. "We haven't been in touch for years. He never answered the wedding announcement you sent him."

Against Pete's advice. Ali had sent the card anyway, though Walter Jakes hadn't acknowledged it or any of her other notes – the birth announcement of their daughter Nevra, the annual photos. Pete didn't know about those either.

She had hoped for some kind of reconciliation, to heal that hurt in her husband's heart. But then, she would never have wished for that meeting to take place in a hospital. There was no reconciliation taking place here. Only a baffled man looking at his unresponsive parent. It was surprising even that Pete had been listed as next of kin. But the ambulance crew or hospital must have found the name somewhere, in his wallet perhaps. Certainly Walter Jakes hadn't been able to give them the information himself.

Several cups of weak vending machine coffee later, they decided to leave. The doctor said that Walter was sedated and would sleep for hours. Ali was heading back to their home on the Island, back to their daughter, and to her teaching job at the elementary school.

"Are you sure you don't want me to stay?" she asked Pete. "I'm sure that Miranda will gladly stay another night with Nevra."

"I'll be O.K." he said. "I'll stay at the apartment. There are things to arrange tomorrow with the insurance company, and I'll have to talk to the property manager. Lots to do."

Not *at Dad's apartment*, she noticed. He couldn't say it.

He attempted a smile. "You'd better get back to Nevra, she'll be missing you. Kiss her goodnight for me."

"We'll both miss *you*," she said.

They embraced in the hospital waiting room, their youth and health creating a brief spark of warmth amidst the drab walls and utilitarian plastic chairs. When Ali looked back, she found it hard to keep on going.

*   *   *

Pete drew into the building parking lot and sat there for some time watching the sun sink behind the city skyline. The building itself – six storeys, twenty-four units – held no significance for him. The Jakes had never lived there as a family.

Where had they ever lived as a family? Came the unbidden thought.

But best not to go there. That was an unproductive avenue and he had work to do.

Still, he was reluctant to go in. To stir it all up again.

When had he last talked to the old man? When had he even *written?*

Pete's mother Jean had died when Pete was fourteen. Josh, his older brother had left for the army soon after. For the next five long, lonely years Walter and teenage Pete had lived like two separate satellites in the house. Rattling around the rooms, no comfort to each other. The death of Josh in a skirmish in Bosnia brought them no closer.

As Pete's high school graduation neared, they talked stiffly of his future. College, or an apprenticeship where he could get his trade papers, as an electrician perhaps. Pete had worked summers as a swimming instructor at the city pools, then at various jobs on construction sites. That June though, with his diploma in his pocket, he realized what he wanted most in the world was to get away. So at nineteen, he had come home to report that he'd joined the army. If Walter showed any emotion at all, it was relief that Pete had found a solution for their problem.

Pete wrote a couple of times from various postings and then even that slight contact tapered off. His last actual trip back to Ottawa was after he'd completed his first tour of duty. At the time, he was wondering whether he should sign up again. He had a thought of looking for another kind of work in the city. Though he didn't voice or ask it aloud, he had been looking for some sign from his father, some encouragement, such as an invitation to stay with him, till he got settled. He got neither encouragement or backing, so he re-enlisted and was sent to Afghanistan. Which turned out to be a good thing, the best thing, because that's where he met Ali.

Now here he was, back in the city again. He felt as if eons had passed.

He sighed and left the car, careful to lock the doors. This was the big city and he was driving Walter's car. Ali had taken the Jakes' SUV back to the Island.

He used Walter's keys to get into the building. The lobby was featureless, furnished with a dully patterned couch and a couple of armchairs. It was clean though, and looked quiet and secure. There was a security camera over the entrance and a connection so that people could screen visitors from their individual apartments. He opened a door to the stairwell and saw a camera there as well. He would ask the apartment manager tomorrow whether there was footage of Walter's fall. The insurance company would want to know.

He took the elevator up. The sixth-floor hallway was empty, all four doors shut. Tomorrow also, he would talk to the tenant who had found Walter on the stairs. Luckily she had heard his moans of pain or he might have lain there undiscovered for hours.

Reluctantly, he put the key in the door of 604 and opened it.

He let out a long breath. Ridiculous! What did he expect to find – to feel?

He stepped gingerly into the room, feeling like an intruder. He looked about him at the beige couch and chair, the beige walls. A pallid painting of a mountain range. The kind that furniture outlets sold along with the couches.

You'd like to buy a painting sir? How big? About 24 inches by 36? And what colour would you like, sir. Beige? Perhaps a hint of blue sky?

He found himself missing his own living room in the house on the Island. The warm red couch with gold and copper coloured throw cushions, Ali's Middle Eastern touch. The painting of a peony he'd got for her birthday, the first painting he'd ever bought. He was thankful anew at how she had lit up his life in every aspect.

He dropped his overnight bag by the door and carried his other supplies into the kitchen. The counters were empty, one clean mug on the draining board. He found a glass in the tidy cupboard. He usually just drank beer but figured he'd need something stronger if he planned to stay in the apartment that night, warding off painful memories.

He poured a shot of rye, and then carried his take-out burger back to the living room where he slumped into the beige armchair and clicked on the television remote. It was set to the Canadian national news channel. On the *News From the Hill* segment which covered parliamentary activities, the coverage was of a brewing political financial scandal. Big whoop, nothing new there. He tried a sports network to check on the baseball scores – the Toronto team was doing well this year -- but he had too much on his mind to concentrate. He turned the set off and looked uneasily around the silent room.

Looking for what – clues to his father's life? That too, seemed pretty beige. Walter now in his late sixties, had retired a few years ago from his job with the internal revenue agency of the federal government. About as beige as you could get. The apartment wasn't very big, the kitchen area was only separated from the living room by a counter. There was a bedroom and a smaller boxy room that Walter apparently used as his office. He supposed he should check in there for Walter's insurance company phone number and other information that he might need.

His mind veered away from the image of that still form on the hospital bed, or the thought of Walter lying broken on the stairs. In the kitchen he poured another drink and carried it with him to the door of the office. The furniture was minimal but efficient. There was a desk and chair, a two-drawer metal filing cabinet and a five-tiered bookshelf of what looked like various tax information binders. He realized he'd been bracing himself for photographs, and was now irrationally rattled that there weren't any.

From a quick look into the filing cabinet, he guessed that Walter was keeping his hand in, running at least a part-time, home-based accountancy business and carrying out some tax work for individuals. There was no file marked personal though, so he moved to the desk. Hopefully Walter was still of an older generation who didn't store absolutely everything on the computer.

And yes, after a short search in the desk drawer, Pete managed to find a telephone/address book. On the opening page there was a place for emergency numbers. Police, ambulance, etc. He noted too, that his own name was there, listed as Next of Kin and his Middle Island address and telephone number. The Old Man must have at least looked up that much at some time. Pete didn't stop to analyze his feelings on discovering this.

Walter had entered in a doctor's name and the name of the apartment property manager. Pete found the insurance company listing under 'i'. He was about to close the drawer when he noticed a tattered looking brown envelope jammed carelessly to the side. The envelope was bulky and the corner of a photo stuck out the top. He stopped, his hand hovering indecisively for a long moment, over the drawer.

"What the hell," he said. Taking a deep breath, he grabbed up the envelope and began spilling the photos over the desktop. He looked at the first one and sank to his knees on the carpet. *Don't ask for what you want, you just might get it.*

The top photo showed a young couple, the man with his arm resting lightly on the woman's shoulders. His parents looked to be in their early thirties, Pete's age now. They stood smiling in the sunlight, on a residential city street. Walter, tall with a rangy build and lean, sharp features, wore slacks and a short-sleeved shirt. Jean had soft brown hair and wore a flowered summer dress and sandals. In the picture, she held baby Pete in her arms while five year old Josh grinned under a baseball cap.

She looked happy.

He looked bleakly around the room. Maybe this was a mistake, to stay here tonight. He should have gone back to a motel.

2

"Where the hell is Jakes?" Halstead demanded.

Jane Carrell, manager of the Middle Island Police Station, smallest police force in the province, waved the telephone at her boss to *shush!*

Or else I'll hand Vern over to you, was the implied threat. And she would carry it out. Chief 'Bud' Halstead got the message. The mood he was in, the last thing he needed was a reminder from the Island clerk that he hadn't yet submitted his financial stats for August.

He scowled at the only other person in the room. Young Jory Stutke, the newbie recruit. Most of Halstead's recruits came from the provincial police academy, reluctant lads who made it plain they had been expecting to train in Toronto, not in the miniscule hick force of Middle Island (pop. 4500). A farming community with fishing and beach tourists in the summer, the Island hosted only a few small hamlets and one village of 1200 inhabitants. Summer could be a busy time on the Bay waters, with even the occasional traffic jam on Main Street. In the off-seasons though, most businesses closed up and the hub of village life was the Island Grill which served up home-made fries and home-made gossip.

Stutke was a bit of a switch. He had actually been raised on Middle Island, attended the Island elementary school, taken the bus across the causeway to high school and spent his summers working on his parents' farm. The kid could tell the difference between a heifer and a steer, played on the Island hockey and baseball teams.

Turned out though that he was likely *twice* as teed off for being assigned for training to the Island force. Thought that when he went away to college for a couple of years, then to the police academy that he'd managed to escape to a more exciting life. Now his frustration knew no bounds. He complained openly at every assignment and Halstead was finding him a royal pain in the butt. He'd be happy to hand over the responsibility to Jakes, his second in command. If Jakes would stop lollygagging around in Ottawa.

He felt immediately guilty, thinking of the senior Jakes' fall. So he vented again at Jane, who had finished her phone conversation with the clerk.

"What did old misery face want?" he grumped.

Jane grinned, looking more like the desktop picture of her four year old playful granddaughter, than a woman in her fifties.

"Oh, we had a lovely chat," she said. "I bet you didn't know that a high grade gravel road costs about $60,000 per kilometer."

"So?" he asked, though he hadn't known. "The causeway is a kilometer long. That doesn't sound too bad." The causeway connecting Middle Island to Bonville the city across the bay, was undergoing some serious shoring up

"That's $60,000 on a flat surface. Apparently it's about ten times that much for this sort of project. Even so, Vern says that Bonville is asking for too big a share from our Middle Island side."

Halstead grinned sourly. "Yeah well they've kind of got us over a barrel, unless Vern and Council are planning to find us a ferryboat somewhere."

He twisted restlessly in his chair, remembering the issue at hand.

"Has Jakes even called?"

"You talked to him yesterday," she reminded him. "He said he'd be back on Wednesday. This is only Tuesday," she added tartly. Even her granddaughter knew that.

Halstead reluctantly turned to address Stutke. "We haven't heard from Bonville public works yet, so you're back on traffic duty at the causeway this morning."

He held up a warning hand. "And no complaints, please. Or I'll bust you back to road crossing guard in front of the school."

Stutke didn't seem to appreciate the joke. If Halstead remembered rightly, the kid had actually done that job ten years ago, when he was about twelve years old. He even looked the same too, only bigger. The same round face under the same sandy cowlick. Halstead thought that even if Stutke did end up in the city some day, his colleagues would suss him out right away as a country boy.

Now he just growled under his breath, grabbed his cap and left.

Jane raised her eyebrows at the quivering door, just short of an insolent slam.

"That's going well," she commented.

Halstead glared. "Somebody's got to supervise the traffic. I suppose you could go if you'd prefer, and Stutke could answer the phone here."

"Maybe I *should* switch with him," Jane said tartly. "Sounds better than working with a grouch."

Halstead felt he had a right to grouch. The roadwork, though necessary, was a real headache, reducing the traffic flow on the causeway to one lane for an entire month. This was a major disruption for Island folk who had to get to jobs or medical appointments in Bonville, or for anyone wanting to leave the Island for any reason at all. Then there were incoming supplies and deliveries to stores and farms. And the mail of course, there was even half-serious talk of bringing it in by boat.

The construction work was the complaint topic of the month for sure. On the street, at the post office, in the Island Grill. Even though the work schedule was posted on signs at both ends of the causeway and there was a schedule in the Bonville *Record* every week, residents still phoned daily into the station to complain about delays and to demand when the work would be done. And today marked the beginning of the new school year, so the big yellow school bus carrying its load of kids over to the high school in Bonville would be navigating the narrow lane as well.

Halstead had been looking forward to a quieter autumn. The busy influx of summer visitors had receded and with it the job of enforcing boating traffic, which always took at least one full-time officer. There should have been a brief hiatus before hunting began with its inevitable conflicts between hunters and property owners with their No Trespassing signs. But apparently, no such luck.

He had to admit that Jane was doing a stellar service, keeping her temper this past week. But he didn't feel like admitting anything. It didn't help either that his wife Stephanie was away. She'd gone to Japan of all places, to visit her daughter Livy who had been working for the summer in an English as a Second Language exchange program. Kids today, restless as water bugs! In his time, it had seemed a big deal to hitchhike over the border to the States for the afternoon.

He hadn't really suffered too much yet. In fact had been having pleasant suppers jawing with old buddy Gus, proprietor of the Island Grill. Chicken in a basket and a brew, like his old widower times, before he met Steph.

But there was a long day to go through yet before suppertime. He was sick and tired of being a nursemaid to Stutke. It was like looking after a big, cranky baby.

Jakes couldn't get back soon enough!

*   *   *

Ali Jakes stood in the yard of Middle Island Elementary School and talked to the elderly maple that had presided over decades of recesses.

"Don't you even think of dropping your leaves yet, " she ordered. "We have the whole month of September to go."

After two years of teaching in Afghanistan's sandy arid landscape, she hadn't yet got her fill of trees.

"My sentiments exactly," said Eileen Patrick, good friend and principal of the school. "Maybe we could start a project, have the children climb up and glue the leaves on."

"Sure," Ali laughed. "Then we'll do all the other trees on the Island. That would keep the little monkeys busy."

"Only briefly," Eileen commented drily, with the knowledge gained from years of dealing with primary school students. "That's a gorgeous scarf you're wearing by the way," she added, admiring the bright red and gold swath of silk. "You've got the autumn colours right there."

"My mother sent it. She's been travelling in India this summer."

"It looks wonderful on you," Eileen said with the good-natured resignation of a perfectly nice-looking woman who had an exotically gorgeous friend. Ali Jakes, with her light honey Middle-Eastern colouring and shiny mane of ebony-black hair would have looked great wearing a paper bag. But in fact, she was stylish as usual in her red wool jacket, knee length skirt and black leggings.

"Thanks!" Ali smiled, then gave a mock sigh. "I guess we'd better go in. Our young mistresses and masters await."

But the truth was that both women were utterly dedicated to their work of enriching and developing youthful minds and would have chosen no other profession. Ali found it was a pleasure working with Eileen who was always considerate and open to staff input into the running of the small school. The building was a one-storey l-shape, allowing each classroom a wall of windows. There were currently eighty-nine students, ranging from kindergarten to Grade Eight. After that the children took the bus across the causeway to Bonville High School.

"I was sorry to hear about Pete's father," Eileen said.

Ali didn't bother asking how Eileen had heard the news. She knew the Island unofficial news network pretty well by now. Pete often joked that he and the Chief would never get a case solved without all those very willing helpers.

"Yes," Ali said. "No fun at all. The hip injury is the worst, Pete says it will be a long recovery."

"A miserable business," Eileen said. "And I gather they didn't find him for hours." Her tone was dire, as if such an accident could only happen in the big bad city.

She shook her head, her thoughts already turning to the busy school day ahead. "Ah well, I'm sure it's a comfort to have his son around at a time like this."

Ali hoped so.

But she had her doubts.

3

Pete woke up, sort of.

His head was muzzy, he wasn't sure about moving it. And Ali wasn't there when he reached for her. When he did look cautiously about, he found himself on the couch in the Ottawa apartment. Something was stuck to his cheek – he reached up and found the family portrait, luckily not crumpled. He placed it carefully on the coffee table, looked around the room and groaned. Coffee. An absolute necessity.

Driven by this primal need, he managed to lurch to the kitchen, find coffee, electric kettle, filter and cone. That was something to know, his father had the fixings for a decent cup of coffee. The cream was sour though, after a week. He noted that the cupboards were stocked with cans of tuna and soups. Bachelor supplies.

After a couple of grateful gulps of the caffeine miracle, he moved back to the living room and carried his mug out to the balcony. There was no chair, no mat on the concrete floor, not so much as a potted petunia. Only a couple of pigeons on the railing to keep him company. But the balmy September air was fresh and reviving. He looked down six floors to a traffic-clogged city street and missed the morning birdsong of the Island. Then, sensing movement above, he looked up in time to feel the whir of a falcon's wings as the bird veered past. The pigeons fluttered in panic, saved at the last moment by Pete's presence. Pete raised his cup in salute to the magnificent flyer. Better luck next time.

But to work. The sooner he got things looked after here, the sooner he could leave for home. Walter, heavily sedated, hadn't been able to give him any direction the previous night. But the insurance company seemed the logical place to start.

He phoned, was referred to the agent who dealt with Walter's file and explained the situation. The woman expressed shock and dismay and offered her condolences.

"What a terrible thing to happen!" But she moved on quickly to her main concern, assessing her company's share of the liability.

"Why was he out on the stairs?" she asked. "Was there a problem with the elevator?"

"It's a bit of a mystery," Pete admitted. He had checked out the staircase on his way in the night before and seen no sign of garbage or recycling bins on the small landing.

"Any information you can gather would be most helpful in making our report," she said. "For instance if there was any possible negligence on the part of the property owner. Shoddy stair railings or ragged carpets. Faulty light fixtures. That kind of thing."

Come and do your own investigation was Pete's uncharitable thought but he didn't voice it. He was pretty curious himself, about what exactly had happened.

In the hallway on his way to meet the property manager, Pete saw a woman leaving the elevator. Middle-aged and attractively maintained, she wore a plum coloured pant suit that contrasted nicely with her salt and pepper hair. She glanced nervously at him and clutched her small dog closer to her chest.

He smiled in what he hoped was a reassuring manner and introduced himself.

"Oh," she gushed in relief. "I'm Helen Verga and this is my dog Pepper. It was just so terrible what happened to your father. It's all made me quite jumpy. How is he?"

Pete explained and heard shock, dismay and condolences again.

"I'm the one who found him," she added. "Or rather it was little Pepper here. He started barking when we were headed for the elevator. He must have heard your father moaning."

She stopped uncertainly at the unhappy thought.

"Have you any idea why he was in the stairwell?" Pete asked.

She shook her head. "Our garbage and recycling station is in the basement. So there really isn't any reason to go out there – unless we needed an emergency exit of course." She looked nervous again. "And thank goodness that's never happened."

"How long have you been in the building, if you don't mind me asking."

"Five years, and it's very well run," she assured him. "Our apartment manager Jay Gupta keeps everything in wonderful shape."

He looked towards the exit door. "Could my father have been planning to visit someone else in the building and decided not to take the elevator?"

She shook her head apologetically. "I hardly knew the man. I don't know if anyone did. He might nod politely if we met in the hallway. How do the British put it? He kept to himself."

Her tone was a teeny bit put out, as if she wouldn't have minded sharing a cup of tea with a single man in her age bracket.

He thanked her for her help and patted Pepper on the head.

Five years. Walter had been living in the building about the same amount of time. And he knew no one. A quiet man who kept to himself.

Or an invisible man, more like.

He had a quick look down the stairwell. It looked clean, well lit and coldly echoing.

*　　*　　*

"Nothing like this has ever happened before. Not in the two years I've been on the job anyway."

Jay Gupta, the apartment manager looked worriedly around the lobby. In his late twenties, Pete guessed, of East Indian ancestry, second or third generation Canadian. He wore jeans and a jacket from the city university.

"I look after two other buildings for the company as well," Gupta explained. "So I'm not here all the time." He added wrily, "I have a degree in engineering but gotta pay off the student loan somehow while I wait for the real job."

Pete nodded, it was a common scenario these days. He looked again at the camera unit that was mounted in the ceiling over the touch pad of the building unit numbers. Other cameras were mounted in the corridors and stairwells in the building.

"I only check the video once a day," Gupta said, "usually in the morning. And even then, it's just a quick run-through at fast speed."

He shrugged apologetically. "There's never really been any need, until now of course."

Pete frowned. "So if Mrs. Verga's dog hadn't heard my father, he might not have been discovered till the next morning."

Gupta looked embarrassed. "I know that sounds crappy," he said. "But I've got the three buildings to manage. Repairs, plumbing, garbage removal. You wouldn't believe the stuff that can go wrong."

Kudos to Pepper, Pete thought. *Walter owes him a box of Milkbones.*

Possibly to assuage his own sense of guilt, Gupta made a helpful suggestion. "Maybe if your father is prone to stroke, he should wear a pager."

"The doctors said there was no evidence of a stroke." Pete said. "Nor heart attack either," he added, staving off Gupta's next suggestion.

"Still, elderly people, living on their own..... My mother telephones my grandfather every day. Maybe you could make a similar arrangement with your father."

Sure. Wouldn't Walter love that. Besides, sixty-seven wasn't elderly was it?

"Thanks," Pete said. "I'll think about it. Could I look at the video now please?"

The manager led the way to a small, windowless office in the basement. The corridor smelt of detergent from a nearby laundry room. Gupta had some difficulty in starting the video on his laptop, which made Pete doubt that he checked it daily or indeed very often at all.

When he did get it running, the footage didn't show the actual fall. The camera had a static position and there was a dogleg in the stairs. Walter had fallen in the upper half dozen steps. So, not a lot of use in determining what had happened.

Gupta clicked end. "Show's over," he said lightly. Then quickly apologized, "Sorry. I hope your dad is doing O.K."

But he looked relieved too. "I didn't see any junk on the stairwell when we found him. Nothing that your dad could have tripped over. Maybe he just got dizzy or something."

Pete thanked him and left. Jay Gupta must be right. A misstep, a miscalculation, could happen to anyone. It was just extremely unfortunate that Walter Jakes' misstep had occurred at the top of a flight of concrete stairs.

And that he had been there at all.

*   *   *

"What plans have you made for your father?" the doctor asked.

"Plans?" Pete echoed feebly. "I haven't had a chance to ask him yet what he'd like to do."

The doctor, baggy-eyed from a night time emergency surgery, said tiredly. "I doubt if you'll get much of a conversation. The man's still in shock, likely even a bit traumatized."

He checked the chart. "We'll be releasing him from the hospital in a day or so though and he obviously can't go home on his own. We've put a pin in that hip and he's going to need physiotherapy."

Seeing Pete looked taken aback, the doctor added sympathetically. "If you talk to the city community services, they can help you contact a home care service. Though there's usually a long waiting list."

Pete looked warily at the sleeping man. There seemed few options.

"I guess he'll be coming with me," he said doubtfully.

When the doctor had left, Pete approached the bed.

"I'm taking you to the Island," he said. Adding drily. "You can meet the family."

But Walter under heavy sedation, slept on. Just as well, Pete thought.

He pulled out of the hospital parking lot into a golden September afternoon. Even the city street seemed bathed in the soft glow of the sun filtered through the red and orange leaves of a nearby maple tree. A few blocks further on, he stopped at a crosswalk where a young safety-jacketed guard steered children across the street. Lunchtime on the first day of school. He had always been glad to go.

To get away from the chill shell of the house where he lived.

4

"**H**owdy handsome," Jane greeted Pete. She'd been happily married for thirty-five years, but that hadn't spoiled her appreciation for a good looking young fellow. Besides, it was fun to see if she could make Pete Jakes blush. He could be such a serious fellow at times.

"How was the city?" she asked.

"Big. Busy. Full of cars."

She grinned. "Yes, well it's official, you're an Island boy now fella. It took a couple of years for us to grow on you, but the transition seems complete."

He doffed his cap. "What do I get, a certificate of honourary citizenship?"

"I'll get on it. Right now you'd better go talk to the chief."

She tskked. "He's in a merry old mood these days. The causeway construction is a real headache, with folks phoning to complain all the time. And it's not as if we can do anything to speed up the work."

The Middle Island Police Station was compact to put it kindly. A one-storey brick 'bunker-style' building, with a parking lot outside for the two cruisers and employee personal cars. Inside, there was Jane's reception counter and area, an interviewing room, a coffee-lunchroom and a couple of cubicles grandly called offices.

There was also a functional holding cell, used rarely for offenders en route to the provincial jail in Bonville, the city across the causeway.

Pete knocked warily at the chief's cubicle door.

"So you're back," Halstead grumped, waving Pete to a chair.

Pete wasn't daunted by such seeming churlishness. In the four years since he'd joined the Middle Island force, he'd come to know his lanky, greying chief as a fair, thoughtful boss who knew and appreciated his flock of Islanders well. Not that he couldn't be prone to bouts of self-pity, such as Jane had just warned of.

"How's your dad?" Halstead asked belatedly.

"Pretty banged up." Pete gave a brief account of the details.

Halstead winced in sympathy. "Sounds rough."

Pete nodded. "Ali found a temporary spot for him at Taylors' Rest Lodge. They had a vacancy he can have for a month. He's coming down in an ambulance."

"The Taylors are good people," Halstead said. "He'll do fine there."

Pete only hoped the staff could put up with Walter. It had been a tough sell, dealing with his father. Despite his weakness and grey-faced with the pain from his operation, Walter had yet emphatically managed to project his objection to going to the Island.

No old folks place. He'd grunted. *Just go home.*

"It's only temporary," Pete had stressed. "We're not checking you in as a resident."

He added encouragingly. "You'll like the Taylors. And the staff are all nice, friendly Island folk."

Walter didn't bother to comment. He had balked too, at the prospect of an ambulance ride but the doctors had explained he couldn't sit up in the car for the three hour trip to the Island. He would have to lie flat for several days yet for the pin in his hip to set. Once Walter realized that he had no choice but to leave the city, he saw that he would vastly prefer a drive with an anonymous ambulance attendant, rather than being trapped for the journey with his son.

Ditto for me, Pete thought.

"So did he have a stroke or what?" Halstead asked. In his fifties himself, he was uncomfortably aware of the potential fates awaiting him. The media was constantly coming up with another study of what he should give up to relieve stress. He'd found the best preventative was not to read the studies.

"No stroke, and his cardio was fine," Pete said. "The video didn't catch his actual fall."

"A mugging, then?" Halstead suggested. "I guess there are some scum low enough to push an old man down the stairs for his wallet."

"I talked to the apartment manager. It seems a pretty secure building, not many strangers wandering around. And no sign of anyone else on the stairs."

Halstead said the obvious, "What does your father say happened?"

"He still seems a bit confused – the doctors said that wasn't unusual following a traumatic experience."

Thinking of Walter's evasiveness, Pete wondered if he was just too embarrassed to admit he'd simply lost his balance or hadn't been wearing his glasses or any of a myriad problems that came with getting older.

"How are Steph and Livy?" he asked, to change the subject. "Having a good time in Japan I bet?"

Halstead nodded glumly. "They're having a great time. I don't like the bachelor life much though. I usually eat supper at the Grill, instead of rattling around by myself at the Retreat."

The Retreat, Steph's creation, provided a restful getaway haven for high-powered business women. *Our Space is Your Space – Come and Relax,* read her attractive brochure. The combination of private cabin space by the lake, plus communal healthy meals in the attractive common rooms, had proved to be a highly successful lure.

Pete grinned. "You're hardly 'rattling around' chief." He knew that Halstead and Steph had their own comfortable living quarters on the property as well. Still, after five years of living as a widower before he met Steph, the chief was no doubt missing her badly.

"Tried Skype yet?" he teased, knowing the chief was resistant to computer technology.

Halstead ignored the question and swivelled the chair round to his desktop. "I guess you saw the causeway mess."

"They've got a good start on the one lane," Pete ventured optimistically.

Halstead grunted. "Not fast enough for me. It's going to be a long month," he said resignedly. "Vern stops in every day to grouch about Thompson bugging him for a bigger share of the cost from the Middle Island budget."

The discord between the lugubrious Island clerk and the Mayor of Bonville was long-standing and would continue to be so. Though it was a David and Goliath situation between the Island population and the city of 45,000 people, Halstead's sympathies were often with the city Mayor.

"I saw Jory there on traffic duty," Pete chuckled. "He didn't look too cheerful."

Halstead grimaced. "He's teed off to be sent here for training but he'd better get over it or he won't learn a damned thing. I've been giving him small stuff to see if he can write a decent report -- illegal leaf burning, Elmer Hicks driving that truck with no muffler."

An annual complaint. Elmer had something against mufflers.

"At least I can take Stutke off causeway duty soon," Halstead continued. "I told Bonville public works that I can't spare an officer to direct traffic and they're supplying a couple of road workers tomorrow."

He picked up one of Jane's telephone memos from the desk and tossed it to Pete.

"Neal Jamieson on Swamp Road has phoned in another ATV complaint. Says someone almost killed his cat. You can take Stutke with you on that one."

Pete winced. "I don't suppose I can send him by himself"

"He's an island boy, I doubt he has the required tact to deal with newcomers," Halstead said drily.

Pete took the memo and stood up. "I think I'm going to use up my store of tact trying to deal with my father."

"Tough go?" Halstead said sympathetically.

"I haven't seen the man for six years and now I remember why. It was weird to see him so helpless though. And he used to seem a lot bigger."

"Well your old man will be safe enough here on the Island. Maybe he'll even loosen up a bit."

* * *

Walter arrived at the Lodge by ambulance two days later.

"You can't come," Pete told a disappointed Ali. "He's not up to any additional strain just now."

Strain. A wonderful way to describe the man's daughter-in-law.

But she understood, and insisted only on sending a bouquet of golden chrysanthemums for Walter's room.

"Look around while you're there," she said. "If you can think of anything to make him feel more at home, let me know."

"I will," he promised. "But I'm sure the Taylors will have done everything to make him comfortable. That's what they do."

Once he got home, though. Ali pressed for details.

"He looked a bit better," Pete said. "The bruises on his face are fading."

Actually, he'd been shocked. In the hospital bed in Ottawa, it hadn't been obvious how thin Walter had become. Now his clothes hung loosely off his almost gaunt frame. Pete remembered the skimpy supplies in the kitchen at the apartment, some canned goods and packages of instant powdered drinks. He'd thought that Walter must eat out a lot but now that seemed doubtful as well. His short iron-grey hair framed a face as bony and severe as a mountain top hermit.

And like that hermit, Walter sure didn't have much recent experience with people. Even struggling with pain from the surgery, he had rudely refused Pat Taylor's help with the wheelchair.

"It's O.K." Pat mouthed to Pete over Walter's head. "We're used to this at first. He'll settle in."

Pete could only hope she was right.

Ali asked curiously, "Did he say what happened on the stairs. Why he fell?"

"Not a thing. I guess he doesn't want to talk about that yet." He held her close. "Don't expect too much honey. He hasn't changed overnight. He might not have changed at all."

She touched his cheek. "Don't say that, Pete. Something good has to come out of this. Maybe you two will finally open up to each other after all these years."

He winced. "*Open up.* I hate that expression, it sounds like ripping open a scab."

She laughed and twisted out of his arms. "Come on, it isn't that bad. Women open up every day, we generally call it conversation."

"Ha, ha."

"Here, have a seat." She patted the couch. "I'll get the drinks and you can tell me what you've learned about your father in the last few days."

"This is comfy," he agreed, after a long welcome home, after being away two whole nights smooch. "But there's not much to tell. After I left to join the army, Walter sold the house and bought the apartment. He stayed at his job, in the accounting division of the federal government."

Now it was Ali's turn to wince. "Ooog. That sounds deadly. But now he's retired, right?"

Pete nodded. "I assume so. Although from his office set-up at the apartment, it looked as if he might still be handling a few clients on his own."

"He probably likes to keep in touch with his workmates."

"I doubt it. He hasn't made any friends at the apartment, that's for sure."

He told Ali about Mrs. Verga and Pepper.

Ali took a thoughtful sip of wine. "Your mom died years ago. Walter would have still been in his fifties -- and he never met up with another woman in all that time?"

He shrugged. "I wouldn't know. I'm the wrong person to ask. We pretty much lived separate lives when I was in high school. Especially after Josh was killed."

Ali nodded sadly. Pete had talked about Josh before, but not much. His brother was several years older and Pete felt he'd never got to know him as an adult.

"Walter is nice-looking in the pictures," she said. "He has a friendly smile." Pete had brought the few photos home so that Ali could at least see that glimpse of Nevra's grandparent.

"Yeah, well that was a long time ago. That's not the man I remember at all."

She was still considering the pictures. "I don't see a lot of resemblance though. He's thinner and maybe a bit taller than you. He hasn't got your hunky shoulders."

He laughed and mockingly flexed his biceps. "Glad to please, ma'am." Then his smile dimmed. "I'm supposed to take after my mother's side of the family."

She put the pictures carefully back in the envelope.

"It's sad though that Walter never found another person he could connect with."

Pete shrugged, "He used to be away occasionally but he certainly never brought anyone home for supper, never introduced me to anyone."

"Maybe he thought you'd find it difficult, that you wouldn't like having some other woman there in your mother's place."

"He might have. But I wouldn't know that either. I wouldn't know anything that he thought about."

"That's a long time to be alone," Ali said.

She was right of course. Pete had school, his hockey buddies. The team won the city championship in Pete's senior year. He hadn't thought about how lonely Walter would have been.

"We couldn't talk to each other," he said. "Except to argue."

"That sounds terrible."

Pete shook his head. "They were just stupid little arguments. Snapping and snarling over nothing. I was hurting, he was hurting – which I didn't give him credit for at the time. We were no help to each other, that's for sure. And mom wasn't there any more to smooth things over."

"It's unfortunate you two didn't have some kind of counselling. That might have helped you talk to each other at least. You'd think the school would have suggested it."

Pete smiled sadly. "I doubt that we would have gone, my sweet. Wouldn't have been the manly thing to do."

"So how do you feel about counselling now?"

"I have to open up and talk about feelings too? Both in one session?"

She tossed a couch pillow at him, then picked up the empty glasses.

"Walter will be comfortable and safe on the Island," she soothed. "That's what's important for now. That's an important start."

Pete watched her walk out of the room.

A start – or just another ending?

5

Acer saccharum. The sugar maple. The annual turning of the tree's leaves in the fall is one of the world's acknowledged natural wonders. The spectacular display occurs only along one thousand square kilometers of northeastern North America and people travel great distances annually to 'see the colours'.

Pete crunched the cruiser along a gravel road lined with maple trees and staghorn sumach bushes that blazed like a line of crimson fire in the sun. But the spectacle obviously held no charm for young Officer Stutke, who seemed lost moodily in his own thoughts.

He was a sullen fellow altogether, Pete thought.

"The chief doesn't like me much," Jory said suddenly.

There's not much to like.

Aloud, Pete said. "Then stop grousing about every job he gives you."

Jory looked stung. "He had me on traffic duty at the causeway for a week! He doesn't give me anything but joe jobs."

Pete shrugged. "Everybody has to work their way up. You should try the army for a taste of how bad joe jobs can be."

Jory settled back grouchily in his seat, "I shoulda been sent to the city. That's what I applied for."

"Things wouldn't be any different there," Pete said. "You better believe that the chief and I have done our share of directing traffic. Still do occasionally, and we smile while we go about it."

They drove in silence up to the Jamieson house. The owner was waiting for them by the mailbox, his face set in aggrieved lines. Oh great, Pete thought, another grouch. The two police officers followed him to the back of the property which abutted an old farm lane.

"Just look at those ATV tracks!" Jamieson pointed. "Look how deep they dig in the mud. That shows you how fast those louts were going."

This was Jamieson's third complaint, Pete could understand his frustration. His wife Celia had come out on the back porch, clutching a big grey cat. New retirees from the city, the couple had come to the Island a year ago with stars in their eyes about 'country' life. Unfortunately the heritage farmhouse they had bought and expensively restored, backed on this farm lane that was used as a regular travelling route by teenage farm kids or 'louts' as he called them.

"I'm terrified even to let Max out," Celia Jamieson said angrily, as she stroked her pet. "He was safer in our yard in the city."

Pete nodded. It was a running battle and there was bound to be more conflict as more urban escapees sought the bliss of rural Island life. Then when they arrived, they seemed surprised that the quaint rustic neighbours had some unpleasant drawbacks. Things like smelly manure piles, noisy corn field poppers that shot all day to scare birds away. And just as in the city, reckless, rude teenagers.

"We all know who they are," said Jamieson. "It's that Trant boy Cole and his friends."

Pete looked over at Jory. The Trants were Stutke cousins, Jory had gone to school with one of the older brothers.

"What about the by-law?" Celia demanded.

"The by-law just says they have to stay off the roads," Pete said.

Jamieson snorted in disgust. "Then the by-law should be changed."

"You're welcome to come and make a presentation to council," Pete said. "They meet once a month."

"I can imagine how that will go. Us against the locals."

Celia looked unhappily back towards the lane. "What about disturbing our peace. Can't you at least fine them or something?"

"I'll talk to the parents again," Pete said.

Jory shook his head as they drove away.

"That guy just makes it worse, you know. Putting out his little signs, saying *Go Slow and Watch out for Cat.* Cole and the others just laugh at them."

"That's really grown up," Pete said drily "Those folks have a right to safe enjoyment of their property."

"It's just a cat," Stutke said mulishly.

"Could be a kid – they might have a grandchild visiting some time."

Stuke was quiet, likely dreaming about his next day off. Pete drove, content to let the peace of the sunny September day wash over his thoughts. Personally he was happy to be back home on the Island where a major crime was an ATV by-law infraction and a political scandal amounted to a complaint about the purchase of a new road grader from the municipal clerk's son-in-law.

Walter had been living at the nursing home for two weeks now. His surgery wound was healing but the doctor said that he still seemed emotionally traumatized by the fall. He was withdrawn and unwilling to talk about the experience, so there hadn't been much progress in communication. And likely never would be, Pete thought bitterly, despite Ali's hopes. She was terribly disappointed that she hadn't yet been able to visit. Or to introduce Nevra to her grandfather.

Grandfather! It was so crazy, to even think of Walter in that context.

He'd told Ali that Walter wasn't up to visitors yet. It was easier than telling her that Walter had unfortunately, been vehement on that subject.

In fact had said, "No fake reunion, meet the family stuff, please. Too much water has gone under that bridge."

From some old impulse to goad, to get *any* reaction, he'd said, "I picked up some pictures at the apartment. I thought I'd make some photocopies for myself if that's alright with you. Ali's always been curious to see what Nevra's other grandmother looked like."

Did Walter wince?

Ah well. To the problem at hand. Cole Trant, nineteen. A problem looking for a solution. Trouble looking for trouble. Nothing major yet, but jail time could definitely be on the horizon for this kid. The chief said that one of these kids turned up every few years. There would be a rash of petty vandalism, windows broken at the elementary school, garbage pails overturned, pot shots at the roadside mailboxes.

"I've seen them come and go – some straighten out, some don't."

Pete wondered what direction the Trant boy's future would take. As they turned down the side road that led to the family farm, he thought of what he would say to the parents. Unfortunately Trant senior, a successful dairy farmer, held a 'boys will be boys' attitude. He thought the problem trivial, even amusing. On this third visit Pete would stress that Gordon Jamieson coud press charges. That a charge of disturbing the peace wasn't trivial and brought fines and penalties.

But as it turned out, they never even got to the house.

Jory who was fiddling with the cruiser radio, called out in excited shock.

"Holy crap, listen to this. Finally something happening! There's been an explosion at Taylor's Lodge."

*   *   *

Jane Carell heard the cups rattling on the shelf in the coffee room.

"What the heck was that?" Halstead asked, coming out of his office. "Now those idiots are blasting on the causeway?"

He was semi-serious. The way this September was going, anything was possible.

"I don't think so, chief," Jane said warily.

The phone rang. Every phone in the station started ringing, land line and cell phone alike. They each grabbed one up. Stared at each other as they got the news.

"An explosion *where?*" Their voices raised in unison, like a chorus of disbelief.

"At the *Lodge?* And now there's a *fire?*"

Halstead could hear Jane trying to calm her caller down, as he did the same with his own. "O.K., thanks," he said finally. "Gotta go. Lots to do."

"Cut them off," he said impatiently to Jane. "I'm heading out there. Call the fire hall and the ambulance. Call Jakes and Stutke. Call Bonville station. Call them all!"

He grabbed up his keys and began pulling on his jacket as he headed out the door.

"The ambulance is going to have one hard time getting over the causeway."

Dad!! The old man!!

D Pete drove as fast as he dared on the gravel road, the cruiser siren wailing a warning to any oncoming traffic. Five kms to go, he cursed, another ten minutes!

Getting closer, he could hear the fire engine siren coming from the village. The cruiser and the pumper arrived at the same time. The scene that met his eyes was daunting. A cloud of black smoke was billowing out the far end of the building.

"Looks like it's the kitchen," Jory shouted, as he reached for the door handle.

The firemen, all Island volunteers, were already unreeling the hoses. Pete noted thankfully that the nursing home was on town water. As the locals put it, the firemen saved a lot of basements out in the country. He could see the other cruiser too, though the chief was nowhere in sight.

"Go help them!" he yelled to Jory. Then, heart in mouth, he leapt out of the car and ran towards the section of the home that housed the residents.

The staff had already been helping patients out onto the lawn. Now they huddled, confused and disoriented, a ragtaggle group in pyjamas and housecoats in a melee of wheelchairs and walkers. One woman was crying. Pete scanned the group anxiously, looking for Walter and finally spotted him on his own, under a tree in his wheelchair.

"Dad. Thank goodness, you're O.K."

An odd expression flickered in his father's eyes, some unaccustomed vulnerability. Pete even wondered whether his father was actually glad to see him. But it passed so quickly he thought he'd imagined it.

"I'm alright," Walter said. But he moved his head dazedly.

A staff member approached to check on Walter and Pete gratefully handed him over. "You'll be O.K. Dad with Lucy," he said. "I've got to go help over there."

He found Halstead in urgent conversation with Jeff Waverly, chief of the Island volunteer fire department. Waverly ran a successful market garden farm when he wasn't putting out fires but today his cheerful ruddy face was tensely serious.

"What the hell happened?" Pete asked Halstead.

"We think some kind of gas leak. The blast blew the propane tank clear across the yard."

Pete wasted no more words. "Where do you want me?" he asked the fire chief.

Waverly pointed. Jory had already taken a spot with the men working the big hose from the truck and Pete ran to join them. The crew were concentrating on the side of the kitchen attached to the main building, to stop the fire spreading. Other volunteers were arriving and leaping out of their own vehicles. As Pete hung on tightly to his section of the unwieldy, bucking hose, he scanned the scene on the lawn. The ambulance had arrived and two attendants were lifting someone onto a stretcher.

"Who is it?" he called to the man working next to him.

The man shouted back over his shoulder, Pete could barely hear him over the roar of the fire.

"Young Cameron Parks, he does the yard work here. It looks bad."

Pete saw another young man sitting on the scorched grass. He was comforting a blonde girl who was wrapped in a blanket and sobbing.

Two, long exhausting hours later, the crew had beaten the flames back to reveal the charred outlines of the former kitchen. The firemen would remain for some time yet to check for possible flare-ups. Pete sluiced off his blackened face and arms and went looking for Halstead. He found his chief talking to the fire chief.

"Great job!" Halstead said. "You've trained a good bunch of men."

Waverly grinned tiredly. His boots and yellow safety jacket were drenched in watery soot. "Yep, and the old pumper came through once again. But she's twenty years old and if we ever run into anything bigger, I don't know. I've been bugging Vern and the council for a year now to buy us a new truck."

"Good luck getting money out of that bunch," Halstead said sympathetically. "It took me three years to get them to crack open the bank account for a new cruiser."

His expression sobered, "So, what do you think happened here Jeff? You said some kind of leak in the gas line?"

Waverly nodded. "The gas would have built up in the basement and something set it off. Don't know exactly what yet. Then that drum of cooking oil caught fire – that didn't help."

He shook his head. "Would have been even worse if it had happened at night. Thank god for small mercies. The whole place might have gone up with all these old folks in it."

Halstead nodded towards the unharmed section of the home. "As it is, looks as if there are a fair number of minor injuries that the staff nurse is treating. Mostly cuts and bumps from the hasty exit."

"And my father's room was the first in line, closest to the kitchen," Pete said feelingly. "It was just a lucky break that he was outside."

"That Parks boy needs some luck now," Halstead said. "We'd better head over to the hospital."

*　　*　　*

The scene at the Bonville emergency department was quiet and grim. Two different ambulances had transported the injured young people to the hospital. Now Halstead identified various sets of parents, waiting anxiously in the room.

There were the Chambers, parents of Kristy the young woman who had been weeping on the lawn. And Benny and Maria Sorda, parents of Zak who was doing the cooking at the Lodge this summer. He'd known the Sordas for years, Benny was a retired plumber who now owned a popular chip truck. These people looked up to nod a somber hello at Halstead's entrance but the Parks family stood apart, by the door that led to the interior of the hospital. Gord Parks paced restlessly with Cameron's two older brothers while their mother was bent with grief on one of the uncomfortable chairs. Another woman, perhaps a relative, had wrapped a consoling arm round her shoulders.

Halstead took a seat by Benny Sorda.

"How is Zak doing?" he asked quietly.

"He's going to be O.K.," Benny said. "He wrenched his shoulder pulling Cameron out. We're just so grateful he wasn't in that kitchen....."

"Shhh," Maria said, touching his arm and looking across the room. "Others weren't as lucky."

She smiled at Halstead. "Thank you for coming."

He didn't mention that he would need the doctor's information for his report because of course there was much more to it than that. The Island people were his friends, his flock, his responsibility. His community. And tonight that community had been hit a terrible blow.

"Any news at all yet?" he asked, indicating the tense Parks family group.

Benny shook his head.

Pete Jakes asked the same question when he arrived an hour later, after settling his father down. And got the same answer. By that time, the Chambers had left with their daughter Kristy.

"The girl was just badly shaken up," Halstead said. "Her mother can do more for her at home, than staying here for the night."

Next to leave were the Sordas, wheeling their son out to the car in a hospital supplied chair. Zak, wearing a sling, was white-faced and groggy on pain killers,

"It's like a ruddy war zone," Halstead said feelingly as he watched them drive away.

Pete looked over at the Parks family group. "Is there anything we can do for them – coffee? Food?"

"I noticed the boys went out for awhile," Halstead said. "They likely got some supper. But Gord and Sharon haven't left at all."

"I could use a coffee," Pete said. "I could get us some sandwiches from the cafeteria."

"No, I'll come too," Halstead said.

In the cafeteria, they made weary choices from the various vending machines, then carried their trays over to a table.

"How's your father?" Halstead asked, over a styrofoam cup of tomato soup.

"He's pretty shook up," Pete said.

"An explosion will do that to you," Halstead said drily.

"Of course," Pete said. "The nurse had to give him a sedative. It's odd though because I don't remember him being an over-anxious type of person. I guess he's still weak from falling down the stairs."

Halstead shook his head. "Two big shocks so close together, that's got to be really hard on the system."

Pete unwrapped his sandwich. "So, what exactly *did* happen? Any more news on that front?"

Halstead frowned. "I couldn't talk to the girl, Kristy. She'd been given a sedative before her parents took her home. And Zak Sorda wasn't in much better shape. He did say that he'd been away in the village, picking up a regular bakery order for the lodge. I gather he arrived back just before the gas blew. Kristy was coming out the door to help carry in the order, when all hell broke loose. She was pushed down the step by the force of the blast."

"Lucky girl though," Pete marvelled.

"For sure. She had the wind knocked out of her but as Zak dragged her away, she screamed to him about Cameron. Jerry Taylor had arrived by then, so they left Kristy safe on the lawn, then ran back to the kitchen. The two of them hauled Cameron out as the fire was starting up. Said his face was all bloody."

"Pretty brave of them," Pete said. "So Zak doesn't know anything about the gas leak or what caused it?"

"I pass the Sorda's place on my way in in the mornings," Halstead said. "I'll stop in and talk to him then."

On returning, they found the Parks in conference with the doctor and waited for their own chance to speak to her. The news was devastating. Though Cameron Parks' other injuries were superficial cuts and abrasions, the damage to his eyes was potentially the worst. The young man could permanently lose his sight.

"We've bandaged him up for now," the doctor explained. "But these cases of blast-related ocular trauma can be very tricky."

Halstead winced, "It even sounds bad."

She nodded. "There can be rupture or hemorraging damage from the stress of the shockwave itself. Or more commonly, lacerating and perforation from flying debris such as glass."

"Commonly?" Pete asked.

The doctor grimaced. "Unfortunately, what with the use of mines in warfare and now the terrorist activity, there's a growing body of data on these types of injuries. I suppose the plus side for your friend here, is that we have more information to work with."

She dropped her clipboard to her side, looking tired. "But we can't even assess the damage until the swelling goes down. That may take a couple of days, and there may be infection as well."

She looked over to the doorway where Gord Parks was leading away his quietly weeping wife.

"There's nothing to do but wait and see what tomorrow brings."

7

Temporary emergency stoplights flickered on both ends of the causeway, marking the safe lane to drive. Below the gravel embankment, the dark Bay waters lapped quietly. The causeway was barely a kilometer long but as Pete drew away from the lights of Bonville, he often felt a psychological distance as well. As if he was leaving behind some of the larger world with all its troubles and complications.

He'd felt that way almost as soon as he and Ali had arrived on the Island. He was still experiencing nightmares then, of the roadside bombing in Kandahar, a tragedy in which several of his army unit buddies had died. Pete had recovered from his physical injuries but the other scars were harder to erase. To Ali of course went the main credit, but four years of Island life had helped a lot too.

However, tonight the trouble had moved the other way, from the Island to the hospital. A reminder that disaster could crop up anytime, anywhere and never to take peace for granted. Main Street looked reassuringly normal on this warm September evening. Several cars were parked before the Island Grill, folks walked their dogs under the streetlights, while a small group of teenagers were horsing around in the parkette by the marina. Pete drove the few kilometers out of town and steered into his own driveway.

From the yard across the road, came the friendly woof of their neighbour Miranda's dog. Ali had found Miranda Paris intimidating at first. An elderly but vigorous woman, with a stern face and unbending manner, she hadn't seemed thrilled at the arrival of the young couple. However, through mutual aid in various life situations, such as Miranda's sprained ankle and Nevra's arrival, they had all become close friends. Miranda's two story frame house was similar to the Jakes, though painted a celery green to the Jakes' plainer cream coloured woodwork.

As he left the car, he heard the kitchen door open and saw Ali framed there in the light. She was in bare feet, with her housecoat wrapped tightly around her. They hugged closely for a moment, then he sighed and drew back.

"I'd better have a shower, honey. I washed up as well as I could at the hospital but it was a pretty patchy job."

As he stepped into the kitchen, she could see his reddened eyes, and soot streaks on his shirt. "O.K." she said. "But then I'll expect a full report. I'll make some coffee."

When he reapppeared in clean jeans and a t-shirt, they took their cups into the living room.

"I heard about Cameron," she said. "How awful. And frightening for the boy and his family. When will they know more?"

He told her what the doctor had said. "Kristy and Zak will be O.K. though."

"Thank goodness," she said. "But how does such a terrible thing happen?"

"The fire chief thinks it was a gas leak," Pete said. "He can't have a proper look round though, till the place cools down. They're still dousing out flare-ups."

"And how is Walter?" her dark eyes were lit with sympathy. "The poor man! What a terrible shock for him. And so soon after his fall! He's barely been here two weeks."

Pete nodded. "He was pretty upset."

He didn't go into detail, how Walter had been dangerously pale and for a time seemed to have trouble breathing. The nurse had been harried and busy, checking up on all the other displaced residents but Pete had finally got her attention. A panic attack, she'd thought and had given Walter a sedative till the doctor came by on his rounds in the morning.

"It's strange seeing him like this," Pete said. "So weak and not in control of things. There were so many angry times when I was younger, that I would have been glad to see him brought low. But now it doesn't feel good at all. Not that I can do anything about it, he doesn't want anything from me, that's for sure."

Ali clucked her tongue. "Oh it's just ridiculous that I can't be of any help. I feel so useless Pete, isn't there anything I can do for him?"

She brightened. "I should take Nevra there to see him," she said. "Surely that would cheer him up."

"Sorry honey," Pete was definite. "Take my word for it, right now that would be a very wrong thing to do. The whole place is in chaos for a start. It looks like a war zone, and the staff are overworked tending to the residents. I think one lady fell and broke her arm in the rush to get out."

Ali sighed. "When is Walter to meet his granddaughter then?" she asked, "Once he goes back to Ottawa, we'll have lost our chance completely."

"I don't know Ali. I just don't know."

"Do you think it might be racial?" she asked hesitantly, hating the thought. "Is that the reason he doesn't want to meet me?"

"Nothing so simple," Pete laughed bitterly. "I'm his own flesh and blood and he can't stand me either."

He kissed her. "I told you what he was like though. Please don't let yourself be hurt. He's not worth it."

"I'm not giving up yet," she said. "There has to be some warmth, some feeling in the man. And I'll find it."

He shrugged. "Good luck honey. I never have."

"What's that?" he asked, turning at a sound from the porch.

"Nothing," Ali said quickly.

"I heard something." He got up to check.

"It's just a cat," she soothed, "a stray. Nevra's been talking to him out in the yard. We call him Kedi, that's the Turkish name for a street cat."

"And he's in our porch?" Pete looked out the window, not opening the door.

"For now. I think he needs a bath, though."

"That's a cat?" Pete said, looking out at a big battered fellow with dirty fur and chewed ears. "He looks more like an orange raccoon. You let Nevra go near him?"

"She likes him," Ali said. "And we need a pet, we're ready for a pet. You know the old rhyme …. First comes love, then comes marriage …. Then you buy a house, have a baby and get a cat."

"That's not how the rhyme goes," Pete objected. "Anyway why *this* cat. He's likely diseased and full of fleas. He might scratch Nevra. If she wants a kitty, we can get a clean little *new* one – there are advertisements at the supermarket all the time."

"Kedi won't scratch anybody," Ali said. "He's a sweetheart." She opened the door and knelt down. "Here boy, come get some milk."

"Yuck," Pete said, spotting a mess on one side of the cat's face.

Ali stroked the rough fur. "We'll have to take him to the vet."

He looked at the leaking sore with distaste.

"How are we going to get him there? He's a wild animal. He's not going to sit quietly on the car seat beside me."

"We'll put him in a box," Ali said. Now she was scratching the mangy thing behind his ears. She smiled happily, "I always wanted to have a cat. I could never have one at the boarding school."

"We'll probably both get rabies," Pete said. "Are you willing to leave our daughter without parents, just to save a mangy old cat?"

She gave the animal a final pat then closed the porch door. "You explain that to your daughter then. How you threw her cat back out into the wilderness."

He started to protest that, judging by his size, the beast had been foraging handily out there. But he gave up, he knew an ambush when he saw one.

On his way to bed, he peeked in Nevra's door. The little girl lay curled on her side, amidst a pile of stuffed toys. On the wicker rocker beside the bed, Ali had laid out clothes for the next day. Tights, a dress, a little pink hoody. It never ceased to make him smile, that miniature wardrobe, like clothes for a pixie, a fairy.

Parenthood!

He'd thought a lot about it before Nevra was born. Had been awed and at times overwhelmed at the prospect. He wondered if Walter had ever had such doubts. Tried to imagine a conversation in which he could bring up the topic. Couldn't. Never in a million years. It was difficult to imagine any conversation at all. During his teen years, Walter never had a good word to say to him, and then he stopped talking to Pete altogether.

He thought of the parents he'd seen tonight in the waiting room. Apt term. The place where people waited for news that would affect their entire family unit, all their intricately woven lives. Bleakly he carried on with the logic. If Walter hadn't been concerned when his son was born, would he have cared if Pete had been killed in that road-bombing in far-away Afghanistan. A chilling thought. Ali cared more about the darn cat.

He realized that for years now, he had practically considered himself parentless, an orphan. And judging by the way Walter was behaving, it looked as if things were going to stay that way, forever.

8

Gas Blast Mystery on Middle Island.
Young Lawn Maintenance Worker May Lose Sight
(Bonville Record)

Jane came into the station, wearing trim black slacks and a new red belted cardigan from the village wool shop. Working in an environment of uniformed men, she felt obligated to 'colour the place up.'

She plunked the newspaper down on the chief's desk. "Some reading for you."

He skimmed the headline. "How is the lad?" he asked.

Never mind the radio or television for news of Island folk. Never mind the local paper. He knew where to go for the latest update, to his own office manager. Through her wide network of children, daughters and sons-in-law, nieces and nephews, Jane had her finger on the pulse of Island life. One daughter-in-law, for instance, worked at admitting in the emergency department of Bonville General.

Today she gave a serious shake to her head. "No news. They're keeping Cameron as quiet as possible."

"Damn," Halstead said. There were subdued conversations and sadness everywhere in the village. In such a closely-knit community, news of the tragic event affected a lot of people.

"Such a terrible accident," Jane said. "It's a wonder more people weren't hurt."

She handed him a sheaf of yellow memo notes. "Sorry, but the rest of life's petty business grinds on. Two complaints of leaf burning violations and Hilda Becker says that Mr. Perkins hasn't cleaned up his yard yet, despite last week's order."

Halstead grinned and pressed the memos back in her hand. "Sounds like some work for Stutke. And tell him I'll expect full reports."

She tutted. "Don't be so hard on Jory. He may be a bit of a grumbler but Jeff Waverly told me he was right in there fighting the fire."

"He'll be happier once he gets off the Island," Halstead said. "And that will suit us both."

Jane left to start her busy day, while he frowned at the newspaper and left his coffee mug untouched. The coffee was decent enough, though he'd had to fight off innovations such as cinnamon flavouring in the past. He just missed sharing his morning brew with Steph, preferably in a deck chair looking out at the mist rising over the lake. One of the pleasures of being married again. But she was now in Japan on the other side of the world and having a wonderful time according to this morning's e-mail. And here he was, poor neglected fellow, already at work.

He turned at Jakes' arrival and did a double take at the sight of Pete's face.

"That's some wicked scratch, " he said. "I hope you didn't get that in the line of duty."

"I hope I never run into a suspect with claws like that," Pete said fervently. He detailed the hair-raising start to his day. How he had finally lured the cat with a can of tuna fish into the shed, then boxed him up. That was the scratching part.

"I dropped him off at the vet's on the way to the station."

Halstead guffawed. "Lucky that all us cops have regular tetanus shots."

That was to be the only light moment in a long day.

"We'd better go out to the Taylor's and have a look," Halstead said. "Those ashes will have cooled down by now."

A depressing sight greeted the two officers. A large section of Pat Taylor's pretty flower beds had been ground into dirt by the heavy emergency vehicles and the eastern end of the building was now a blackened ruin. The damaged gas tank lay a distance across the lawn, where it had been blown by the blast. Stutke's strips of yellow plastic police tape marking off the area, added no cheer.

Jerry Taylor stood holding a cup of coffee as he morosely viewed the site. Red-haired and stocky and organizer of the local 'Our Kids are Terrific' annual bicycle marathon, he was normally a cheerful fellow.

"Morning fellas," he greeted them. "I gotta say, this is a miserable start to a day. Did you hear about Cameron?"

Halstead offered commiserations. "And how are you doing?" he asked.

"I'm O.K. thanks. Zak was the one who wrenched his shoulder getting Cameron out. He did most of the lifting."

"And Pat," Halstead asked. "How is she bearing up?"

"She's pretty upset," Taylor said. "Of course she's most concerned about Cameron but several of our residents also needed treatment for shock and stress. We're lucky no one had a heart attack."

He shrugged, "But Pat's throwing herself into her work, as usual. There's a heckuva lot to do. Not least figuring out a way to feed all the residents when we don't have a kitchen. Benny Sorda, god bless him, brought over urns of coffee from the chip truck and some bagels first thing. So that was breakfast taken care of. Lunch and supper for thirty people to figure out next."

Halstead clapped him on the shoulder. "This is a good community, Jerry. Everybody will pitch in."

Taylor nodded. "I know, Bud and we're grateful for that. Still, it doesn't help that we just upgraded that kitchen equipment a couple of years ago. But I guess that's why we all pay a fortune for insurance."

He tossed the dregs of his coffee into the ashes. "Ed Bell from the gas company is coming at ten. It's the damndest thing. He was just here last week, doing the monthly maintenance check and that propane tank was fine. Come on, we can wait in the office and I'll show you the records."

The normally quiet, efficiently-run home was in chaos. The elderly residents clogged the corridors, like distressed bees who had lost their hive. Seeking comfort, instead they only hindered the staff. Pat sped along the hallway, ignoring the clamour. As Taylor had said, his wife was a harried woman.

"We've had to double up your father with another resident for the time being," Jerry explained to Pete. "His room still smells of smoke and we may have to paint to get rid of it. But he's O.K. there, and his roomate is a nice old fellow."

"I'm sure he's fine," Pete said. "We appreciate everything you're doing for him." Privately he had his doubts that Walter would react well to having a roommate, but complaints could wait. He had other things on his mind just now, such as why that gas pipe had leaked.

In the office Taylor showed them up to date maintenance charts for all the systems of the home. Electrical, plumbing, and gas.

"We have the whole place inspected top to bottom every month," he said.

"Provincial regulations and insurance specifications require it."

He looked out the window at the bright orange van coming along the torn up driveway. "Here comes Ed now."

Bell, a competent looking fellow in a standard brown work overall, approached carrying a bag of tools. "Let's have a look," he said grimly. If he had missed something crucial in his recent inspection, his job could be on the line.

The fire chief had turned off the outside gas tap on arrival the day before but no one had yet been able to inspect the basement. Now the four men looked down a short flight of concrete steps below the charred remnants of the kitchen floor. The others stood at the top while Bell cautiously descended.

"Be careful down there," Waverly warned.

Bell had switched on his portable trouble light and found something to hang it on. They heard him swear as he banged into something. Then nothing for a time as he crawled around in the debris.

"How are you doing down there?" Waverly called finally.

The light was returning to the stairs. Grunting, Bell emerged and stood for a moment catching his breath and wiping off a cobweb.

"See anything?" Jeff asked.

"There's no split or ruptured pipes," Bell said. "The gas leaked from the outside tank."

"How long would it have taken to build up down there – enough to explode?" Halstead asked.

Bell shrugged. "A couple of hours likely."

"How come the kids didn't smell the gas?" Halstead asked, referring to the well-known rotten-egg smell that was added to the gas for that very purpose.

"Likely they did," Bell said. "By then it was too late.'"

"And what set it off?"

"You'd be surprised. If there's enough of a buildup, even using a cell phone or turning a light on could do it. Or maybe one of those kids lit a smoke."

He nodded toward to the blackened *No Smoking* sign on the lawn. "Kids never pay attention to those things."

Halstead considered this, then returned to the salient point. "The valve connection on the outside tank was open, you say."

"Yessir," Bell said. "Once that bleeder valve was open, gas would have flowed down the window well into the basement. Lucky that tank was only a quarter full or the whole lodge would have been blown to kingdom come."

The men were silent for a moment, contemplating such a disaster.

"How does that happen?" Halstead asked carefully. "That the valve was open?"

Bell shook his head. "Usually somebody turns the handle."

"Is that easy to do?"

"No sir," Bell said even more soberly. "You'd need to get at that sucker with a wrench."

Halstead took a breath. "Could somebody do that by accident? Just make a mistake? What about kids doing a prank?"

Bell frowned. "Take a wrench and yank at that handle? I doubt it. And why the heck would anybody do a thing like that?"

Exactly what Halstead had been asking himself.

He turned to the fire chief. "Well this is a nasty curve, Jeff."

Waverly nodded somberly. "Yep, it sure is."

They watched Waverly drive away. Across the road a bright yellow tractor droned lazily, readying the field for winter wheat. A flock of gulls followed the machine, looking for grubs in the freshly plowed rows. That was the normal way of things, Halstead thought. Not this dreadful charred kitchen, that struck such a sinister note in the pleasing country landscape.

"This explosion business isn't getting any better," he said sourly. "It was bad enough when we thought it was an accident."

The fact that the gas valve had likely been tampered with changed the whole focus of the investigation. They were no longer just looking into the causes of a tragic accident. Halstead scowled at the offending propane tank, as if wishing there was a way to make it give evidence.

"Roger Huma is sending over an assistant from the forensic lab in Bonville to check the valve handle for prints. Of course Waverly's will be there, he had to turn it off. But there might be traces from someone else. There's also a couple of wrenches from the Lodge toolbox to check."

Pete didn't comment. Neither officer was holding much hope of finding anything conclusive. Any workperson could blamelessly carry a wrench. And thanks to television and movies, everybody knew about wiping off fingerprints.

In the field, the tractor begin another row, the gulls rising and shreiking objections. "So, what are we looking at here?" Halstead asked. "What the hell's going on, some kind of insurance scam by the Taylors?"

The words felt absurd, even as they came out of his mouth. Pat and Jerry were a hard-working couple, cheerful volunteers and supporters at many community events.

"It wouldn't make much sense," Pete agreed, "not if they just upgraded the kitchen a couple of years ago." He considered. "Though they could be in some kind of financial trouble. It happens."

"I'll talk to the bank," Halstead said, "but I can't see either Pat or Jerry taking the risk of injuring any of those old folks, even to save their own financial skins. I just can't picture it."

He shook his head, "Any other ideas? There doesn't seem to be any benefit to anybody, just disaster all round. Jeesuz it better not be a prank. I hope not."

Then he voiced the even tougher question. "So forgetting *why* for a moment – if that's possible -who could have jimmied that valve?"

"The tank was around the side of the building," Pete said. "It wouldn't have taken more than a minute. Almost anybody working there could have done the job. And if they were seen, they could say they were going for a walk or a smoke."

"I doubt that Pat Taylor had any wish to blow up her own kitchen," Halstead said. "Then there's Kristy and Zak."

Pete raised his brows. "That sounds as crazy as the insurance scam idea."

Halstead nodded. "Kristy was working in that kitchen too. She doesn't look like the suicidal type to me."

Pete leaned back, crossing his arms. "So, Zak?"

"He wasn't even there before the explosion," Halstead added. "Not to mention he helped pulled Cameron out of there. Probably saved the guy's life. Now we just have to hope that the docs can save his eyesight."

He thought for a moment, then said reluctantly. "I'll go talk to the bank about the Taylor finances. See what you can find out from

Pat about who else goes in and out of the kitchen. We've got to find out exactly what happened that day and when."

*　　*　　*

Pete found Pat Taylor in the laundry room. Short and sturdy as her husband, she wore the same colorful lime green scrubs as her staff. "Makes it easy for the residents to spot us," she would laugh.

She came towards him now, wiping her hands on a towel. "Just a small crisis this time, thank goodness. One of the clothes washers is leaking." She looked down the hallway. "I think your father is in his room. He's calmer today."

"Actually I'm not here to see my father this visit," Pete explained. "I just had a few questions for you about the scheduling in the kitchen. Who works there, how a typical week goes."

"Come into the office for a minute," Pat said. "I've got the schedules there."

He looked over her shoulder at the chart on the wall. "You can see it's pretty well just Kristy and Zak and me," she said. "Kristy comes in at eight in the morning, helps me with breakfast and stays to help prepare supper. She leaves around four-thirty. Zak comes in at ten and does supper and clean-up after and leaves around eight."

She smiled, "We've been lucky to have such talented help. Kristy is working on her dietician's degree which helps with meal planning, and the residents all love Zak's cooking. I think he's got a great future as a chef."

"And no one else goes into the kitchen?"

"Not really," she explained. "The staff room has a coffee maker and a fridge. All that's needed for snacks and a break. That's what we're using now as a prep room, though it's pretty cramped."

"And what about Cameron?" Pete asked.

"He works for his dad's landscaping business. We have a contract with them and Cameron's been coming by regularly to cut the grass and trim the hedges. He didn't come as much in high summer but the grass always starts to grow again in the fall."

She smiled. "On his breaks, he preferred to see Kristy in the kitchen."

"They're an item?" Pete asked. He wasn't surprised. The petite blonde was very attractive.

"Cameron would certainly like to be, " Pat said. She frowned. "Kristy and Zak used to date. Frankly, when I was hiring for the summer, I was worried there'd be too much atmosphere in the kitchen. But they both said that was just a highschool thing and were sure they could work together. And so far, it's worked out great for me, as I said they're both very professional."

She looked across the lawn to the blackened remnants of her kitchen and her expression sobered. "Maybe I was right in the first place though. Now look what's happened."

"What do you mean by that?" Pete asked curiously.

Pat shrugged, "Oh I don't know. Like I said, sometimes there was *atmosphere*. Once in awhile I got the impression that Kristy enjoyed being the centre of attention between the two fellows."

"You think Zak still cared? Could he have been jealous?"

Pat led the way out of the office. "No, please forget I said anything. I'm just being silly, I think I'm still a bit in shock."

*   *   *

Back at the station, he compared notes with the chief.

"Todd at the bank says that the Taylors are in decent financial shape," Halstead said. "Business is good. As you know, there's a waiting list for the rooms."

Although ironically the Taylors had taken out a loan two years earlier.

"Let me guess," Pete said. "For the renovations."

Halstead nodded. "Yup. They've paid it off already though."

Pete reported on his conversation with Pat Taylor.

Halstead sighed. "Well there's a wrinkle. Guess we'd better have a conversation with young Sorda. Have Jane call him to come into the station. If he isn't driving yet, pick him up."

10

Zak Sorda carried his parents' Portuguese heritage in his handsome colouring, dark liquid eyes and black hair. Like many second or third generation Canadians, he was taller and bigger built than his parents. He had been an all-round sports star in highschool and now in jeans and a red windbreaker draped over his injured shoulder, he still looked in great shape.

"Hi there hero-boy," Jane greeted him brightly. "How's the shoulder?"

"Coming along, thanks. It won't stop me from going back to college next week."

"Glad to hear it," Jane said. "The chief's in there with Pete, waiting for you."

"Hey chief, hey Pete," Zak greeted the two officers cheerfully. Pete coached Zak's younger brother on the Island hockey team. "What's up?"

"We just want to go over a few details about the fire," Halstead said easily. "It's been a pretty disturbing time for all of us."

"That's for sure," Zak said fervently. "Man, I sure wouldn't want to go through another day like that for awhile. We drove past the Lodge on the way in, what a mess. The whole kitchen is going to have to be rebuilt."

"There's going to be a lot of other fall-out to go through too," Halstead said. "Legal business."

Zak nodded. "You mean like insurance and all that stuff."

"Right," Halstead said. "So they'll need accurate reports – from us, from the fire chief, from the Taylors. We're just trying to get the picture straight in our minds, particularly right before the explosion."

"Can't help with that," Zak said. "I was getting the bakery order."

"Was that usual, was that a regular routine?"

"It wasn't *un*usual," Zak said, "if that's what you mean. I generally pick up the buns from the bakery Wednesday morning. We get ten dozen, freeze some of them."

"But you don't necessarily go at that time."

"No, just sometime in the morning."

Halstead nodded. "Pat Taylor says that Cameron usually came into the kitchen around ten for coffee."

"Yeah," Zak said. "The kitchen is quiet around then. We've cleared away all the breakfast things, loaded up the dishwasher, cleaned the counters."

Halstead looked at Pete, *over to you.*

"Pat Taylor said that Cameron might also be visiting Kristy." Pete said.

Zak looked surprised. "Yeah, I guess he might."

Pete pressed, "Didn't you used to go out with Kristy?"

Zak shrugged, "That was in high school, a long time ago."

"Jory Stutke thought you two were pretty serious. He said you went to the prom together."

"Yeah, well Stutke wouldn't have minded going with her either. She was the prettiest girl in the school. Prettiest girl on the Island. Every guy on the team wanted to date her."

"So why did you two break up?" Pete pressed.

Zak shrugged again, "Like I said, it was a high school thing, a kid thing. We weren't going to get married or anything. We both had things to do, like college."

"So you haven't found it difficult working with Kristy this summer?"

"Nah, it's O.K. Kind of fun really. It's a big job preparing meals for forty people. We work well together and it's an important accreditation for me, towards getting my college chef's certificate."

He straightened, suddenly wary "Why are you asking all these questions anyway – is it something to do with that gas pipe? Dad said the gas inspector was talking about it at the diner."

Halstead looked at Pete - so much for keeping a lid on information.

"Exactly what do you know about the gas pipe?"

"Just what the guy said. The outside valve was open. That's what caused the gas build-up in the basement."

"Did you smell any gas before you left for town?" Halstead asked.

Zak shrugged. "I didn't notice anything. But I was sort of in and out that morning. Checking the menu with Pat in her office, then going to town."

"Any idea what could have happened to that valve?"

He shook his head. "Hell of a thing. Poor Cameron."

* * *

Halstead swivelled in his chair. In the field behind the station, a half-dozen geese still cruised the rows of dried up cornstalks, gleaning the occasional kernel.

"So, what did you think?" he asked Jakes.

Pete considered. "Seems pretty believable to me. Like he said, it's been a few years since the break-up with Kristy."

Halstead nodded. "And even if he did have some wild idea about blowing Cameron up – not to mention Kristy - there was no guarantee that the leak would blow at ten-thirty. Whoever jimmied that valve either didn't know when it would blow or didn't care. And that doesn't fit with Zak trying to revenge himself on a rival who was only there between ten and ten-thirty."

Pete shrugged. "Maybe he just wasn't very good at it. Or he got the wrong information from the Net about how to cause an explosion."

But Halstead didn't look comforted by the joke. "He did rush in to save Cameron, remember."

"He couldn't do much else, with Kristy and Jerry Taylor there."

"Jakes!" Halstead said in mock horror. "I didn't realize you could be so cynical."

Pete grinned. "Comes from being around you, I guess."

Halstead pushed a file folder across the desk.

"Waverly's preliminary fire report. It describes the loose valve."

"What's the conclusion?" Pete asked

"See for yourself," Halstead pointed to the top sheet.

The gas valve was opened in some manner by person(s) unknown.

He sighed. "Now it's definitely in our ball park. We'd better talk to the *femme fatale* in this little drama."

*   *   *

Pete drove into the Chambers' driveway that led to a well-kept red brick house. A plaque proclaimed a heritage farm, in the family for several generations and there was a hundred year old maple on the front lawn. The barn was modern though, one of the new hooped type steel buildings. Not picturesque and not yet proven to be better lasting than the old wood barns. Time would tell. Parked in the rutted lane was an enormous combine, yellow and green, like some irradiated insect escapee from a godzilla movie.

An aging St. Bernard dog rose stiffly from the house steps to bark at their arrival.

"Hello Martha," Halstead called to the woman who came to shush it.

He knew the senior Chambers well, good hardworking folks who were proud of their daughter's recent graduation as a registered dietician, as reported with photo accompaniment in the Bonville *Record.*

Mrs. Chambers was slender, even thin, and dark-haired, Kristy's luminous blond looks must have come from her father's side, Pete thought.

"Hello Bud," Martha said. "I guess you're here to talk to Kristy." She frowned, "I wish you didn't have to bother her. Not so soon. She's still pretty shook up."

"We'll be careful," Halstead assured her. "But it's best to get the facts while things are still fresh in her mind."

Martha grimaced. "Oh it's fresh alright."

She hugged her arms tightly round herself. "It still gives me shivers. To think we could have lost our baby girl."

She opened the door and lead them to the sunporch, a pleasant room at the side of the house. Kristy sat or rather huddled there on a cushioned white wicker couch. She wore jeans and a blouse and despite the warmth of the afternoon, she was wrapped in a flowered quilt. She looked fourteen, not twenty-four.

But she looked up with well-mannered politeness and said "Hello, Mr. Halstead."

Martha pushed two chairs forward and said "I'll leave you to it. Mind you don't upset her Bud."

The officers sat while the dog settled himself at Kristy's feet. "I know I talked to you before Kristy," Halstead said. "But I think we were all pretty upset then."

Kristy nodded. "You know it!" She shivered, as her mother had.

Halstead smiled sympathetically. "I know it's hard but I'd like to go over the sequence of events again, see if there's anything more you remember or can tell us."

Kristy sighed. "I'll try. Some of it's pretty hazy."

"Just cast your mind back to say ten o'clock, a half hour before it happened. When things were 'normal'." He paused. "Were they normal by the way?"

She thought, chewing her pink bottom lip.

"I think so. It was the quiet time in the kitchen. I was reading the paper, waiting for Cam to come. I had saved some lemon tarts for him – his favourite."

Her voice quavered for a moment but she shook her head determinedly and went on. "So yes, it was normal."

"But Zak wasn't there," Halstead said. "Was that normal?"

Kirsty nodded. "He always went to the bakery to get the buns on Wednesday. Pat has a standing order."

"Didn't he mind leaving you and Cameron alone?" Halstead asked.

She frowned. "Of course not."

"We heard that you used to go out with Zak." Pete said.

"High school," she scoffed. "We were kids. We've both dated other people since then."

Halstead leaned forward in his wicker chair. "So, Cam arrived. Then what happened. Did you have time to get him his lemon tarts?"

She shifted on the couch and pulled the quilt tighter. "I don't want to think about it. Do I have to?"

Halstead smiled sympathetically. "I'd appreciate it Kristy. You could help us figure out what happened."

"Cam hadn't started his tart," she began haltingly. "He was telling me something funny...."

"Did you smell any gas at that point?" Halstead interrupted.

The girl looked blank for a moment. "No, I don't think so."

He motioned for her to continue.

"Then I saw Zak arrive with the boxes, so I went to hold the door open for him. Then there was this awful..... sensation I guess. As if something had kicked me in the lungs.... I couldn't breathe...."

She stopped and took a breath now, remembering.

The two officers waited.

She looked up, apologetically. "I must have passed out. When I woke up, Zak was dragging me across the lawn. Then he fell on the grass too. We looked up and saw the smoke and then I realized Cam was still in there. I started screaming ...."

She shuddered. Stopped. "That's it," she said numbly. "That's what I remember."

Halstead looked at Pete. Frightening as the girl's experience had been, there wasn't much in her account to help the investigation.

"Just a couple more questions, Kirsty," Halstead said sympathetically. "Can you think of anything, any little detail that might help us figure out what happened that day?"

The girl pulled the quilt more tightly around her shoulders and bent to pat the dog. "They say there was a broken gas connection pipe somewhere," she said softly.

Neither Pete nor the chief had to ask about the ubiquitous 'they'. The pronoun was a catch-all description for all Island gossip. The girl went on, not looking up and still petting the big dog. "They say that maybe one of the staff broke it, maybe even Zak."

"Why would Zak do a thing like that?" Halstead asked.

"They say he might have been jealous because Cam liked me."

"What do *you* say?" Halstead asked. You knew him well once. People don't change much, do you really think Zak could do something like that?"

She sighed. "Zak was kind of a wild guy in high school, my parents weren't crazy about me going out with him. Nothing really bad, wind-surfing and boating stunts, a couple of speeding tickets, things like that. He was the guy that always pushed the envelope a little farther." She smiled wanly. "I guess that was part of his attraction."

Her pretty face hardened. "So if you had asked me that question a week ago, I probably would have said no he couldn't do something so horrible. But now with Cam in the hospital and maybe going to lose his sight, I have to say I honestly don't know."

11

"What think?" Halstead asked when they were back in the cruiser.

"Zak could certainly have got at that valve handle," Pete said. "He had unlimited access really – he could have nipped out there at any time and nobody would have thought anything of it."

Halstead frowned, the idea obviously unpalatable. "I get it that he might not have wanted to see Kirsty with Cameron but I just can't see him doing something that could have hurt all those other people. Kristy most of all of course, but what about the Taylors who have been great employers and are friends of his parents? Then there were all those helpless old folks … I can't see it."

Pete nodded. "O.K. then If not Zak, who else? And for what motive?"

"Beats me," Halstead said. He looked silently for a moment at the passing fields, said finally, "Jane told me something a little disturbing"

Pete raised an eyebrow. "More disturbing than an explosion and a fire?"

Halstead nodded. "Jane said that Zak and some partying friends once almost burned down a barn. It was when I was away for a couple of years, working off the island. They set some hay bales on fire and it spread. It was lucky a neighbour spotted and reported it."

"Were there charges?" Pete asked.

Halstead shrugged. "They were all minors. Their parents paid the fines."

"Well, shoot," Pete said. "How come nobody thought to tell us yet?"

"It was nearly ten years ago and Jane said that even she'd forgotten. But Tom got in last night from one of his long-distance hauls and when she filled him in on the news, he remembered the barn incident."

Tom Carell was a truck driver, often away from the Island for several days at a time.

"What about Kirsty? She didn't mention that."

"She was just a kid, she wouldn't have been in high school yet. And the story probably just became another local rumour."

"I guess we'd better have another talk with Zak." Pete said.

"Yup."

*　　*　　*

Zak Sorda wasn't so cheerful on this second trip into the station. No breezy talk of baseball scores.

"That's the trouble with living on an Island," he said disgustedly. "Folks have memories like elephants. Every little thing you ever did, it's out there forever. Might as well be written on my forehead."

"The incident is also written up in a police file report," Halstead said reprovingly. "You and your friends nearly torched a barn."

"I thought that kind of report on minors was closed or sealed or something," Zak protested.

Halstead shook his head. "Not from a chief of police."

"I was fourteen," Zak shrugged. "We were just having a joint. You know, like kids do. Trying the stuff out. The fire was an accident."

"The report says that you had a beef with the farmer. One of the other kids said that you were out to get him. That setting the hay on fire was your idea."

That stung. "The lousy bastard shot my dog!" Zak spat out rawly. "Said that Casey was worrying the lousy sheep. Then he found out it was a coyote but it was too late."

Halstead was silent, waiting for Zak to calm down.

"That was a rotten thing to happen alright," he allowed. "But you still can't go around burning barns when you're mad at someone. It's against the law."

Zak slumped back in his seat. "I never set that fire, no one did. Like I told you, it was an accident. We would have called for help but the neighbour beat us to it."

He looked moodily around the cubicle. "Anyway, why are you bringing that old stuff up now. Who cares what a bunch of nosy gossips say?"

"Maybe we're thinking about another fire, Zak. Something more recent."

The light dawned. He looked doubtfully from Halstead to Jakes.

"Jeezus. I hope nobody's saying I started that explosion at the Taylors!"

"Well, did you have anything to do with that explosion, Zak?" Pete asked. "Now would be the time to tell us. Maybe you just had another accident."

Zak jumped up. "I pulled Cameron Parks out of that fire, Chief. I'm a goddamned hero. So now you're accusing me of *arson*?"

"We're not accusing you of anything Zak. We're just having a little conversation here."

"Yeah well, I'm not interested. So if you're done, I'm outta here. I'm going home."

Halstead nodded. "You can go lad. For now."

Zak stormed out, leaving two thoughtful police officers in his wake.

Halstead swivelled into thinking posture. The geese had left the field for now, perhaps were out on a practise flight for the big fall journey.

"The lad's a bit of a hot-head all right.,"

"Understandable," Pete said. "Arsonist has a bad ring to it."

"Arson is bad all round." Halstead sighed. "You'd better go over Zak's movements that morning."

"We already checked with the bakery. He was definitely there, and left about ten fifteen. It would have taken him ten minutes to get back to the Lodge."

"He could have left home for work much earlier. Sneaked into the yard and turned that valve. Then just arrived as usual, and left for the bakery."

Pete grimaced. "Pretty cold-blooded. That's not my impression of Zak."

Halstead mused silently over this.

"They're still one more witness to see," he said finally. "Trouble is, the boy is in intensive care and not up to talking to anybody yet. Let's just hope that Jeff Waverly comes up with some other suggestion about what happened there."

*   *   *

The Middle Island Auxiliary Fire Station consisted of two truck bays in a renovated garage behind the Island municipal building. Halstead had called ahead to arrange a time to see the fire chief, who like everyone else in the volunteer department, had another full-time occupation.

When Jeff Waverly wasn't being called out to fight a fire or to use defibrillator equipment to save someone suffering a heart attack, he owned and operated a large market garden business. But the growing season was pretty well over now, except for squash and brussel sprouts and like most farmers who spent a lot of time alone in the fields, he never minded coming into town for a chat.

When Halstead arrived, he found the big red pumper truck outside, freshly hosed down and gleaming glossily in the sunshine.

"There's a fine sight," he called to Waverly. "Makes me feel excited as a kid again."

Waverly, about five nine and muscularly built, today wore jeans and a sweatshirt, marked with the station logo. He grinned. "I bet you wanted to be a fireman."

Halstead nodded. "It was a toss-up between that and an astronaut."

"And here you are, a policeman."

Halstead looked regretfully at the pumper truck. "I must have taken a wrong turn somewhere."

He followed Waverly into the cool interior of the garage. There was no pole for sleepy firemen to slide down but there was a row of long yellow slickers on hooks, lots of boots, and impressive helmets. Waverly led the way to a small office, where the walls were plastered with official looking notices. He poured coffee and invited, "Park yourself."

The desk was stacked with paperwork, similar to Halstead's own. He knew that during the winter, Waverly devoted many hours to studying government-issued manuals and updating training courses. Currently he had a force of eighteen men on call.

Waverly offered milk from a small fridge and pushed a chipped cup of sugar cubes across the desk.

"So, what's up?"

Halstead poured milk and stirred a couple of cubes into his cup. "I've read your report on the Lodge fire – several times. There's not much in the line of forensics."

"Gee," Waverly said. "It's a good thing we're friends or I might think you were being critical of my report."

"Not critical," Halstead protested. "Maybe disappointed. *'Perpetrated by some human agency. Person(s) unknown'* What good is that to me, Jeff?"

Waverly frowned. "You might consider that an explosion and resultant fire tend to wipe the slate pretty clean. If there's a slate left at all."

"You're right, of course," Halstead acknowledged. "But it's a damned unsatisfactory situation, you have to admit. Particularly for Zak Sorda and his family, as the gossiping has already begun. You've known Zak as long as the rest of us, Jeff - what do you think, is he an arsonist?"

Waverly waved a hand, "You mean is he paranoic, asocial, and bitter about what life has handed him?"

Halstead's eyebrows rose. "Sounds as if you've been doing the same reading I have. But that's not a very good desciption of the Zak Sorda we know. He comes from a good, loving family, was a star high school athlete, seemed – at least before this happened – an enthusiastic, ambitious fellow."

Waverly sighed. "We can all have cracks in our systems. Cracks that can show up in a crisis, either physical or emotional. I'm sure that young Sorda isn't immune."

"Well yes, he's had a rough spot or two," Halstead agreed. "Like you said, so have we all. But we don't all run out and blow up a building when we feel low."

"Fortunately," Waverly said drily. He looked out at the street.

"Actually I'd be a lot more comfortable if whoever did this, *did* have a motive. The last thing we want is to have some lunatic setting off explosions in the community."

"You've got that right," Halstead said fervently.

"I've been looking up some stats," Waverly said. "They're pretty chilling. Nationally, about five thousand cases of arson a year. Now, a lot of those are fires set in abandoned buildings or other acts of public mischief. And there are the insurance scams of course, but that doesn't account for all of them. So, given the options, we'd better hope someone else with a motive shows up real soon."

But Halstead's thoughts were with Benny and Maria Sorda. Parenthood could be a rocky road. It was a good thing that young folks had no idea what they were getting into when they planned to have a child. Otherwise no one would have the courage to go through with it.

He was grateful that his own daughter was happily married to a stable, hard-working man. But it had a lot to do with luck, really. You did your best and then just crossed your fingers.

12

The Lodge was looking less like the scene of a disaster. In the days since the explosion, the contractors had demolished the ugly remains of the destroyed kitchen and cleaned up the site. Pete found Pat in the front garden, kneeling among her plants. In her lime green scrubs, she looked like a garden gnome herself.

She rose, wiping dirt off her knees.

"Your flowers survived," he said, noting clumps of orange and white.

She smiled, "These are chrysanthemums. I bought them at the nursery."

"They look nice anyway," he said.

"Thanks, they do help a bit I think. And I'm so glad the kitchen is gone. It was awful for the residents to have to look at that whenever they were out on the patio."

Pete nodded sympathetically. "How long before you're back in business?"

Pat sighed, "About a month unfortunately. Rick and the boys are doing the best they can. They had other work slated to do during the day but they're squeezing us in evenings and weekends."

She slapped dirt off her trowel. "We've set up a temporary kitchen of sorts in one of the storerooms. There was an extra fridge there already and we've added a couple of microwaves, kettles, and grills where Kristy and I can prepare breafasts and lunches. So far we're making suppers at the United Church kitchen and trucking the food over here."

She shrugged her shoulders. "It's an experience. And people are so helpful. Tonight I don't have to cook at all. Gus is sending over pizza from the Grill."

"Sounds as if you're coping very well," Pete said. "I'm sure everyone appreciates your efforts." He held up a large shopping bag.

"I've brought some clothes for my father, I figured the ones from his room will be all smoky. And he didn't bring that many from the city."

"That's good thinking! We've been running things through the laundry but it's a big task."

"Is he out on the patio?"

Pat looked hesitant. "Actually, Pete, he rarely leaves the room. We've been a bit concerned about him. He was just getting used to us, but the explosion seems to have set him back."

"How so?" Pete asked.

She had stopped inside the doorway and considered her words. "He's been a bit … difficult to know, if you don't mind my saying. Never that friendly or at ease with the staff."

"No offense taken," Pete said resignedly. "I know what you mean."

"We're used to a period of adjustment," Pat explained. "It's a big change for most of our residents, giving up their homes and all. But that's not the case for your father, he'll be leaving at some point."

She shook her head. "But the explosion seems to have upset him terribly. He's very nervous and anxious, he barely touches his meals and he's thin enough already. He never comes to the common room, only wants to sit by himself watching the news."

She added a little crossly, "I'm afraid that's the only time of day that he perks up at all, to watch *News From the Hill*. Staff tell me that he won't let anyone talk or even tiptoe around the room if the television is on, without grouching at them to be quiet."

Pete could only say inadequately, "I imagine the explosion was unsettling for most of the residents."

Pat smiled. "You re right of course. Hopefully it will pass."

Pete continued on down the corridor, his thoughts on what Pat had said. He didn't remember Walter as a particularly anxious person, but then his father seemed to have repressed all feeling long ago. The doctor on the last visit had reported that Walter's hip was healing as expected, so there shouldn t be any new anxiety on that score. He had been even been attempting some strengthening exercises. Odd then, he should be getting better, not worse.

Girding himself, he opened the door of the room. The other resident, a quietly friendly octagenarian, was out and Walter was alone, sitting in the wheelchair. The T.V. was on but he wasn't looking at it. He seemed to be staring absently into space.

"Hi Dad," Pete announced himself, the words still feeling awkward on his tongue.

Walter started and almost jumped in the chair. As if he'd been galvanized by an electric shock.

Pete quickly crossed the room. "Sorry to startle you like that."

Walter sank back in the chair. He looked dazed and Pete made a mental note to ask Pat about the strength of his medication. A little daunted, he dropped a hand on the older man's shoulder, the first physical contact in how many years?

"It's a great day," he said. "How about I take you to the patio for a spin?"

Walter shook off the hand with a twitch of his shoulder.

"I'm alright here," he said brusquely.

Pete looked out at the lawn, where other residents chatted in the late afternoon sun under a giant flame-leafed maple. Walter seemed oblivious. Pete felt the familiar clench of tension in his chest but he kept his tone chatty.

"I've brought you some fresh clothes, smoke-free." He spilled out the bag's contents on the bed. A couple of pairs of chino trousers, two modestly striped shirts and a tan cardigan sweater.

"Hope they fit - I had to guess at the size."

Walter made no reply to this witty sally. Pete pressed doggedly on, putting the clothes on hangers as he talked.

"The doctor says you can advance to a walker soon. Then you can take yourself out to the patio."

"I'll be taking myself a lot further than that."

"All in good time," Pete said. "You've still got more physiotherapy ahead of you."

Walter twisted frustratedly in the chair. "I've got to get out of here."

"The explosion's over Dad. You're safe. Are you taking those anti-anxiety pills the doctor gave you?"

"You don't understand. I've got responsibilities. I've got clients, work that I have to finish."

Pete tried not to sound exasperated. "You broke your hip falling down a flight of stairs. They'll understand if their bookkeeping will be a bit late."

Walter snorted. "I doubt it. They'll be looking for another accountant."

"So maybe you'll lose a client or two. Sometimes you just can't control events Dad. Stuff happens. Besides, aren't you supposed to be retired?"

"I've got responsibilities," Walter repeated agitatedly. "You don t understand."

Pete sighed. "I understand. If you'll make a list, I'll phone or e-mail them and explain."

Walter seemed not to have heard him. A stand-off. Like so many others through the years. "Maybe one of your colleagues in the Revenue department can take on the work temporarily or suggest someone who can." Pete suggested.

"I've got to get out of here," Walter said stubbornly.

Pete shut the closet door. "Sometimes you just have to accept that the world has stopped for awhile, Dad. Right now I m going home for supper. You're welcome to come with me by the way. It's a standing invitation."

But Walter had already returned to a moody contemplation of *News From the Hill.* Likely the federal financial scandal again, he seemed to be obsessed by it. Pete shrugged, at least it was a diversion from the recent traumatic events.

*   *   *

It was a lovely September night, with a bit of a breeze soughing through the dry, rustling leaves. Normally Pat Taylor would have left her office window open but the horrid burnt odor of her ruined kitchen still hovered in the air, a reminder of that awful morning.

"You can't still smell it," Jerry protested. "It's just your imagination."

"Doesn't matter," Pat said. "I can smell it."

"They'll start building soon," Jerry soothed. "The kitchen will be even nicer than before."

She sighed and turned back to her desk.

"Are you coming up soon?" he asked, not very hopefully.

She frowned. "You know I've still got to write out the work schedules for next week."

"I know, I know. You're like a hen who has to safely bed your chicks for the night."

"Yes and let's hope it's a quiet night." She cast a dark look towards the hallway, in the direction of Walter Jakes' room.

"He's had his medication, he should be alright," Jerry said.

"I hope so."

He pecked her on the check. "I'll see you later, then. Don't work too late."

She looked a bit ruefully after him.

A long day. It seemed that lately all the days were long. Jerry was always saying they should take a holiday. They could afford it, he said but that wasn't the problem. The truth was she would find it difficult to leave the Lodge, even for a couple of weeks in Cuba. He was right, she had to learn how to delegate.

"What if you broke a leg or worse?" he would say. "The Lodge wouldn't shut down. The rest of us would manage somehow. We'd likely manage just fine."

"Gee thanks," she said. "I love the 'or worse' part."

But he had a point. And she had almost reached the point of agreeing with him.

Till this recent upheaval. An explosion, who would ever have expected anything like that to happen! She couldn't possibly leave now, no way. Jerry had reluctantly agreed.

She frowned and averted her gaze from the shut, curtained window. Although she presented a calm, rattle-proof exterior, as sturdy as her figure – Jerry called her his rock -- she too had been quite shaken by the explosion. She felt a great responsibility for the health and safety of her residents and though it wasn't logical, she felt an almost personal negligence for what had happened. Even though she could have done nothing to prevent it.

Irrationally too, she felt a rush of anger towards Walter Jakes. Such an unpleasant, unfriendly man. Despite all the efforts of herself and the rest of the Lodge staff, he had made no effort to fit in. Normally she rode through all the many problems involved in running the place. But this month, with Walter Jakes and then the explosion, had been especially difficult.

Of course the explosion wasn't Walter Jakes fault either. And yet ......

Though Pat wouldn't have called herself a superstitious woman, except for the obvious safeguards regarding spilled salt and walking under ladders, she couldn't shake the feeling that this unpleasant visitor from the city had brought bad luck with him. It wasn't very charitable of her but she wanted Walter Jakes *out* of her Lodge. She wanted him gone.

With a shiver, she returned to the more manageable tasks of staff scheduling and meal planning.

13

Report from Officer Stutke to Chief Halstead, September 18.
Responding to complaints from two citizens, of a disturbance caused by a vehicle with a faulty muffler. Officer overtook and questioned suspect driver.
Suspect was belligerent and uncooperative.

I'll bet! Halstead grinned, picturing the scene. Whenever given the opportunity, Elmer Hicks liked to complain about the 'police state' that supposedly wanted to control every aspect of his life. When really he just begrudged having to pay for a new muffler.

Served suspect with a notice to repair the vehicle muffler within ten days or pay a $200 fine.

Halstead chuckled and showed the report to Pete.

"I'd better tell Stutke not to hold his breath. He'll be making at least a couple of trips out to the Hicks residence to try and pick up that fine."

But the report was concise enough, Halstead acknowledged. The lad might make a police officer yet. He was less pleased with the other report on his desk. This was also concise, disappointingly sparse in fact. The forensics assistant from Roger Huma's lab in Bonville had found only a few oily smudges on the valve handle.

Hardly surprising. Ed Bell said that he always wore work gloves while on the job. And Jeff Waverly had been wearing big rubber firemen's gloves. The area around the tank was well-travelled grass, so had revealed nothing useful regarding footprints.

Pete was absorbing this when Jane came hurrying in. She was out of breath and hadn't even paused to shut the station front door.

"Somebody's vandalized the Sorda's chip van, " she gasped. "I saw it on my way in. They painted 'Murderer' and 'Firebug' all over it in white paint. They even kicked over Maria's flower vases."

"No," Halstead said disgustedly. "Dammit. We'd better get out there."

The Canadian Tire store was at the west end of the village. Benny Sorda rented a space in the parking lot for the truck and a half dozen picnic table for diners. A retired plumber who liked to stay active, Sorda opened for business in the first warm days of May and kept serving burgers and fries till Thanksgiving weekend in the fall.

The truck and surroundings had always been scrupulously neat and inviting to travellers and locals alike. The magenta coloured vehicle perched like a small ship on the tarmac, ringed by Maria's vases of geraniums and the tables, packed with happily munching customers. When combined with the striped red and white awning over the serving hatch, Benny's cheerful welcome, and the tantalizing aroma of frying potatoes and vinegar -- irresistible!

Not so cheerful a sight this morning, though. A small group of on-lookers milled about uncertainly in the lot, most of them undoubtedly sympathetic. Nevertheless, Halstead pushed them roughly aside.

"Police coming through folks, that's enough gawking."

They found Benny standing in silent contemplation of the damage. He looked up at their arrival. "Hello, Bud, Pete. Here's a mess."

The white-painted letters sprawled unevenly across the front of the truck, some right across the serving hatch door which hadn't been lifted open yet.

The message was ugly enough, as Jane had reported. FIREBUG. MURDURER. DONT EAT HERE.

Benny attempted a small smile. "They couldn't even spell it right."

Halstead patted Benny's shoulder. "They probably couldn't spell arsonist. Just stupid idiots."

Sorda shook his head sadly. "Tell that to Zak. Tell that to his mother. Look at her flowers, ruined."

"Where exactly is Zak?" Halstead asked, looking around the parking lot.

"He took Maria to the city to see her sister, " Benny said. "I thought it would be good for her to get away. And now she's got this to come back to!"

He grabbed angrily at one of the big stone vases and tried to prop it up again. Pete bent to help and they managed to right the two vases that were still intact. The third lay in pieces, the geranium stems broken, the red petals spattering the pavement.

Benny straightened, catching his breath. He eyed the hateful slogans. "Maybe the store has something that will take that paint off before I open up. The stuff is still sticky, couldn't have been done more than a couple hours ago."

He seemed about to head for the store directly. Halstead took his arm.

"That can wait a bit Benny. Got any coffee fixings in the truck? I could use a cup. Looks like you could too."

Benny looked confused. "Yeah sure," he said finally.

More cars and gawkers had pulled into the parking lot, attracted by the sight of the police cruiser.

"Better put up the closed sign," Halstead advised Pete. "And tell them all to get on about their business."

"I'll be open for lunch," Sorda protested.

"I doubt it," Halstead said.

Pete dragged one of the picnic tables behind the truck for privacy and left the chief with Benny while he tried to get some answers as to who had done the mean deed. The store and parking lot were at the edge of the village, empty fields on one side and only one house on the other. Still, the perps must have decided not to work in the dark, as flashlights could have been noticed either by the neighbour or by passing cars on the road.

So they had worked with their paint and brushes and carried out their crude art in the early morning while the mist rose in the nearby fields. The job wouldn't have taken more than twenty minutes.

"Well?" Halstead asked when Pete returned. He gestured to the coffee urn on the table. "Pour yourself some java. Benny's gone to get some paint thinner and cloths. I couldn't hold him back any longer."

Pete sipped the brew gratefully. Though the September days were warm by noontime, they could start off a bit chilly.

"The neighbours didn't see or hear anything out of the ordinary," he said.

Halstead expected that. The Hardins were both in their eighties and likely went to bed by nine o'clock. Even if they awoke early, both had been deaf as posts for years now.

"But Carl Hope, the store manager came in earlier to open up for a delivery from Montreal. Said that a blue pick-up truck barrelled past him about a mile out of town."

"That's a big help," Halstead said. "Every second vehicle on the Island is a blue pick-up. I've got one myself." He tossed the dregs of his cup onto the grass. "But the information will leak out somewhere on the grapevine. It's just a matter of time. Too bad Benny will already have cleaned up the truck by then. I'd love to set the jerks to painting over this crap. And to paying for it too."

"It's a nasty business," Pete said.

Halstead nodded. "I'll send young Jory over to give Benny a hand. It's good that Zak is away at the moment."

Pete grimaced. "Benny said he called and told Zak the news. He wanted to prepare Maria, spare her the shock."

"Shoot! He'll be hot-footing it back home." Halstead shook his head. "Damnation, that was dumb of Benny."

He looked frustratedly around the parking lot. "Keep an ear out then. Hopefully we can head him off before he does anything stupid."

*　*　*

But when the call came a couple of hours later, they were too late to head off Zak Sorda.

"He's out at the Parks' place," Halstead called into the lunchroom. "Raising a ruckus. Take Jory with you."

They used the siren on the cruiser. Not because there was much traffic on the road, but in hopes that Zak would hear them coming. The Parks lived a couple of miles out of town. A sign at the driveway advertised the family landscaping services and a pair of heavy duty mowers were drawn up before the open door of the steel sided garage.

Mr. Parks senior and two of Cameron's brothers were out on the front lawn facing Zak in what looked like a stand-off. But the siren and the arrival of the police officers, instead of quelling Zak, seemed to ignite him into action. As the two officers left the car, Zak leapt forward with an angry yelp and took a swing at Kyle Parks. The two of them fell struggling to the grass and Dan Parks looked ready to jump in.

By this time Pete had reached the group. He pushed Dan away and yanked at Zak. Meanwhile Jory had caught hold of Kyle. Both he and Zak were sputtering angry obscenities and Kyle was wiping blood away from his mouth.

"Bastards," Zak spit out. "Picking on my Dad. On my parents." He turned and twisted in Pete's grasp. "You should be arresting them!"

"Goddamn it," Mr. Parks said. "Lock that crazy maniac up and throw away the key. You should have done it when he blew up that kitchen and near killed our Cameron." Mrs. Parks had now come down from the porch and was crying, which upset her husband even more.

"Come on now Zak," Pete said. "These people have enough trouble on their plates right now."

"You think *they've* got trouble? What about my family." He seemed ready to attack again.

Pete gave his arm a hard twist. "Do I have to put the cuffs on you Zak? Come on, let's leave these people alone. You need to cool down."

Even then, he and Jory had to half push, half drag Zak to the cruiser.

"There will be charges," Mr. Parks shouted after them. "You'll be hearing from us."

Pete shoved Zak, none too gently, into the vehicle.

"You haven't helped yourself with this stunt, Zak," he said as they drove away. "You're just making things worse, showing people that you can't control your temper. You've got no proof that the Parks vandalized the chip truck."

But Zak had subsided sullenly behind the wire barrier to the back seat. By the time they arrived at the station, Halstead met them out in the parking lot.

"Don't bother stopping," he said to Pete. "You might as well take him straight over to the jail in Bonville. Gord Parks has already called."

He leaned down to look into the back window. "This is a fine mess, Zak. Now you're going to rack up an assault and battery charge. That's really going to cheer up your folks."

Zak didn't look at him, didn't say anything. Pete left the car for a moment to confer with Halstead. "He won't get a bail hearing at least until tomorrow. Maybe not for a couple of days. Have you called Benny?"

Halstead sighed. "I will. I haven't exactly been looking forward to the call." He looked over to the car, "It's probably for the best if he has to stay over there for awhile. Keep him from any more idiotic behaviour."

Zak was silent on the drive over the causeway. Pete had seen the effect before, he'd felt it himself after intense physical activity. The adrenaline subsiding like a tide water and leaving behind an actual physical depression. And too, Zak must be beginning to think of the enormity of what he had done and its possible after-effects. Stutke was quiet too. Pete wondered whether Jory had every arrested anyone before, let alone someone he knew. It could be a strange experience. So it was a sombre ride altogether, in contrast to the cheery view outside the car of the sun-glinted bay waters.

The detention centre, a low slung block of featureless concrete with an outside exercise yard surrounded by a barb-wire topped fence, was definitely a cheerless place.

Pete thought that Zak's bravado wobbled a bit as the two officers escorted him out of the car and up the sidewalk. The daunting atmosphere and booking procedure were designed precisely to do just that, particularly the identification photograph.

"Don't I get my one phone call?" Zak asked.

"You'll get it in there," the Bonville officer said, indicating the door to the cells.

"Chief Halstead will already have called your folks," Pete said.

Zak looked back once, as the Bonville officer led him away.

"What a dope," Jory said as they waited for their return lane to open on the causeway.

"Zak has been under a lot of pressure the past week," Pete said. "Think how you'd feel if anyone trashed your parents' business. And called you a murderer."

"Well sure, trashing the chip truck was a low blow. It's not his parents' fault if Zak got jealous and blew up that kitchen."

"Now you're acting as badly as Zak," Pete said. "Assuming a thing without any proof."

Stutke shrugged. "I don't see any other suspects turning up. And today he acted like a real jerk at the Parks place. Mrs. Parks was even crying."

"But what if Zak isn't guilty of hurting Cameron?" Pete asked. "It isn't a matter of whether you like Zak or not. You're a policeman, or at least in training to be one. It's your duty to keep an open mind."

Jory made a face, as if this was a new concept.

"O.K.," he admitted. "I guess I liked him when I was a kid. We all did. Zak was always kind of wild, the type of guy you told stories about. The first kid to jump off the Simpson Road bridge into the creek in the spring. Kayaking, water ski-ing, he was always the dare-devil, pushing the envelope more than anyone else. You could even say we looked up to him. He was a sharp dresser too, not like us farmboys in feedcaps and overalls."

Pete nodded. There was always one of those fellows in any group, of any age. He remembered his own pals in high school and later in the army. There was always a daredevil for whom even war sometimes wasn't enough action, enough excitement.

Jory looked out the window, remembering.

"But the stunts got crazier and more dangerous, especially after he started driving. He had some real close calls. None of us would drive with him anymore. Except Kristy, I guess he slowed down a bit when he started going with her. When they split up though, he went back to being a maniac."

Jory turned and said seriously, "So if you're asking me whether he would risk blowing up a whole nursing home full of people, just to get back at Cameron. Yeah, I think he could. He's crazy enough to do that."

Pete nodded. It was a fair enough personal assessment, based on first-hand evidence.

"At least Sorda's out of the way for the time being," Halstead said when they got back to the station. "Gives us a bit of a breather to figure this thing out."

14

"How's it going, Bud?" Gus asked, pushing a beer across the counter.

Halstead noted that summer was now officially over. Never mind the solstices, the proprietor of the Island Grill and Motel sartorially recognized only two seasons. From May on through the summer, he wore a singlet and cargo shorts, but had now donned his winter wear, faded jeans and a lumpy blue checked lumberjack shirt. His ponytail was a little thinner and greyer too, Halstead saw, which did not affect the man's cheerful outlook. Once a happy hippy, always a happy hippy.

"When's the little woman get back?" he asked now, always keen for a chat.

"Not for another few weeks," Halstead said. "Mother and daughter are having too much fun seeing the sights, I guess."

"They're likely picking out one of them fancy kymonas for you," Gus laughed. "You can wear it at Hallowe'en."

"Har de har," Halstead gratefully started on the beer. Fried chicken in a basket would follow, what the hell. While the Steph's away, the chief will eat grease and salt. and burp too if he feels like it. It didn't seem fair that if a man reached middle age in his own lean condition, that the women could still be at him about a host of other health threats.

"Tough day?" Gus asked more sympathetically. He'd known Bud a long time.

"Better off than some folks anyway," Halstead said. "I was over in Bonville today, dropped in at the hospital to see how Cameron is doing."

He shook his head. "He's out of intensive care at least and the specialist has had a look. It's what they call secondary ocular damage, from fragments of glass and the like. Particularly his right eye."

Gus winced, "That doesn't sound good. I guess they'll be operating to get that stuff out?"

"Not sure," Halstead said. "Apparently in some cases it's better to wait and let the eye scar and heal itself."

"And then Cameron would be able to see?"

"That isn't sure either way, surgery or not."

"Damn," Gus said, his gaze taking in the assorted patrons of his busy restaurant. "Unofficial poll here would be running at least two to one that Zak fixed the explosion to happen. Folks say that he has a grudge against the Parkers and that jail is the best place for him."

"Shoot. I'd expect more loyalty than that. Benny and Maria Sorda have done a lot for this community."

Gus pulled the metal basket of chicken pieces from the hot fat, shook them free of grease and popped a batch into the basket on the counter.

"Course that's mainly the fellas who come in here to watch the games."

He nodded towards the back room with the mounted television. By general customer consensus, the set was pretty well always tuned to the sports channel. Any female customers were resigned to the fact and preferred to dine in relative peace at the front of the establishment. Especially now, when the Jays were looking to win in their Division.

"And they'd never say anything to Benny's face," Gus added. "Their wives are probably nicer to Maria. Word is she's a wreck."

Halstead sighed and picked up a fork.

"Something like this is really tough on the parents. Tough on the whole family."

He'd stopped at the chip truck yesterday. Had been surprised that Benny was even there, but Benny said it was too hard to be at the house doing nothing. That the doctor had to give Maria something for her nerves. Otherwise she was crying all the time.

Gus put a couple of rolls beside the basket and leaned forward confidingly on his elbows. "Yeah but Bud, you gotta admit it looks bad for the kid."

"Hey!" Halstead raised a warding hand. "He hasn't been tried yet. Nor even arrested."

Gus shrugged. "I'm just asking like everybody else. If it wasn't Zak Sorda who tinkered with that valve – who did?"

*　　*　　*

It was the same everywhere the chief went. Gus had said the Island Grill's unoffical poll was running two to one against Zak and he'd bet the results would be the same with the general public. By nine o'clock in the morning he'd already fielded a call from Bob Denys, editor of the Bonville Record and incidentally a fellow player in the local curling league.

"Just calling for an update on the investigation," Denys said cheerfully. "Is there going to be an arrest any time soon? An inquiring public wants to know."

Halstead snorted. "An inquiring editor wants to sell newspapers you mean. Haven't you had enough already this week? I know I have."

"Come on Bud. You know it's a battle for print newspapers these days. We're all losing ground daily to the internet. Give me a break."

"I will, when I get one myself."

"O.K. be that way. We'll flip for lunch on Tuesday. Heads you pay, and tails you pay too."

Lunch or not, he sure as hell wasn't going to tell Bob Denys the newshound about the visit he'd had from Sorda senior later that morning.

*   *   *

Benny looked as if he hadn't slept since the trouble began. His normally well-fleshed cheeks hung limply on his face, his once-cheerful gaze held no sparkle. Halstead noticed new greying in his dark hair.

"Come on in, Benny" he invited, standing to greet him.

Benny sat down heavily, like an old man. "You know why I'm here, Bud. I need your help in clearing my son."

"I'm doing what I can, Benny," Halstead said sympathetically. "You know that."

The chip truck owner thumped the desk in frustration. "Zak should be getting a commendation for bravery for dragging Cameron out of there. Instead..... this!"

He fought for control. "Damn it Bud, this is all so wrong. I know Zak has had some trouble in the past, but that was just youthful carelessness. High spirits, drinking foolishness. Since then, the boy has got two years at college under his belt. He's only got another year to get his chef's certificate."

Halstead shook his head. "We're not talking youthful hijinks here Benny. Cameron may lose his sight. People could have been killed."

Benny leaned forward, his voice urgent. "Zak would never do anything like that." His face twisted with pain. It's not right, the way people are talking. Zak doesn't believe that the Taylors will ever hire him back. It's a hell of a cloud hanging over the kid, hard for him to go off to school this way. I hate to see it."

"I hear you Benny but the gas valve didn't open itself. That's the problem I'm faced with. Have you got an answer for me?"

"I don't know Bud – I can't imagine who would do a rotten thing like that. I only know it wasn't Zak."

"Then who, Benny? Give me some ideas."

Benny shrugged, offered listlessly. "One of the other kids?"

"Not Cameron, certainly," Halstead pointed out. "Look how he ended up. Surely you can't mean Kristy. What did she get out of it?".

Benny looked dazed. "I don't know, you read stories, see movies. Maybe she wanted to get Zak in trouble….." he stopped. "Sorry Bud, of course she didn't. If I wasn't so desperate I wouldn't even suggest such a thing."

Halstead sighed. "I know it seems desperate but we haven't laid any charges yet."

Benny looked bleakly across the desk. "It's almost as bad this way, Bud. Like we're all living under that black cloud."

Halstead hesitated, then said it anyway. "I hate to say it Benny. But you should be thinking about talking to a lawyer."

He didn't say that he'd been checking on the legal background regarding arson. It seemed that even if the act was prompted by recklessness, the law viewed the crime in the same light as premeditated intent.

*   *   *

His heavy lunch had made Halstead dozy, but just as he'd put his feet up, Jane announced gleefully from the front counter,

"Here's Vern, chief. Coming through!" Gleeful because she knew darn well that he liked to grab a few winks sometimes in the afternoon.

Vern Byers was just about the only man Halstead knew who still wore a suit to work. Perhaps he felt it was required of him to live up to the dignity of his office as Municipal Clerk. A harmless delusion. He folded his skinny shanks into the chair where Benny Sorda had that morning poured out his heart, and launched into venting over his current woe. At least, Halstead reflected, Vern now had some real worry to take his mind off the causeway wrangle with the Bonville mayor.

"People are upset, Bud. They don't like the idea of having a hothead like Zak Sorda walking around free in the community.

Some folks are out and out calling him an arsonist. He's got history, you know."

"He's hardly walking around free, Vern. Last I checked, he was occupying a cell at the Bonville lock-up."

"Yeah but Benny will bail him out at the arraignment."

The clerk shook his head dolefully. "The courts don't keep anybody in anymore. Murderers getting out on day passes after serving only a year. Government crooks in Ottawa making off with millions. Makes you wonder what this country's coming too."

Though he shared some of Vern's sentiments, Halstead felt compelled to point out that Zak Sorda hadn't yet been charged with arson, let alone tried or convicted.

But Vern went on. "And then there's the question of insurance. It's going to be big. Jerry Taylor says he had a talk with their agent. If the Parks lad does lose his sight, he'll be handicapped for the rest of his life. I ask you, is it the Taylors' fault if some crazy boy with a bad temper blows up their kitchen?"

And if someone was criminally responsible, Halstead thought, would there be any money at all? He stood up dismissively, enough of this.

"I guess we can just count our blessings, Vern, that we live in a country with free medical care for all."

Even Vern Byers couldn't think of anything bad to say about that.

15

Middle Island Community Library.
Open noon to four, Thurs & Fri. Children's Library Sat mornings.

The library was a small, one-storey converted house, barely more than a cottage. There were late-blooming roses along the walk though and a view of the Bay from the porch at the back. Ali found her neighbour Miranda at the desk, Emily the border collie at her feet. The dog wagged her tail and followed as Nevra scooted off to the children's section of the room.

"I've saved a new curious monkey story for her," Miranda confided, pulling the book out from the desk drawer. She'll be the first to read it."

Ali stowed it in her bag. "I'll save it for the bed-time story."

She dropped gratefully into the comfy armchair by the window, a gift from a library patron's living room. "We just finished a busy session at the park," she explained. "Up and down the slide, mostly up. How's the blogging going?" she added.

"Busy," Miranda said reprovingly. "I think I saved a half dozen chicks today."

Ali got a kick out of watching seventy-five year old Miranda at her new internet venture, a blog about raising chickens. She had begun in response to a news story from Vancouver where some residents had successfully won the right to raise the birds in the city. Miranda, who kept a dozen Anaconda hens herself, was concerned about the fate of the birds in the hands of novices. She had written a letter to the Vancouver newspaper and people had replied asking for advice. Now she had quite a few young urban followers on her blog. An interesting cap to her forty years of teaching schoolchildren in the Canadian Arctic.

"I need a cozy book," Ali sighed. "Something to take my mind off these recent sad events."

All over the island, people were taking sides, even at the school. Ali didn't know whether Zak Sorda was innocent or guilty, but she admired Benny Sorda's passionate defence of his son. She couldn't help but contrast that with Walter Jakes' cold treatment of Pete.

Miranda nodded. "I scolded Morley Bevan in the post office this morning. He and some others were talking about Zak Sorda as if he was some kind of monster. I told them, "Shame on you. We've all watched that lad grow up."

Ali winced and scrunched further down in the chair. "I know. I hate what's happening, the things people are saying. I try to excuse them by thinking they're just worried what's going to happen with Cameron."

"I don't excuse anyone," Miranda said stoutly. "I say get your facts straight before you open your mouth. And then be kind."

"Right on," Ali agreed, then grew pensive, looking out at the village street. "But it is a tricky puzzle, you have to admit. If Zak didn't set off that explosion, who did? And why, for heaven's sake? That's the biggest puzzle of all."

"What does Pete think?" Miranda asked.

Ali frowned. "I don't think he and the chief are any further on than the rest of us. Pete says it's not an insurance fraud on the Taylors' part. I know, I know, it's awful that they even have to consider that possibility but that's what the police do, that's their work."

Anyway, the Taylors are apparently in decent financial shape. In fact, it's the other way round really. If the investigation doesn't come up with someone to try for setting the explosion, the Taylors could be involved in a legal battle regarding Cameron's expenses."

Miranda sighed. "I keep hoping that it will turn out to be some accident after all. An alignment of awful coincidences."

"But what if it *was* Zak, Miranda?" Ali persisted. "Maybe he's more mixed-up than anybody guesses. Things happen to people. Maybe he's depressed, or angry. All good reasons to get him into care, if he needs it. His next eruption might be even more serious, he might hurt even more people."

She broke off. "Oh, I do hope it wasn't him! Think what that would do to his parents. I imagine they'd move away, off the Island." Her eyes brimmed with pity. "What a sad thing that would be."

Changing the topic slightly, Miranda said, "I saw Pat Taylor the other day and it sounded as if she and the staff had done a Herculean job getting things back to normal at the home. And your father-in-law, is he adjusting?"

Ali shrugged. "Frankly Miranda, I wouldn't know. He and I don't have a lot of communication. In fact, not any."

"Oh," Miranda said.

Ali sat up, looking miserable. "The whole situation is a disaster. For Pete, certainly. I wouldn't know what Walter Jakes feels."

"Walter's injuries...." Miranda suggested. "Maybe when he feels better."

Ali shook her head. "His ribs are mending by now, though the hip will be slower of course."

She subsided again in the chair. "Oh Pete tells me that the doctor thinks Walter could be suffering a psychological relapse since the gas explosion. But I'm afraid there's no way around it, Miranda. The man just doesn't want to know me or his granddaughter."

"That's too bad, dear." Miranda said sympathetically. "I know you were hoping to heal the breach."

Ali looked disconsolately out at the street. "I'm baffled and beat. Promise you won't tell Pete, but I went to the Taylors yesterday with a beautiful fall bouquet. Purple asters, goldenrod and silver teasel stems that I collected along the roadside. When I got there, I stood in the hall nerving myself up to go into the room.

But then a helper came to take Walter for a walk. I tried to walk along with them but he just brushed me aside."

She didn't tell the rest of it. How Walter had asked her to leave him alone and not come again. But Miranda looked as if she could guess.

Ali shivered. "He had such a cold way of looking right through me. I had thought about taking Nevra there, but now I think she'd just be frightened."

"Best not to," Miranda agreed.

"And it would probably make things even worse for Pete. I can only hope he has a better chance of a breakthrough if I'm not there."

She looked across the room at her daughter. "It breaks my heart to think that they could have known each other. Of course I would never have wished an accident on the man. But I did think something good might have come out of it."

"His choice," Miranda said briskly. "Some people will cut off their nose to save their face. Up to him to come around."

"I don't think he will, Miranda. He won't even come out for a ride with Pete to tour the Island. And apparently dinner at our house is out of the question. Walter Jakes is a closed book," she said sadly. "He shut himself up long ago, and he won't let anyone in. It's a mystery to me what he's locking in, what he's protecting. He seems almost like a man in hiding."

She petted Emily who, as if sensing her upset, had come over and put her nose in Ali's lap.

"Dogs have no problem loving," Miranda said. "But sometimes people do."

Later, when Ali and Nevra had left, Miranda tskked. "Well wouldn't that just frost your corns," she said to Emily. "I'd like to go over to the Taylors' and shake some sense into that man."

Miranda was very fond of the young Jakes family, newcomers who had already proved to be a wonderful addition to Island life. She thought that some afternoon soon, she might just go out to the Lodge to visit her friend Muriel Patterson, who she hadn't seen in awhile. And while she was there she might just ask Pat Taylor if there were any self-help books on family relationships in the common room. And suggest that she leave a couple in Walter Jakes' room.

$*$ $*$ $*$

Island Arson Investigation Remains a Mystery
Police Stumped – Residents Nervous

Halstead tossed the *Record* on the restaurant table.

"Having fun?" he snapped at Bob Denys.

Denys didn't bother opening the menu, they both knew it well. "Hot beef sandwich?"

"What's the soup?"

Split pea. The Riviera cook made tasty soups.

Denys crumbled crackers into his bowl, and took an appreciative spoonful. He had a rumpled face under a thatch of thick greying hair, and he wore a rumpled corduroy jacket. Like Halstead, he was enduring middle age with rueful bemusement.

"Phil Pruit's had carpal tunnel surgery. He won't be able to rejoin the Stormonts till December."

This was good news. Halstead and Denys curled for the Bonville Redpolls. Last year, the Stormonts had taken the Oldtimers trophy cup away from the Bonville team but now without Pruit, their top scorer, the Stormonts would be at a decided disadvantage. Still, Halstead wasn't going to let Denys go changing the subject just yet.

"I'm glad to see that fear-mongering gives you a good appetite," he said drily.

Denys objected. "I'm not creating the fear, I'm just reporting that it's there."

"Bull," Halstead said. "You probably heard about Alita Harrison's calls to the station. You should know that one old biddy's worries are hardly a terrified populace."

"I hear she's demanding night patrols of the village," Denys snickered.

Halstead shot him a baleful glance.

"O.K. Denys relented. "But have you got anything new to tell me? Anything to clear the Sorda lad? Any other suspects?"

Halstead stirred his coffee glumly. "You're right," he admitted. "I've got nada."

Denys shook his head. "Tough."

Halstead said earnestly, "But we don't need any innuendo in the press, thanks a lot. There's enough of that going on in the village. Gossip at the post office, at the Island Grill, around the dinner tables."

Denys looked serious too. "I just report the facts, Bud. You bring me some and that's what I'll write. And the facts are that an arsonist is a scary prospect."

"Now are we going to win that curling cup this year or not?"

16

CONSTRUCTION AREA – DRIVERS WILL EXPERIENCE DELAYS

Usually it was only a ten minute drive to the Bonville courthouse, but now there was a ten minute wait merely to get on the causeway. Pete didn't mind, he'd left in good enough time to get to the courthouse in time to attend Zak Sorda's arraignment. He leaned back in his seat and enjoyed the spectacle of the noisy gulls rising in the air currents over the Bay, no traffic tie-up for them. He waved sympathetically to Parsons the flagman, and the burly man in the bright yellow safety jacket came over to the cruiser.

"How's it going?" Pete asked.

Parsons shrugged. "No one's thrown anything at me yet this morning. We had some fun here yesterday though, with the courier guy."

"What happened?" Pete asked. He knew that the courier had to drive across the causeway several times a day to make deliveries on the Island. "He must be getting plenty ticked off."

The flagman laughed. "Sure is and then yesterday he took the bump too fast and almost wrecked his axle. He blocked the causeway for a half hour till we could get the tow-truck here. Jeez, he was mad."

This morning's trip was without incident, though and Pete arrived at the courthouse in plenty of time. The Sordas were getting out of their car as he arrived in the parking lot. Benny looked grim and Zak who had been out on bail for the past week, looked pale. He wore a suit and tie and had slicked back his dark hair.

Benny nodded an understandably terse greeting. Although Pete coached the younger Sorda's hockey team, this was not a friendly occasion. Pete was attending at the hearing as the arresting officer. The three men entered the courthouse, a cavernous century old building. Their footsteps echoed in the gloomy corridor and the massive mottled windows managed to dull even the bright outside sunlight. Construction had begun on a grand new courthouse that would service the surrounding three counties but the complex wasn't expected to open for business until the next spring. It was supposed to be roomier, lighter and more energy efficient.

A small knot of people filed through the door of courtroom three. Pete recognized the usual suspects, a motley crew of traffic offenders, probably a shoplifter or two, and a pale-faced fellow who was obviously suffering a serious hangover. Pete took a seat on a bench apart from the Sordas who were sitting with their lawyer. There were two other cases before Zak's. Traffic violations, as Pete had guessed. One DUI and an illegal parking job in a loading zone. The judge, who Pete hadn't seen before, looked like somebody's strict grandmother. He doubted that boded well for Zak. She suspended the DUI's license for six months and issued a fine to the illegal parker.

Next up was Zak. He stood rigidly while the court clerk read out the charges

"Causing a disturbance, unprovoked assault, resisting arrest."

The judge studied her documents for a moment, then looked at Zak and the lawyer. "How do you plead, Mr. Evans?" she asked, directing her question at the lawyer.

"Guilty, your honour."

Zak twitched and seemed about to say something but the lawyer quelled him with a steely look. Pete knew the judge could pronounce sentence that day or could reserve judgement till after a pre-sentencing report. The report could contain testaments to the defendant's good character, and future intentions. For instance, Zak's near-completion of his culinary courses could work in his favour.

The judge looked out at the courtroom. "Is the arresting officer here?" she asked.

Pete stood. "Yes your honour."

"The defendant is asking to be released on his father's recognizance. What is your opinion on whether he is a dangerous offender and a risk to society?"

Pete looked at Benny. "The defendant comes from a good family, your honour. They stand behind him."

The judge studied Zak for a long moment.

"I'm going to release you on your father's recognizance and a promise to appear when called for trial. Count your blessings and be grateful for your family's support."

"There will be conditions," she continued. "You must stay away from all members of the Parks family. You will abstain from the consumption of alcohol or drugs, and you will not travel out of the vicinity."

She rapped her gavel. "$5000 bail stands."

Pete knew that the eventual fine on the assault charge could be twice that amount. If Zak didn't get jail time. Then there were the lawyer's fees as well. Hefty sums that would eat into any funds that Benny and Maria had managed to put aside for retirement. He hoped fervently that Zak wouldn't let them down.

Outside in the parking lot, Benny waited to thank Pete.

Zak was less grateful. "What about those Parks brothers," he demanded. "When are you cops going to lay charges against them for messing up the chip truck?"

"It wasn't them," Benny said quietly. "The whole family were away in Hastings that weekend for a wedding. They didn't get back till later that day, just like you did."

"Yeah, so they say," Zak said trucently.

"It all checked out," Pete confirmed. "Everybody except Mrs. Parks, she stayed home to be near Cameron."

Zak made a disgusted sound. "Who did paint the truck then? I know that Kyle Parks was involved somehow. He probably got some friends to do the job for him."

Benny turned to face his son and said in a steely, not to be brooked, tone. "We'll have no more of that kind of talk. I know you're going through a very tough time right now, but so are your mother and I. We've no time for unhelpful, belligerent behaviour, not to mention sheer stupidity. If we're going to get through this, we need to be thinking clearly."

He paused to unclench his hands. "What I need from you, is a promise that there won't be any more foolish action. That we're going to go home, sit down like rational human beings and have a quiet supper with your mother and your brother. Later we'll talk about how we are going to proceed to prepare the pre-sentencing information, getting letters from the college administration head and so forth."

Zak seemed about to protest but wisely didn't.

"O.K. Dad," he nodded. He looked back at the court though and said bitterly, "But you might bettter have left me here in the jail. I'm not too welcome on the Island these days. The cops will just be dragging me back soon to try and nail me with the explosion."

Benny patted his shoulder. "Let's just take it one step at a time, son."

They headed for the car.

"How did it go?" Halstead asked.

"Benny gave him a good talking to – really read him the riot act," Pete said.

"Good," Halstead said. "We could use a little peace around here. I hope that gives Benny and Maria a little break too."

*　　*　　*

But the next morning, Jane rapped on the office door. "Benny Sorda to see you chief. I'll get coffee."

The chip truck owner looked tired, his face drawn. He thanked Jane politely when she brought in the cups but obviously had other matters on his mind. When she left, he leaned forward urgently.

"Thanks for seeing me Bud. I've come to ask you whether Zak is going to be able to leave for the start of term at the cookery school. Our lawyer tells us it could be months till the assault trial, maybe not till Christmas. So Maria and I have talked things over with Zak and we think it best to keep moving ahead. It will look better for Zak if he continues with his studies."

He paused. "Hopefully by then, the Parks will have had good news about Cameron and their anger will have settled down. With luck, the judge will just fine Zak and sentence him to some community service."

"I thought the judge said Zak couldn't leave the vicinity," Halstead said carefully.

"That's true," Benny agreed. "But the lawyer says we could get around that, ask for a special dispensation, as long as Zak reports in and comes home on weekends."

"Well then you're all right," Halstead said.

Benny looked down at his hands, clenched tightly in his lap. "The lawyer said I should talk to you first to find out what you were planning to do…. you know, about the gas explosion. Whether you would be 'contemplating an arrest', is the way he put it."

He looked up. "What do you say, Bud? It's been a couple of weeks now. A couple of weeks of torment for my family, I can tell you."

Halstead nodded his sympathy. "You know the situation Benny. We're doing all we can." He didn't add that unfortunately as time went on and the never-long list of possible suspects dwindled, Zak became the ever-more likely choice.

"I'll phone Carl Curzon the Crown Attorney," Halstead said. "Find out which way they're leaning. Whether they think they have a case."

He saw Benny out, then made the call.

After a few pleasantries, Curzon ticked off his points. "Sorda's lawyer is going to say the case is circumstantial. There's no fingerprints, no witnesses, a chancy plan that couldn't guarantee success."

Halstead played the devil's advocate. "Zak knew his way around the kitchen, he had knowledge of the gas system."

"The lawyer will say he's a good worker, a dedicated student."

"What about motive?" Halstead asked.

He could hear the shrug in Curzon's voice. "Pretty far-fetched. And even if Sorda was overcome with jealousy, the plan wouldn't guarantee to hurt his rival."

"If he was overcome with jealousy he might not have been thinking rationally." Halstead pointed out. "Then there's the previous charge of accidental arson and the recent assault charge. Doesn't exactly indicate a stable individual."

"They'll argue youthful hi-jinks re the barn-burning. For the assault they'll argue that he was understandably upset at the vandalism on his parents' truck. I wouldn't care to go before a jury with this Bud, not if we're going for reckless endangerment or gross negligence."

"Thanks, I hope the Sordas' lawyer is as good as you."

"You asked. Now tell me what *you* think?"

"I don't know. I like the family and I thought I liked Zak. I hope he didn't do it. But I know the other family too. And if Zak did do this, he has to be stopped. What's he going to do next time he's thwarted. Who else might he hurt?"

Curzon was silent for a moment. "Then keep on with it. And get me a witness."

"Sure, I'll do that. I must have one kicking around here somewhere in my filing cabinet."

"Ha ha. Just get on with it, and good luck."

Kyoto is a much more restful city than Tokyo. We have seen many beautiful temples and gardens.

Halstead wondered how restful a city of one and a half million people could be. Though compared to Tokyo's nine million folks, maybe so. And he'd heard that the Japanese cities had a low crime rate too, he wouldn't mind learning more about that. Especially as he was currently dealing with a stalled case himself, and warding off Islanders' concerns about harbouring a possible arsonist in their midst.

The picture attached to the e-mail showed Steph and Livy in a garden of flowers and trees that Halstead couldn't name. Mother and daughter were radiant and smiling at the camera.

We are going to try a Skype call on the weekend. Here are the instructions, I'm sure Jane will give you some help. You can do it!,

Miss you, Steph.

Halstead clicked escape. I miss you too,

In the staff room, Stutke was eating donuts. Homemade, another of Jane's many stellar attributes.

"I fed five growing children for years," she laughed. "I can't just turn off the baking instinct now."

"Haven't you got anything to do?" Halstead barked at Stutke, aware of his own unreasonableness, even as he spoke. Pete, who was eating donuts too, looked up in surprise. Halstead thumbed through a thin sheaf of memos. "We've got a hunting violation down at Snake Point and what about the chip truck vandals?"

"Why are you looking at me?" Jory bristled. "I didn't paint that truck."

"No but you might know who did," Halstead said. "You could be some use here, Stutke. You're supposed to be in touch with the youth element as they say."

Jory looked uncomfortable, as if he didn't quite know how to take that. Was the chief actually asking for his help?

"You hang out with these characters," Halstead said. "They might talk to you."

He knew that Jory was no bar fly, but his crowd liked to go to a Bonville bar from time to time. They also hunted and fished together in season. And he'd gone to Bonville High with most of them too.

"So what exactly do you want me to do?" Jory asked.

"Mingle my son," Halstead said, impatiently. "Ask questions, but discreetly."

Stutke looked dubious. "Yeah sure. Discreet."

Halstead made a shooing motion. "So get going, Stutke. You can take the donut with you."

Jane poked her head in the door. "Sorry to interrupt but there's a call for you, Pete. Pat Taylor from the home, she says it's urgent."

"Thanks," Pete said, excusing himself. *Now what?*

Pat did sound concerned. "Hi Pete, I don't mean to interfere. But a taxi has just arrived here, and the driver is looking for Walter Jakes. He said he got a call asking him to pick up a fare and take him to the train station in Bonville."

What the hell?

"I suppose it's not my business," Pat said apologetically, "but I did ask your father if you knew that he planned to leave. It didn't seem right when he hadn't given me any kind of notice. I asked who was going to take care of him up there in Ottawa, when he can still barely get around by himself, let alone make a meal or take a shower."

"Where is he now?" Pete asked tersely. "You didn't let him go!"

"I could hardly chain him up," Pat said, now sounding a bit indignant. "But the taxi is still there in the driveway. It's taking them quite a while to pack the walker and suitcase into the car."

"Do you know the driver?" Pete asked.

"Yes it's Jimmy Harris," Pat said.

"Then please get out there and tell him not to leave," Pete said.

"He's not going to like that," Pat warned. "He'll be expecting the fare to Bonville. Your father will be angry too."

"Tell Jimmy I'll pay him. Just don't let them take off, I'm on my way."

Pete grabbed his car keys and dashed out with a quick over-the-shoulder explanation to Jane. Ten minutes later, he arrived at the home and swung into the driveway on screeching tires, blocking the route out. He leapt out and ran over to the taxi. A quick glance showed Walter in the back seat.

Pete took a calming breath. "Hey Jimmy," he said leaning through the driver's window.

Harris, an over-heavy fellow who had taken up cab driving after a job injury on a construction site, looked teed off.

"Pat's already been out here telling me not to go. So what's next officer, are you going to get your pop out of the car or what? I'm losing money here."

"Hold your horses," Pete said. "You'll get your money."

He opened the back door and leaned in. "What the hell's going on Dad?" he started angrily. "You know you can't …."

Walter sat rigidly with arms crossed. "Leave me alone. You can't keep me here."

From the driver's seat, Jimmy tapped his hand in an irritated tattoo on the car dashboard. Pete changed tactics. "Don't make me haul you out in front of everybody, Dad. Come on back inside and we'll figure out a proper plan."

"I have a plan," Walter said obstinately. "I'm leaving."

"Sure you are," Pete said. "And what will you do when you get to the city. Check into some men's shelter downtown? Don't be ridiculous. Anyway I'm not going to let you go. So unless you plan to spend the night here in this cab, you'd best get out."

Harris turned around, rolling his eyes.

Pete ignored the driver and watched Walter decide. His father didn't look good at all. His skin was pale and clammy, he was breathing shallowly and his eyes seemed unfocussed. Pete wondered if he was missing some medication.

However, Walter did have the sense to bow to the circumstances. He sighed tiredly and nodded a reluctant agreement. Even then, Pete found it was an awkward business to manoeuvre him out of the taxi. Walter winced in pain at one point and Pete hoped the hip healing hadn't been set back.

Harris had the grace to help with the walker and suitcase.

"Figure out your time and I'll drop by the dispatch office and pay you tomorrow." Pete said.

Pat Taylor and a helper had been hovering on the porch through the episode and now the helper wheeled a silent Walter away down the corridor.

"Thanks for calling me," Pete said. "He doesn't look good at all."

"We're taking good care of him here," Pat said. "But if he's that unhappy …." Her voice trailed off.

Pete nodded. "Frankly, I don't know what else do with him right now. I'd be grateful if he could stay on here while I try to find something else."

Pat looked doubtful. "We'll do our best, but we can't chain him to his chair and I can't have him upsetting our other residents. It's been difficult enough coping with the explosion and all the changes in routine since."

"I'll talk to him," Pete promised.

In the room, he found Walter sitting slumped on the bed, punching frustratedly at the buttons on the TV remote. "Damn thing doesn't work."

Pete snatched the remote away. "It's the green button you want. You can turn it on after I leave. Now are you going to tell me what the hell that stunt was about?"

Walter lay back wearily against the bed pillows, his hand shading his eyes. His breathing was shallow. "I'm over twenty-one. I'm not a prisoner. I was going to leave."

"How were you going to do that?"

"On the train," he said. "I was going to take the train."

Pete could have pointed out the total unfeasibility of the plan. But Walter wasn't listening. "I've got to get back at my work," he insisted. "My clients, all that confidential tax information..... I should never have left."

Pete knelt before him. "Look Dad, it's not that bad. I told you that we can contact your clients and tell them about your accident. They'll understand."

Walter twisted away from the contact. "You don't know anything about it. Just leave me alone."

Pete rose to his feet. *O.K. old man, here's an approach you're not going to like.* "The doctor says you've been through a lot of trauma lately. He suggested you might see a psychiatrist, get some help with your anxieties.".

"That's ridiculous," Walter scowled. "I just need to get back to the city. I don't need to see any shrink."

"You think you're acting rationally?" Pete asked. Despite himself, his voice came out in bitter mockery.

"You think you're acting like a normal person? You want to get out of here, but you won't co-operate with the therapist to get your hip working again. You're rude to the staff who want to help you. Instead, you sit hunched in front of that damn news channel. Why not watch the baseball game like everyone else in Canada. Or a comedy for a change? Afraid you might crack a smile or a laugh?"

He plowed on, knowing it was pointless. "Or here's a thought, instead of following the criminal activities of some Ottawa politicians on *News From the Hill*, why not spend some time mending fences with your own family?"

"I'll watch what I want to watch," Walter said obdurately. "And I'm getting out of here when I want to leave."

"Unfortunately, you can't leave yet," Pete said. "Not in a wheelchair, trying to manage completely on your own. How would you get to your medical appointments for a start?"

"I thought you were going to find me some help up there."

"I've checked with all the agencies and there's a long waiting list for home help."

Walter hissed in frustration. "You're not trying hard enough."

Pete bit his tongue, wondering that it wasn't black and blue lately through all the workouts. "I put you on a couple of lists. Now you'll just have to wait, like everybody else."

Walter looked desperately about the garden, as if he was a wild animal seeking a way out. "I'll hire my own help," he said doggedly. "I'll advertise in the newspaper."

Apparently he found the willing and voluntary assistance of his own family much too high a cost.

"I'll get you out of here," Pete said through gritted teeth. *And there's a promise that I'll keep.*

"But in the meantime, please behave yourself. The Taylors are getting pretty fed up with you and your next stop will be my house. We both know how you'd feel about that."

*   *   *

"Maybe he *should* go," Ali said. "He seems so anxious and upset. And he's certainly not warming up to me!"

"The doctor says not yet." But he too, was beginning to wonder whether there was any point in keeping Walter on the Island. Whether it was doing him any good. It was a relief to spend some pleasant time with his daughter. Story-time and bed, the comforts of childhood. Apparently now with a new listener, the big orange cat.

"Kedi's purring because he likes stories too," Nevra chuckled.

"Yes well he doesn't need a pillow," Pete said, scooping it up for himself.

They were working their way through a sumptuous collection of the Beatrix Potter books, a present from Grandma Nuran,

Ali's mother. Nuran, a noted sociologist and author, traveled extensively in search of material for her books on women's lives in other cultures. Although Nuran hadn't been present through most of Ali's growing-up years and in fact had disapproved of her marrying at all, Nevra's arrival had brought about a *raprochement*. Now, instead of the occasional sparsely-worded e-mails of the past, there were warm telephone calls and a stream of parcels for her granddaughter.

Tonight's volume was *The Tale of Johnny Townmouse* and his country cousin Timmy Willie. The story began when the country mouse fell into a basket of vegetables slated to be delivered in the town. Nevra listened wide-eyed while Pete read of Timmy's scary adventures there with traffic and people. His mouse cousin only wanted to show him wonderful treats but Timmy was terrified by the town noise and bustle and begged to go home. Then the story was turned about and poor Johnny Townmouse was frightened of country terrors, such as big cows and noisy lawnmowers. In the end, each mouse decided he was happier at home.

Pete had grown up in the city and found a home in the country. Tucking Nevra into bed after the story, he wondered what life his little daughter would choose.

18

Across the Island from the Jakes' home, a bonfire crackled merrily on the beach at the bottom of the Stutke farm. The fire pit, a ring of strategically placed stones, had been used countless times in this and other summers. The setting for many a party, as the hunks of blackened driftwood scattered about the sand, could attest. As Jory grew up, the drinks might have changed from freshie to beer, but the friends had stayed the same. They had travelled together first through Middle Island primary school, and then over the causeway on the yellow school bus to the high school in Bonville.

Tonight, the friends were gathered at what was likely the last bonfire of the summer. It was rarer now, to be all together. People were going off to university or college, some to travel in countries on the other side of the world. They'd wolfed down the burgers and potato chips, washed that down with brewskies and were now toasting marshmallows on sticks. As the sinking sun streaked the lake water with bands of purple and orange, a mood of nostalgia settled over the scene.

A chorus of 'We're going to miss you guys', 'Be sure to send lots of pics on Facebook,' "It's not that long till Christmas' rang out over the marshmallows.

Then a girl said, "It's weird here without Cameron or Zak."

Uncomfortable silence. A marshmallow oozed off a stick and fell hissing into the fire.

"Geez," said one of the guys. "Why'd you have to bring that up? What a downer."

"Sooorry," she said. "Anyway, it *is* a downer. Are we just supposed to forget about them, as if they don't exist?"

"Well not Cameron of course," the guy said. "But I wouldn't mind if Zak Sorda just disappeared."

"I wish he'd disappeared before he'd blown up that kitchen and put Cam in the hospital," said a fellow called Curtis.

"I wish he had to face what Cameron does," said Jory's girl friend Gayle. "See how he'd like having a bomb blow up in his face."

"Hey!" Jory roused himself from peaceful contemplation of the fire and thoughts of reaching into the cooler for another beer. "Nobody's been arrested for the explosion yet and you guys have already got Zak tried and sentenced."

"You're the cop," challenged Curtis. "Get to it. Sorda shouldn't be wandering around free as a bird. Not when Cameron is in the hospital."

There were nods and assent from around the fire.

Jory looked at his girlfriend Gayle, wrapped snugly in his jacket. She looked torn. *What the hell?* He felt betrayed.

Curtis who had had one too many brews, was now standing. Or weaving.

"So what is it, are you afraid of Sorda? He's not that tough."

Jory stood up too. "Oh yeah, how tough are you? Tough enough to mess up Benny Sorda's chip truck? That was a real class act. And I've got a pretty good idea who helped you."

He looked over at Brad Jackson, the pair usually hung out together.

"F off," Curtis sneered. "You got no proof. Anyway, what's the diff? So some foreigners get their truck decorated. Maybe they'll get the point and leave."

"Zak Sorda was born in Bonville General, just like you and me," Jory said. "That's how foreign he is."

Stumped for an answer, Curtis tossed the beer bottle at Jory. It fell short and bounced harmlessly on the sand.

Jory took a step forward. "I'm off duty tonight. But that wouldn't stop me from taking somebody in for threatening an officer. Why don't you just sit down before you fall down."

Curtis' girlfriend dragged him back to the blanket. The bonfire flickered on merrily for a bit, but the mood of the group had soured and people started to pack up.

Jory checked that all carloads would have a designated driver. This won him no points either, he acknowledged ruefully. There was definitely a downside to being a police officer in the place where you grew up. If this kept up, he'd soon be a total outcast and might as well not bother coming home at all.

Later after the other kids had left, Jory and Gayle sat by themselves on a blanket looking out at the strip of moonlight on the water. Gayle shivered despite the warmth of the night. Jory wrapped his jacket more tightly about her shoulders, leaving his arm there too.

"What a mess," she said, leaning back against his chest. "Cameron in hospital, Zak out on bail. Who would have thought things could end up like this?"

She twisted to face him. "And how could you defend Zak?"

"I'm a police officer, remember," he said, Pete Jakes' words echoing in his thoughts. "And even if Zak is a suspect, he's innocent till proven guilty. Everybody gets the same rights."

She made a face that he could see even in the dusk.

"What about Cam's rights?" she asked.

He grimaced. "I'm just doing my job."

"It's more than that. You talk as if Zak didn't do it. That somebody else did."

"At least I admit that it's a possibility. You've known Zak forever too, Gayle. Don't we owe him that much?"

She stood up and tossed a handful of sand into the embers in the pit. "Then prove it Mr. Policeman. Or the rest of us are never going to believe it."

They walked up to the house, then he drove her home through ten minutes of stony silence. She kissed him goodnight, but it was just a measly peck.

He drove off, squealing gravel.

She was right though. If not Zak, then who? He'd better come up with something. Maybe he'd go back to the Taylors and have a look around. Pete Jakes was a good guy and smart but he couldn't talk to Island folk like a boy who'd been raised here.

Still, it was a lonely drive home along the familiar moon-white road. This business of being a cop could be tough. He remembered the books he'd read as a little kid. The cats and dogs and other animals in their various uniforms. Doctor, fireman, mailman and so on. He'd always wanted to be the policeman. In the stories, policemen seemed always to be bravely rescuing or defending the other animals. They played an important part in the life of the village.

Then in his teens, he'd watched all those movies with the car chases. The life of a policeman looked exciting, adventurous, even dangerous. What guy wouldn't like a taste of that? The gun wasn't such a big deal to him. He was a country boy, his dad and brothers had been taking him out to hunt since he was twelve. But that wasn't the same as going down some city alleyway and having another guy shooting back at you. Of course that wasn't too likely to happen here on Midde Island.

So, what else was there. Prestige? Being a big shot? People having to do what you said. He'd met some guys like that in training, real bullies. No he didn't think he was like that. Though he didn't mind the respect the uniform sometimes brought. But only sometimes – because other times like this, friends seemed to see him as a traitor.

Training had been a revelation. He'd learned there was a lot more to the job, all kinds of different things you could do eventually. And he'd learned of the responsibiity involved in the job.

One thing he hadn't learned yet though, was how you knew if someone was telling the truth.

He wondered if he ever would.

19

Halstead had managed to navigate the on-screen Skype instructions, but he didn't know if he liked the experience or not. At first it was great to actually *see* Steph. But then it just seemed to point out how much he was missing the real woman. And he couldn't even pretend that she wasn't having a good time – she looked so great. Her dark hair with that dazzling silver streak. A red sweater. Her wonderful 'back at ya' smile.

"Hi darlin'" she greeted him so happily that as usual, he decided he did like Skype after all.

"Hi," he said, with a wealth of feeling.

"You sound tired," she said.

"It's a worrisome time here." He told her of his chat with Carl Kurnek about Zak.

"So it's looking bad for him."

"It's bad either way for the Sordas," he said. "If Zak would just fess up, he might be able to get off with a gross negligence charge."

"But then he'd never get work in a kitchen again," Steph said indignantly. "It would be a terrible blot on his record, his career would be over before he really got started. And what if he's innocent! Surely the Taylors will vouch for his work at the home."

"I'm not so sure, Steph. There's Zak's past record, it's not exactly comforting, even for his friends. You're lucky to be away right now, doubt and mistrust are hanging like a black cloud over the Island. People are choosing sides, not talking to each other. It's not pleasant."

"And how are things going with Cameron Parks?"

"Still waiting to hear what the specialist will say."

They talked of the day's sightseeing, how Livy was doing and her new friend, a young Japanese man named Haruto who had been a co-worker on the school project.

"But enough about us," she said. "How are you? How is it going with Pete's dad? Have you met him yet?"

Halstead looked towards the lake where dawn was just beginning to pinken the water. Six a.m. to catch Steph at 2 p.m. "Nobody's met him. According to Pete, the man just wants to get the hell out of here, as quickly as possible."

She whistled. "He won't even crack for Ali and Nevra?"

"He hasn't even met them yet. Pete doesn't want to risk getting Nevra's feelings badly hurt."

"Poor Pete!"

"It's weighing heavily on him, I can tell you."

"And you," she said sympathetically. She thought for a moment. "I've got an idea."

He listened. "That might work," he agreed. "I'll run it by Pete."

She blew him a kiss. "In the meantime, go fishing. That always makes you feel better."

"I know what would make me feel better," he said. "But I guess fishing will have to do for now."

*   *   *

Jakes shook his head. "It's a nice offer, chief. But I can't let you take Walter out to the Retreat. I wouldn't inflict him on anybody. Besides, what would Steph think?"

"It was her idea," Halstead said. "He can stay in one of the cabins. Steph's away for another couple of weeks and there's no one out there but me. I should have thought of it sooner."

Pete didn't look convinced. "You don't know the man, what he's like."

"You said he isn't happy at the Taylors. That he doesn't like sharing a room."

Pete nodded, thinking. "True. His roomate is pretty quiet but I'm sure he'd rather have his privacy. And he's not going to get his own room back for awhile."

He slumped back in his chair. "What a disaster. He doesn't like me, he doesn't like being in the home, he isn't interested in being a grandfather." He sighed, "So you can see, turns out it wasn't exactly a brilliant idea to bring him here."

Halstead shook his head. "That's a shame. How he can resist knowing your two lovely ladies, beats me. He's getting around better now, you say?"

Pete nodded. "He'll be graduating to a cane soon."

"O.K. then," Halstead said decisively. "The Retreat it is. He'll have all the privacy he wants."

"I don't think he could manage," Pete said practically. "You're away all day working."

"You can hire Colleen to make his lunch and help out." Halstead referred to the woman who helped Steph when there were guests at the Retreat. "She'll be glad of the work."

Pete still looked doubtful. "I'd feel bad about landing my father on you. Dealing with him is no picnic."

"I can handle it," Halstead assured. "There's TV in the cabins for him to watch. And you never know, maybe he'll get bored enough to play some cards. Does he play rummy?"

"I wouldn't know," Pete said ruefully. But he liked Halstead's idea of moving Walter out of the Lodge. Though Pat Taylor had always been polite, she would probably welcome the change as well. And who knew, maybe the move would cheer Walter up a bit too. Miracles could happen.

"O.K. what the hell," he said. "I'll run it by him. Nothing ventured ...."

*　　*　　*

Two days later, after work, Pete turned into the Retreat driveway and parked beside Stephanie's flower-bedecked sign. "Here we are," he announced. He enjoyed seeing Walter's tight-lipped reaction to the sign's wording. "Find Us. Find Yourself. Women's Wellness Retreat." But Walter kept quiet, only his head shake implying that this unpleasant chapter in his life just kept getting worse.

"It's a great place," Pete enthused, being deliberately cheerful. "You'll be in your own cabin out back. No roomate. Wait till you see it."

He fetched the walker out of the back of the SUV and went around to the passenger side to help Walter out. Walter accepted with his usual bad grace. He was moving less stiffly, Pete noticed. At least his physical ability was improving, too bad his social skills weren't keeping pace.

The chief, on the watch for their arrival, opened the front door to greet them. They entered the main room of the lodge, lined with varnished logs and a vaulted ceiling over a large fireplace. A south facing wall of windows fronted on the lake, on this evening daubed with dazzling orange and red brush strokes under the setting sun.

"Coffee?" Halstead offered. "I've just finished my supper."

Pete looked at Walter, and said hastily. "No I think if you don't mind, we'll just get settled first."

"Sure." Halstead led the way along a path lined by solar lights, to a clutch of four smallish cabins. He opened the door to number one, revealing a compact sitting room/kitchen, cosily curtained in floral prints. The window overlooked the lake, which added to the pleasing effect of being in a boat.

"Bedroom in there," Halstead indicated where Pete could unload the luggage. He emerged, saying "This is pretty nice, eh Dad?"

He felt as if he was encouraging a four year old to be polite and say thanks to grandma for a present of new socks. At least Walter grunted something that could have been thanks, in Halstead's direction. Halstead paid no notice, blandly pointing out necessary details of light switches, coffee pot instructions, and the television remote. Walter seemed most interested in that and even sat down and tried it out twice. Pete could see he quickly found the news channel. Then he left the set on mute, though still staring at the screen.

Pete glanced at the chief and shrugged. "O.K. dad, I guess we'll go now," he said.

Walter looked up. "Where's the key?"

Halstead looked surprised. "There might be a key in the house, nobody's ever used it. But I'll look for it."

He flipped the lock switch, "You can lock yourself in if you want. But you should open up in the morning, so that Colleen can get in here to clean."

"I'll open the door if she knocks," Walter said.

And that seemed to be that. With no invitation to stick around, they left.

"You're sure he wouldn't rather be in the house?" Halstead asked once outside. "Livy's room is available."

They had already discussed this. The stairs would have been a difficulty.

"He'll be O.K.," Pete said. "He'd rather be on his own."

Dusk was settling over the landscape, striping the sky with wide bands of mauve and pink. Despite his assurances, Pete looked uneasily back at the four cabins that now seemed to be huddling under the dark fir trees. Walter's window was the only light.

He shook off the feeling. The solar path lights were coming on, the chief was living only forty feet away. Even if Walter hadn't had a cell phone, the chief would likely hear his shout.

"He'll be fine," he said again. "Now how about that coffee?"

*   *   *

Pete arrived home, stretching tiredly before getting out of the car. Dealing with his father made him more tired than a full week's work. The lights were still on in Miranda's house across the road. Their neighbour was a self-professed night owl.

"Hi fella," he said to the big cat who was stretched out contentedly on a blanket in the laundry basket. Nevra had given him one of her toy bunnies for company. He called upstairs to Ali and said he'd be coming soon. Yawning as he took off his jacket, he felt something in the pocket.

Walter's address book. It had fallen out of a bag during the hasty move from the Lodge and Pete picked it up. Then he'd forgotten to leave it in the cabin. He would drop it off on his next visit but first he would jot down Jay Gupta's number and that of the insurance agent which he was bound to need again. He began to thumb idly through the pages. The entries were scant, which didn't surprise him. Walter was hardly likely to be part of some big social whirl. Still, aside from the emergency numbers there were a few names. Friends? Pete doubted it. More likely the names of clients.

There seemed to be about a dozen, whether they were all current he couldn't tell. One business name, GL Solar Industries. Likely a small company, which would make sense. Any large companies would have their own accountancy department, and wouldn't be farming the work out.

The few individual names were distributed throughout the notebook. A couple were underlined. One name, LaRiviere, rang a bell. A name Pete had heard recently. But he was too tired to think right now. Maybe it would come to him in the morning and he could check it out on the Net, humanity's handy new universal memory.

Pete nodded at the laptop screen. Yes, he'd been right. No wonder the name had stuck in his mind. It had only been the headliner on every television and newspaper story for the past week.

CABINET MINISTER'S AIDE IMPLICATED
IN CONTRACT SCANDAL

Andre Lariviere, assistant to the Prime Minister's Office, is to testify at an upcoming ethics committee hearing.

Mr. Lariviere, head of the Department of Procurement has been summoned to answer questions related to improprieties in the awarding of construction contracts over the past two years.

As of press time, Mr. Lariviere has refused to take an interview with the Citizen.

So? He asked himself. Maybe it wasn't that common a name, but there were likely dozens in the city phone book. He continued reading the story.

Sandra Arum, a researcher for the News from the Hill television program, says she is pleased with the news. Arum has been pursuing the subject for several months now and her programs have led to the public demand for the ethics hearing.

There that bell rang again.

Pete took the address book out of his pocket. Yes the Arum name was there too, he'd assumed the woman was just another client. But the fact that the two names were in the same address book was beyond coincidence. The LaRiviere listed in Walter's handwriting had to be the same man who was involved in the growing government financial scandal.

But what connection could Walter Jakes have with a cabinet minister's aide in the federal government? Because Walter was certainly interested in the story. Only last night he'd been watching the television coverage in the cabin. Now that Pete thought about it, that was how he usually saw his parent these days. Hunched before the television set, riveted to the news channel. Pete had figured that was just Walter's way of ignoring his son or anybody else who wanted to talk to him.

But was there more to it? Did Walter have a personal interest in the affair, something beyond a mere keen interest in the nation's business? He seemed almost obsessed with the story. Pete tried to remember exactly what the investigation was about. He'd had so much on his mind lately, and like many jaundiced Canadians who had heard far too many similar stories in recent years, he hadn't paid much attention. Every few years there seemed to be another scandal. One party would get voted out and another voted in, promising transparency and honest government. Then the process would begin all over again.

The common thread running through all these scandals was usually money and the investigations were usually prompted by some review of financial records. Such as tax returns! That could be the connection. Maybe Walter had been contacted by the committee regarding tax information about one of his clients.

Or did Walter know something even more pertinent to the investigation -- had he possibly discovered some illegitimate activity involving a client. And now he wondered morally what to do about it?

That would certainly explain his recent severe anxiety attacks. Having retired after forty years as a law-abiding accountant, he would hardly want to cap his career with possible criminal charges. Perhaps he was wondering how to get the information to this Ms. Arum without involving himself.

Pete stared at the screen, mulling over what this could mean, till Jane's voice, calling from her desk, broke into his thoughts.

"Hey handsome," she said merrily. "I thought it was your turn to make the coffee."

He hastily switched the screen back to the weather site. He wasn't sharing these disturbing thoughts with anyone yet. He needed to speak to Walter.

* * *

But nothing was ever easy with Walter Jakes, he was thinking ruefully an hour later. He had driven out to the Retreat under the excuse of delivering some groceries for Walter's lunch. After his customary apathetic greeting, Jakes senior had turned back to the television. Though it was only the sports report, for a change.

Pete figured there was no point in beating around the bush. Walter Jakes wasn't big on small talk. He took the address book out of his pocket and waved it before the screen.

Walter whipped his head around. "Where did you get that?" he demanded.

Pete explained. "I found it in my pocket when I got home from helping you move."

Walter stuck his hand out. "That's my book. Give it to me."

"Not so fast," Pete said, opening the book to a page. "There are some interesting names in here. This Mr. Lariviere for instance, he's in the news a lot lately, it seems he's about to be investigated by a federal committee. A friend of yours? And this Ms. Arum, the television investigator on *News From the Hill*, you've got her number here too. The thing is, do you have something to tell that committee, something about one of your clients?"

Walter made a grab for the book but Pete held on to it.

"I'm a police officer, " Pete said. "And not dumb. Besides, the way you've been behaving since you came here, it doesn t take a lot of brains to figure you have something pressing on your mind."

Walter snorted. "If you were a proper policeman you'd return a man's property, not nose into his affairs."

Pete didn't bother pointing out that most police work was exactly the opposite.

Walter muted the sound on the set and made his longest speech since he had arrived on the Island. "I never knew you had such an imagination. I've been a bit anxious because I've lived through an explosion. Which would never have happened by the way, if you'd left me in Ottawa. End of story."

Pete felt the familiar tide of frustration rising up in his chest. He fought it back, sat down and said as mildly as he could, "O.K. as long as you realize that you can ask me if you ever do want to talk about anything or need any help."

Walter scowled. "There's nothing to help with. And I'd hardly be asking *you*. We've gone our separate ways, so let's not pretend to friendship now."

I could have used some friendship back then. Pete thought. *But you never asked for it and I was afraid to offer it.*

"Ah to hell you with you," he said disgustedly. "Handle your own problems. The sooner you're out of here, the better."

"I can't wait," Walter called after him. "Just call me a cab."

But Pete knew that the mystery of the notebook would nag at him. Like a burr under his collar.

*   *   *

Ali hopped off her bicycle and dropped it to the grass. She picked up her thermos and waved back to Pete, before scrambling down the short slope to the pebbled beach. The water was crystal clear on this side of the island, cold for swimming even on a hot summer day, but the long curved stretch of water-smoothed rocks was one of their favourite walks. It was a treat today too, to be on their own while Nevra spent the afternoon pressing autumn leaves with Miranda. Much as Ali loved her daughter, she did occasionally yearn for some time alone with Pete.

It was one of those hazy, warm September days that, like the red berries of the bittersweet, seemed to mix summer memories with a sense of the coming winter. There was nostalgia even in the beauty. Already the hawks were beginning to gather - kettles of hawks they were called – to catch the thermals and fly south for the winter. But today Ali was resolutely enjoying the summer side of the coin. The lake seemed to stretch on forever, broken only by the bump of South Island that mirage-like, appeared to float magically above the surface of the water.

She arrived at the shore and spread her arms wide in sheer joy to encompass the wide vista of sky meeting water. "And we have it all to ourselves!" she marvelled anew. "Who needs the Mediterranean crowds?"

She spun around, laughing, her long dark hair flying. A vision herself, lithe and leggy in jeans and tank top, a red sweater tied loosely about her waist. Then she frowned, her honey-skinned forehead wrinkling. She didn't seem to be having her customary effect on her husband. The usual frank adoration.

She certainly was adoring, looking at him. He hadn't lost a bit of his army buffness. True, they were in their early thirties and were parents of a four-year old but she thought that only added to his attraction.

She grabbed up his hand, "We could be a photo in one of those glossy holiday magazines," she laughed, pulling him into a mock pose against the cliff.

He hugged her absently, his gaze abstracted as he looked out over the water.

He had been that way ever since coming back from the Retreat yesterday. morning. Ultra-quiet, almost guarded in his responses. Today he wasn't using his binoculars either, even his beloved birds couldn't get his attention.

"A nickle for your thoughts," she teased. Thoughts cost more now, since the penny had been discontinued.

"Sorry," he said. "There's just a lot going on right now. The Lodge investigation. The ATV headache."

He started up the path. "We should start back."

She looked regretfully back at the waves, at the sun on the rocks. What was the rush?

That evening Ali worked at the kitchen table, cutting out paper ducks for a school art project. Pete sat with Kedi in the living room, watching *News from the Hill*. The night's programming was once again a discussion about the growing scandal in the government. The opposition parties had been calling for an investigative hearing and it seemed to be finally happening.

Big whoop Ali thought, same old, same old.

But Pete seemed to be interested and that was good. Maybe it would divert his thoughts briefly from his troubles with Walter.

She would make some cocoa.

21

On the concrete ledge, hundreds of feet above the city pavements, the female falcon stirred. The afternoon was waning early, soon it would be hunting time. It was wet beyond the ledge, and far below the rain shimmered in the glow of amber streetlights that ran for miles in all directions.

The low hum of traffic meant nothing to her.

Unike the high wild places where her ancestors hunted, these new concrete cliffs lit up every evening with hundreds of squares of light. But that meant nothing to her either, she had grown used to the phenomenon of light at night. This was her world, where she lived. She had adapted.

Her prey had adapted too, but not so successfully. The bats fluttered helplessly, blinded by the strange, lit night. Birds were tired and disoriented. She set off, just coasting for now. The building balconies were prime targets for surprising foolish, strutting pigeons.

She heard alarms ringing from one building, a shrill cacaphony of sound, shreiking in the damp air. She veered away. There were plenty of other buildings, plenty of other pigeons.

![22](chapter number 22)

Seven p.m. Though only early September, the evenings were getting shorter. It had been raining lightly for the last hour of the drive and the grey Ottawa streets were glistening with long streaks of car lights. Pete wasn't looking forward to staying at the apartment but he could hardly justify the expense of a hotel.

He tried to push away other thoughts. He wasn't used to not confiding in Ali. Had simply told her that he was going to the city to see if he could hurry up the search for some home help for Walter. She was already hurt and puzzled enough about his father, without adding more wild surmises.

"Steph will be coming home soon," he'd said, "and she doesn't need to find Walter sitting around like a miserable toad at her reunion with the Chief."

"But he hasn't even met Nevra yet."

He shook his head. "That's just not going to work out, honey. We gave it a good shot. We're done."

Reluctantly she'd agreed. And that made him feel guilty too, because that was only part of the reason why he had come to the city. That burr under his collar wasn't going away. He couldn't get the names from the notebook out of his mind. He needed to find out exactly what kind of mess Walter might have stumbed into. And that meant he needed to talk to Sandra Arum, the television journalist and find out if there was anything to his suspicions.

He drove into the apartment parking lot and fetched his bag from the back seat. But he slowed his steps as he opened the door to the lit-up building lobby, which was crowded with at least a dozen agitated people, milling around and all talking at once. He spotted Jay Gupta and Mrs. Verga among them, and others who were probably residents of the building as well. The group were surrounding a pair of police officers, who seemed to be trying to calm them down.

The entire crowd turned at his entrance. Gupta and Mrs. Verga began to talk at once, hailing him as an old friend.

"Officer Jakes….so glad you're here ….robbery….police." The words came flying at him. Mrs. Verga grabbed his arm and pulled him towards the Ottawa officers.

He managed to talk above her and ask, "What's going on here?"

"And you are?" one of the officers asked.

"His father lives here," Mrs. Verga added helpfully.

Wait a second, Pete thought, looking more closely at the other policeman *I know this guy.*

"Hey Braden," he said. "You still collecting icing penalties at the rink?"

Braden turned to him with a surprised grin. "Jakes! How ya doing?"

And yes, it *was* Matt. He was heavier set now, and those shoulders that had pushed his way through the Lynx's defence, were a little broader. But the same large friendly features, under a crop of thick sandy hair. The two clapped shoulders, would have embraced, but for their wondering audience.

"Look after things here for a minute, Lorne," Matt said to the other officer, "I'm going to have a quick catch-up with my buddy."

He waved to the clutch of tenants. "Back in a minute, folks." Then led Pete over to the window.

"*Officer* Jakes?" he echoed Mrs. Verga. "So you're a cop too."

Pete explained briefly.

"No kidding!" Braden seemed delighted. "We'll have to get a beer later and catch up on news." He looked over his shoulder. "Better get back to Lorne though, and figure this situation out." He paused. "That woman said your Dad lives here?"

Pete nodded. "What's happened? Why are you fellas here?"

"Some kind of a break-in to the building," Braden explained. "If we can ever settle this bunch down and get a straight story out of them, we might find out the details. You seem to know some of these people. Maybe you can help."

Pete pointed. "Gupta the manager is your best bet."

The hubbub rose again as they approached the group. Matt spread his hands quellingly.

"O.K. folks, Mr. Gupta is up first. Give us some quiet please."

Jay said that about five o'clock that evening, the fire alarms had sounded. He seemed to be enjoying the excitement. Pete guessed the upset made a welcome change from dealing with plumbers and waste disposal problems.

"Could you pinpoint the initiating alarm?" Braden asked.

"It was coming from the sixth floor hallway," Jay said eagerly. "We have an emergency procedure and everyone followed it. The residents headed for their nearest stairway and assembled here, in the main lobby."

Walter's apartment was on the sixth floor. "And was there a fire?" Pete interrupted.

Jay shrugged. "Doesn't seem to be, and the alarm stopped. But there was definitely something going on. The Coopers who live on the fourth floor saw someone running down the stairs ahead of them. He was faster than them though and was gone by the time they reached the bottom."

Braden looked around the group. "Anybody else see a stranger in the building? On the lobby screen?"

A man nodded. "We got buzzed shortly before the alarm. But we weren't expecting anyone, so we ignored it. Figured it was one of those pizza delivery fellows, they always get the apartment numbers wrong."

Another man nodded. "We got buzzed too."

"Did either of you check the lobby screen?"

Two head shakes. No.

Braden frowned and addressed the entire group. "So did any of you actually order a pizza tonight? Have one delivered? Let the guy in?"

Head shakes all round.

"Somebody might have left the door ajar," suggested a woman. She looked fretfully about her. "Some people are terribly careless. Or if they're expecting a delivery."

"O.K." Braden said. "My partner here, Officer Price, will accompany you to check out your apartments. I'm going with Mr. Gupta here to look at the lobby security video."

He turned to Pete and raised his brows. *Want to come?*

They followed Gupta to his windowless little office. Once again Pete found himself watching the video footage of the stairway where Walter had fallen. Like déjà vu. Only not quite, as a dark shape appeared on the screen and Braden said quickly, "There he is. Stop the video."

But there actually wasn't much to see. The man, or likely a man, moved quickly and seemed experienced in dealing with security cameras. The figure wore dark clothing and kept an arm over his face.

"No pizza," Braden observed.

Jay laughed, "Maybe he ate it on the way down." The figure disappeared, presumably out the side door to the garbage bin area at the back of the building.

"So not a lot of help there," Braden said. "Not that I was expecting much. These pros aren't going to smile and pose for the camera. I'm surprised that this guy even let himself get spotted."

The entrance footage was more daunting, showing various tenants and presumably visitors, entering the building over the past twenty-four hours.

"This could be tough," Braden acknowledged. "Even if we look over only the past four hours, we'll have to ask all the tenants to view the video and and identify their visitors."

"Best have a movie night in the lobby and invite them all," Pete said. "You can bring the popcorn. That way they can all watch it at once."

Braden shook his head. "You heard the lady back there, people get careless and leave the door open. Or this guy will have just waited for his chance, then walked in behind somebody else. Wearing a ballcap no doubt, since he's so security conscious."

Gupta was beginning to look a little worried. "I guess I'm going to have to write an incident report for the company. I've never had an attempted robbery before."

Braden nodded at the screen. "You've been lucky, then. Lately, there's been a rash of robberies in the area."

"In apartment buildings?" Pete asked. "Seems risky. Isn't there always a danger of being spotted by a neighbour?"

Braden smiled tolerantly. "You've forgotten what life's like here in the big city, country boy. People in apartment buildings don't have neighbours. They might as well live on separate planets. There's people coming and going through the doors and on the elevators all the time. Delivery people too, like Mr. Gupta says. Thieves actually like the opportunities afforded by apartment buildings, sometimes they even live in the buildings themselves. Then they can just cruise the hallways and try the doors."

"You've looked into this," Pete said.

"Daily research on the job," Braden said cheerfully. "You wouldn't believe how many bicycles are stolen in any year from lower floor balconies. And of course nowadays there's the positive bonanza of small electronics. The thieves can just go from unit to unit and fill a bag. Cell phones, I pads and pods, video games, even laptops. And gaining entrance is pitifully easy. They'll go door-to-door, posing as a marketing surveyor or a building maintenance worker. Tenants are incredibly trusting, they don't even bother checking with the landlord."

Officer Price was waiting in the lobby with his report.

"It doesn't look as if he had time to do much here. There's some damage on the sixth floor where he tried to jimmy a door. Then when he was seen, he pulled the fire alarm to cover his exit."

"What apartment number was that?" Pete asked.

Price consulted his notes. "604."

"Not your dad's place?" Braden asked.

Pete nodded.

"The lock is pretty much busted up," Price said. "Usually they just look for an unlocked door. At least the guy didn't get in."

"That's good," Pete said. "Dad wouldn't need that, he's already in pretty shaky shape."

He told Braden about the explosion.

Braden clucked his tongue. "Sounds like Walter is having quite a run of bad luck lately."

Too much bad luck. Pete thought. That burr in his mind had just grown into an entire patch of the scratchy plants. He might have some questions of his own about this robbery attempt. But he wasn't about to talk to Matt about it. Not yet anyway.

Helen Verga, clutching Pepper, had been hovering anxiously nearby.

"We were out for a walk," she said breathlessly, hand to her heart. "To think he would have tried my door next! I've been telling Jay I can't bear to stay here tonight. It's been too much of a shock. I'm going to stay with my sister."

Jay watched her leave, then said to Pete. "I told her she would be perfectly safe, there's nothing wrong with her lock. I'll have a locksmith come to fix your door as soon as possible, " he assured. "If you want to stay though, maybe you could push something heavy against the door. Just for the night."

"I'll figure something out," Pete said drily.

23

An hour later at a downtown sports bar, Pete and Matt Braden chinked glasses over a platter of buffalo wings.

"Here's to old times," Matt toasted.

The two, centre and forward, had led their school hockey team to take a city championship in their senior years. But they hadn't kept up, since Pete went into the army and left the group behind.

"Mike King was asking about you earlier this summer," Matt said. "We had a bit of a reunion at my parents' cottage north of the city. A bunch of the guys came."

He hesitated, "I didn't know what to tell them. Didn't want to look up your old man to find out where you were."

Tacit acknowledgement that Pete's friends had never been welcome at his father's house. The old man had not been the welcoming sort.

"So you had enough of the forces?" Braden said.

Pete explained in more detail about his injury in a road-side bombing, and how he'd come to take the job on the Middle Island police force.

"No kidding," Matt chuckled, "That's rich. After all your travelling, you end up only a hundred miles from home."

"What are the rest of the guys up to?" Pete asked.

Braden mentioned familiar names. Several of their team mates had stayed in sports or sports-related jobs. One went into the family business of selling equipment. Another was a part owner in an exercise club. Most were married, most had children. Lucky Mike King was now managing an A level team in Chicago.

Pete remembered his conversation with Jory Stutke about hierarchy in groups. Mike King had definitely been the leader in their team, a dazzling forward and top scorer. A great natural athlete and good-looking like Zak Sorda. Pete and Matt had been stalwart lieutenants and good, reliable players. A couple of the other fellows had moved away and like Pete, had not kept up.

Braden shook his head, "Now we're all dads. Life moves along, doesn't it?"

They showed photos on their smart phones. Matt's pictures were of an attractive blonde woman and two tow headed boys. "That's my crew."

"I met my wife over there in Afghanistan," Pete said. "This is her with our three-year old daughter, Nevra."

Braden brought another round. "So, what's policing like on your Island?"

"Probably much the same as in the city," Pete said. "Only less of it." He shrugged. "The summers are fun, patrolling on the police boat. Otherwise we've got drug busts, robberies, vandalism, hunting violations – even the occasional murder."

Braden's eyebrows rose. "The place sounds like a regular hot bed of crime."

Pete grinned. "Not really. Though right now we're looking at a possible arson, that explosion I was telling you about."

Braden grimaced. "Arson is nasty, one of our least favourite crimes and that's saying a lot. At least the fraud cases don't usually involve injury to people, just to buildings. But the others, the wackos, they often start in their teens. You've got to hope to catch these perps early."

Pete nodded. "It's difficult though, to know." He told Braden about Zak.

"Tough," Braden agreed. "Good luck with that."

"So aside from a busy robbery season, what's going on up here?" Pete asked. "I see there's another scandal in the government. Maybe some charges coming up?"

But Braden didn't seem that interested.

"Same old, same old," he said. "Glad it's not my division."

It was more fun to talk about sports.

"How about those Bluejays," Braden said. "They could make the playoffs this year."

"That would be good," Pete agreed. "It's been awhile."

They dissed some players, praised others. Then as they finished up their coffees, Pete explained that he was looking to make some home help arrangements for Walter. Braden gave him the name of a central agency that oversaw services for seniors.

"They were helpful last year when we were looking for a spot for my mother-in-law."

"Thanks," Pete said, jotting down the information.

"Hey no problemo, buddy." Braden grabbed the check. "If you're going to be around for a few days, maybe you could come and meet the family. Have some dinner."

"Maybe on another visit. I'm only here briefly then I'm back to checking out that arson on the Island."

In fact, he was anxious to return to the apartment to make his own assessment of the bungled robbery attempt. Braden had suggested the drink though and he hadn't wanted to refuse. Besides, it was great to see his friend again.

"O.K." Braden said, "but we'll get the families together soon. Good luck with that investigation."

*   *   *

Pepper hadn't barked at Pete's arrival in the hallway, as the little dog and Mrs. Verga had presumably gone to stay the night in the security of her sister's home. The other residents seemed to be braving it, though whether they had piled up furniture against their doors, he wouldn't know. He stood looking around the empty apartment at the beige furniture and walls, the featureless painting over the couch. The fairly heavy television set that according to Braden, any self-respecting thief would scorn nowadays in favour of the portable electronics.

So, pretty slim pickings. Unless the intruder wasn't on a trolling expedition at all, but was after something specific in apartment 604.

Yep, that would seem to be the unavoidable conclusion.

Time for another check through Walter's office. He turned on the light and pulled up the chair next to the filing cabinet. It was a two-drawer model, the bottom drawer holding only a couple of tax manuals, boxes of paper clips, staples and other office supplies. He thumbed quickly through the dozen file folders in the top. There were names on the labels, but the contents were skimpy. And the last tax records seemed from at least two years ago. The files must all be electronic, he realized. They'd be on the computer.

He turned around, ready to start the hunt. And stopped. Because there was no computer on the desk. How had he not noticed before? He supposed the equipment was so ubiquitous in every home, as familiar as the television screen, that he hadn't noticed its absence when he was at the apartment a couple of weeks ago. And he hadn't exactly been studying the décor or contents then either.

No worries though, there would be a laptop somewhere.

But it wasn't anywhere in the office.

Why would Walter hide his working computer? And when would he have done so. Not on the day he fell on the stairs, presumably just an ordinary day when he was going about his tasks in an ordinary way. He was dressed but still wearing slippers, so he was obviously intending to come back to the apartment.

So dammit, where was the computer?

It took only moments to search the office, then he moved into the rest of the apartment. He didn't enjoy the task of looking through Walter's closets and possessions. A couple of news magazines. An accountants magazine, who would have guessed it? Not many books. Pete wasn't much of a reader himself, though Ali always talked so enthusiastically about whatever she was reading, that he felt he'd read the book himself.

There was a slim stack of DVDs, Eastwood, Stallone, Bruce Willis. Like father, like son in one respect at least. That gave him a strange feeling. On a lower shelf, he found a lamp too, that gave him pause. A round ceramic lamp, with an orange glazed base and a shade in a lively mexican design. He remembered that the lamp had sat on his mother's bedside table, by her books. Walter had bought it for her while they were away on a rare trip, the winter before she got sick.

The shade was dusty, there was no bulb in the fixture. Looked as if there hadn't been for some time. He was surprised that Walter had kept the lamp, and replaced it carefully on the shelf.

But no laptop. So, no answers here, only more questions. He would see what Ms. Arum could tell him tomorrow. Craving fresh air, he opened the door to the balcony, then ducked back quickly as a shadow whirred past him in the dark. He stayed away from the railing, waiting for another glimpse of the bird. It was amazing how the peregrines and other raptors, these wildest of creatures, were adapting to city life. Nesting on the ledges of high buildings, feasting on plump pigeons.

And now apparently hunting at night. He'd read recently that this was a new behaviour, the birds normally hunted at dawn and dusk but now they were also taking advantage of the halo of city street lights to hunt in the dark. Their prey was bats, pigeons, and also certain migrating birds that only flew at night. Still, unike the shameless pigeons, the falcons continued to live a regal existence apart from their apartment dwelling neighbours. The birds were disdainful of human activity and oblivous to the recording cameras and web sites devoted to every aspect of the falcons' lives.

Too bad the internet camera wasn't aimed at the building windows, Pete thought idly. Then a thousand witnesses would have been watching the break-in with their supper. But maybe, just maybe..... Chuckling at his own foolishness, he fetched his I-Pad and googled the Ottawa peregrine website. But the site was inactive, now that the young birds had hatched and fledged. All that remained were some stills of the remains of the scantily-built nest. The pictures reminded him of Jay Gupta's surveillance video. People watching people, and just about as much use.

So much for that idea. Laughing at himself, he phoned Ali to report on his day. She was pleased that he'd met up with an old friend.

"But a break-in at the building!" she was dismayed.

"It's O.K.", he said. "Nothing was taken. But Dad doesn't need to know about this, it would only make his anxiety worse."

"He's not likely to hear it from me," she said resignedly. "Still, it's dreadful, all this happening. But I guess that makes three things, so maybe your father's life will get better from now on."

"Three things?" he asked.

"Haven't you ever heard that bad things come in threes? There was Walter's fall, then the explosion. And now the break-in at his building."

He was going to say that maybe the break-in didn't count since the perps failed. Instead, he simply said, "I hope you're right."

24

Benny Sorda opened his front door. He looked surprised, then wary.

"Hello Jory," he said neutrally. He knew Jory of course, as he knew most of the Island young people who had been coming through the years to the chip truck for lunches and snacks.

"Hello Mr. Sorda," Jory said. "I heard Zak was home for the weekend. I was wondering if I could talk to him."

Benny still looked surprised, but he only turned to the staircase and called up, "Zak, someone here to see you."

Zak came down the stairs, barefoot in jeans and a rumpled shirt, his hair in uncombed clumps, as if he'd just got up. It was two o'clock in the afternoon. He didn't look great.

He recognized Jory, scowled and rubbed his chest. "Oh it's you cop-boy -- what the heck do *you* want?"

Jory raised his hands in a peace-making gesture. "Hey look – no uniform. Off-duty. Just me, not the forces of the law."

Zak sighed heavily. "So what the heck do you want? I doubt you're here to ask me to the Grill for a brew. Nobody wants to be seen talking to the leper."

Shoot!, Jory thought. This is going to be tougher than I figured.

But he persevered. "Just wondering how you were doing, man." He was standing his ground. Finally even Zak felt the awkwardness of not doing the host thing and looked back towards the kitchen.

He shrugged. "We may have some brews here. I guess we could sit out on the deck."

"Sure. That'd be good," Jory said. He followed Zak down the hall. The senior Sordas seemed to have retreated diplomatically to a sitting room where Jory could hear the sounds of the television.

The deck overlooked Maria's pretty garden, flowerless this time of year but on the deck itself there were two huge ceramic tubs of chrysanthemums, one bunch a brillliant orange and the other a deep maroon colour. Zak opened the beer cans and handed one over without comment.

Shoot! Jory thought again. *How do I start?*

He raised the can, said thanks. "How's it going in the city?" he asked. "Where are you staying?"

Zak mentioned a street near the college.

"How are the classes?" Jory asked.

Zak shrugged. "Most of the other students are kids. I'm an old man there." He was twenty-four, two years older than Jory. Somehow the age difference had seemed a lot more when they were kids. Zak drank about half a beer in one gulp and put the can down on the deck rail. "Enough of this phony school stuff," he said. "Why are you really here, Stutke?"

Jory took a breath. "I was thinking about the trouble at the Taylors' place."

"You mean the morning I blew everybody up?" Zak asked caustically.

Jory nodded, "Yeah, that day."

"What about it?"

Jory leaned forward. "I was wondering if you ever go over it in your mind….."

"Only every goddamned day."

Jory shook his head, "I mean if you ever think of anything different, anything strange, anything other than the usual stuff. Not just that day, any time in the week before too."

"What if I did?" Zak asked bitterly. "What difference would it make? Everybody on the whole damn island except my parents, already assumes I did it."

He looked sceptically at Jory. "Don't tell me you believe any differently."

Jory turned his hands up. "I don't know."

Zak raised his eyebrows in surprise. "Well I guess that's something. One vote for doubt at least." Then was immediately discouraged. "But it's not much help. No offense but you guys aren't looking hard to pin this on anyone else."

"What would *you* do to prove it was somebody else?" Jory asked.

"What?" Zak looked puzzled.

"I meant if it's true what you're saying, that you didn't do it, why are you sitting around on your butt waiting for us cops to figure it out? You're the one who has most at stake here."

Jory pressed on. "It was your kitchen, you knew the staff at the Lodge. Who could have done this and why?"

Zak was silent, chewing this over.

"You have to help yourself," Jory said. "Or at least help me. So start remembering, going over that week like a terrier looking for a buried steak bone."

He'd brought his notebook and a pen. "The gas company investigator doubted it would be more than a few hours build-up in that basement before there was enough to blow if sparked," he said. "It went off at 10:30, so that valve handle was turned say sometime between six and seven a.m. What happens at the Taylors around then?"

"You must have got this already from Pat and Jerry," Zak said. "From me too, Chief Halstead and I went over it."

"So now I'm asking you, again." Jory was obdurate "Maybe there's some detail that you forgot. Something that could pin this on somebody else."

Zak shook his head. "I appreciate that you want to try, kid. But I can't think of anybody for this one. Not anyone on the Island anyway."

"Then there has to have been a stranger there that day," Jory said. "And we have to find someone who saw him. *You* might have seen him."

Zak leaned back in his chair and shut his eyes. Jory waited patiently, finishing his own beer and looking out at a grey cat scratching itself in the driveway.

Zak sat up suddenly, startling him. "I've got him!," he said. "He was a short guy with a limp. No, make that a tall guy with a mustache. He was carrying a bomb in his briefcase…"

Jory stood up, crushed the beer can and threw it in Zak's lap. "Jerk!"

Zak was laughing. Finally he sputtered out, "Sorry man."

Jory was still teed off. "I'm glad you find it so funny. You're the one facing jail time."

"I might as well find it funny," Zak said. "It's that or go nuts."

He put out his hand. "I will keep thinking man, I promise. And thanks for your doubts."

Mr. and Mrs. Sorda came to see him to the door.

"Thank you for coming to see our boy," Maria Sorda said, practically wringing his hand.

As he drove away, he wondered if he'd made things better or worse.

Worse for him that's for sure. Gayle wasn't answering his calls.

25

Lunch hour and the burger place was filling up with city workers pressed for time. Last night's drizzle was done but the grey sky had lingered, making the air humid and heavy. Pete flattened his cardboard container and carried the tray over to the recycling bin. He took his coffee with him to the car, where he checked the directions to the television studio and office where Sandra Arum worked. He had phoned ahead for an appointment, stating only that he was a police officer who needed some information on the ethics commission story.

On arrival at the three storey functional office building, he parked the car and reviewed again how much he was going to say. The woman was a noted investigative journalist, skilled at interviewing and nosing out information. He would have to be on his mettle, if he was not to give anything away about Walter.

A young man in jeans and a t-shirt that read Save our Planet was reading the Citizen at a desk. Pete introduced himself and mentioned his appointment. The fellow led him to another door, where he knocked and called in, "Sandra, your ten o'clock is here."

Sandra Arum rose to greet him, a slim woman with a strongly featured face. Smartly cut blonde hair. Tailored trousers and a striped blouse. Her eyes were keen with intelligent interest. She looked efficient and very savvy. Behind her on the wall, there were framed award certificates for excellence in journalism.

"Come in," she said, extending her hand.

She offered him a seat and a can of pop from a small fridge behind her desk.

"So you're from the Bonville area, Officer Jakes, or may I call you Pete. That's a beautiful spot, I've been there in the summer."

But she wasn't the type to waste much time on small talk. She leaned forward on her elbows. "So I'm dying of curiosity Pete. What brings you here to my office?"

"I've seen some of your articles pressing for this ethics committee investigation," he said. "I believe you even caused it to happen."

She nodded with satisfaction. "Occasionally we get one for the good guys, my team and I have been working on this for months. But it's only just begun. There are layers of corruption to sift through yet."

Inwardly, Pete winced.

"Could you tell me a bit about how it works?" he asked. "What's the thread that led you to Mr. Lariviere for instance."

She countered with her own question. "Can you tell me why you're interested? The doings of the federal government seem a little way out of the Bonville jurisdiction."

He shrugged. "I'm a citizen, I'm just interested.in what happens in my country."

She studied him for a moment, her gaze shrewd and assessing.

"O.K. Officer Jakes, for now. But my questions aren't going away."

She settled back in her chair, playing with a pencil as she marshalled her thoughts. "The thread, as you call it, started with the disgruntled owner of a paving company. His bid for a contract was turned down and he happened to know that the winner of the contract had been convicted of bribery in another country."

She nodded to Pete, "Yes, such is the wonderful world of business."

She went on, "However, in our country, this interesting complication is actually in contravention of the government's own rules that say a supplier will be barred from winning government contracts for ten years if it or any board members have been convicted of various offenses – including bribery, money laundering or extortion."

Seeing that she had Pete's total attention, she continued.

"Our disgruntled contractor duly reported the information to Mr. Lariviere's department but didn't hear a word for six months. Then he got a letter saying that the rules didn't apply if there were no other suppliers to do the work."

He wrote back, that was nonsense, that he was ready to deliver. Another month of waiting, then he got some bafflegab that the department felt that his company couldn't handle such a large contract."

He sent more letters crying foul, called the Procurer's office and got stonewalled completely. That's when he got in touch with us. He said he'd heard of other stories similar to his, all centering around this same department."

She pointed to a file on her desk. "I did some nosing around the Hill beginning with chasing up the rumours. For instance, people have noticed that Mr. Lariviere seems to always drive an expensive luxury car of recent make, that he commissioned extensive repairs on his home last year, and that he and his wife take their vacations in Italy and France.

She smiled. "All this of course is meat and drink to an investigative journalist.Where there's smoke, etc. and it certainly seemed there was a history of inequity in that department. When I had talked to some of the people concerned and had my facts, I called Lariviere but he wouldn't talk to me either."

She paused. "And he hasn't yet. However he has obeyed the summons from the ethics committee because he darn well has no choice."

"Sounds as if he's been doing this for awhile," Pete commented.

"He wouldn't be the first," she said cynically. "The government is like a tempting ripe apple. There's so much opportunity for corruption. Especially in procurement. Governments buy everything from paper clips to helicopters. They award construction contracts to the tune of billions of dollars annually. They spend millions on office equipment, advertising contracts, vehicles. They pay to have buildings and grounds maintained. They pay for training services and consultants and pollsters. And there's lots of lobbying for the contracts, sometimes involving goodies to sweeten the pot. Secret commissions and kickbacks. Cash in brown envelopes. Deposits in Swiss bank accounts. Or maybe just a new deck on the cottage."

She tapped the file. "I wouldn't be surprised if the Larivieres own a villa tucked away on some hillside in Tuscany. Too bad they didn't move before the shite hit the fan."

She leaned back and crossed her arms, a formidable opponent.

"Because this could go right up to the Minister herself. Charges of misuse and misdirection of public funds. Breach of trust." She chuckled with frank glee. "And then will follow the frantic cover-up attempts, that can get as bad as the original misdeeds. But I'll save all that for the book I'll be writing when this is over."

"It's been an education," Pete said.

She tossed the pencil on the desk. "Now it's your turn. Why did you want to know all this?"

"Lariviere," he said carefully. "I've run into that name lately. Also some other names that might be connected."

Sandra Arum was interested now, leaning forward on her desk, a gleam in her eye.

"And just where did you get this information?" she asked.

"Let's just say that I'm making enquiries."

"Is it something to do with a case you're working?"

Pete reluctantly accepted the fib. It could be a case, and he was working.

"I have a couple of other names." He'd made a short list from Walter's notebook. "Could I run them by you?"

She shrugged, "Go ahead."

The first two brought no reaction but when he read off the name Gary Lucknow, she raised her eyebrows. "That one, I know that one."

She tapped some keys on the computer.

"Here we go. Gary Lucknow, owner/director of GL Solar Industries. He's in the rogues' gallery all right. He hasn't been called up yet before the committee but he's on the roster and he definitely has reason to worry. His company manufactures solar panels. That's a burgeoning business right now, huge, multi-million dollar contracts are involved. GL Solar is said to have an edge because they've apparently developed a new lower-cost battery for the units, which could make them much more affordable for the average home. The government might invest heavily in them."

She scrolled down further. "But if there's any funny business involving the contract, it could be cancelled. And our records show that Lucknow can't afford to take that kind of hit. The company is out on a financial limb. He'd likely go bankrupt. As it is, I imagine production is being held up until after the hearings."

She turned the monitor screen towards Pete. "Here, I've got a photo of Gary Lucknow at a Rotary dinner." The picture showed a bulky man about forty-five, with thinning hair above round Slavic features. He was flashing a confident salesman's smile for the camera.

When Pete looked away from studying the screen, he realized that Sandra was studying him. "So?" she asked. "Are you going to tell me where you got this list of names? And whether your informant knows anything relevant to the investigation."

He shook his head. "Sorry. I don't know yet whether anybody knows anything at all. But what you've told me could be helpful."

"That's nice to know," she said drily.

"Is any of this going to stick on the big guys?" Pete asked. "Or just on the little fish?"

"Oh, I think we're going to reel them all in," Sandra nodded confidently. "The little fish get quite chatty when faced with jail time. They don't go down alone. For instance the multi-million dollar airbus trial," – she mentioned a huge scandal during the previous government's reign. "That one began when a businessman got into an argument with his accountant. The accountant retaliated by leaking certain interesting documents to the media, revealing a scheme to bribe businesses and politicians."

She grinned. "And don't forget the most notorious case of all – Al Capone was brought down by an accountant who noticed that Capone hadn't paid his taxes. It should be a motto for all aspiring crooks, mounted in a big gold frame above the CEO's desk.

Beware your accountant."

She rose to show him out. "I'll be waiting to hear more, Officer Jakes. Any time you're ready, phone me first."

26

His head buzzing with thoughts, Pete looked dazedly at the downtown city crowds. Directly in front of him was an orange newspaper box. On the plastic window cover was a cartoon of the Canadian Parliament Buildings with steam billowing out the roof and windows, the iconic Peace Tower at the centre, blowing its top. Cartoon politcians were streaming out the front entrance.

The headline revelled in news of the coming investigation. *Minister's Aide to be Grilled Re Financial Discrepancies. Records scrutinized.* Would Walter Jakes also be scooped up in the net? It seemed impossible.

He saw some people on bicycles, headed towards a square of green that glimmered between two buildings. A park, that's what he wanted. The sun had finally come out and he needed some fresh air and time to mull over what he'd just heard. There were benches fronting on the canal, but he kept on walking. Canada geese pecked in the grass, scattering grouchily as he approached. A pair of mallards landed with soft splashes on the water, but he hardly registered the sight.

Beware your accountant.

The words sounded like an ominous echo in his head.

Sandra Arum had outlined the details of some very serious business, with very serious consequences. But how could Walter Jakes be involved in any of this? Walter the beige, Walter the invisible, barely known to his fellow tenants. Walter the government accountant for god's sake. The man was about as exciting as mud. But then as Sandra Arum had pointed out so gleefully, all kinds of people hired accountants. Even crooks. Maybe especially crooks.

He stopped to watch a youth throwing a frisbee for his dog. The dog was young, eager and full of beans, and barking joyously. He caught the frisbee several times in mid-air, and soon a little crowd was gathering to cheer the pair on. But for Pete the diversion was brief. He moved along the path, unable to escape his churning thoughts. He was a police officer, used to considering all angles, turning over all possibilities, even if it involved his own parent. So he couldn't keep out the most daunting question of all.

Maybe Walter's involvement wasn't so innocent.

O.K. the idea was out there. No panic, Now he could mull that over and get rid of it. He sank down on a bench, arms wide along the top, taking a deep breath.

What did he really know about his father?

Or maybe that wasn't the best route to take. He'd been saying for some time that he didn't know his father at all. Now he realized that wasn't just some glib phrase. It was actually true. Pete considered himself an honest person. Where had he learned honesty, who had taught him? His parents, he would have thought. But if asked whether his father was an honest man, he could only answer, I think so, or I have no reason not to think so.

But he didn't *know*.

Walter was an accountant, skilled in preparing tax statements for businesses and governments. He might be quite capable, as are many people, of hiding a bit of income here, adding a deduction there. For an accountant, it might become a bad habit that carried on into other areas of his life. Such as in his work for clients. If that was the case, It would certainly explain his anxiety attacks and his obsession with watching the television news station all day. He was afraid of discovery.

But why would Walter do such a thing in the first place? He had no obvious financial needs. The apartment was modest enough, and Pete assumed that the government pension that Walter had built up over the years would cover his other expenses. But the truth was once again, that he didn't *know* any of this for sure. He hadn't cared or been interested enough to ask, and Walter was hardly volunteering any information.

Maybe he had some secret vice? Not alcoholism, Pete thought. He'd seen no signs. Gambling, betting on the horses? He doubted that. But possibly some bad investments. Even the most financially prudent people could lose money on a so called sure thing on the stock market. It must be something like that.

Jeesuz, though. One thing stood out in stark relief. If Walter was involved in any of this illegal activity, if he had been cooking the books for someone like Gary Lucknow, he would be discovered and punished. Sandra Arum and her team wouldn't give up till the last stone was overturned. She wouldn't be the only one who wanted to speak to Walter Jakes, either. And the other inquiries might not be as polite. For instance, it seemed that somebody had been pretty keen on getting into Walter's apartment the other night. Maybe somebody else was curious about the missing laptop.

Pete shook his head angrily. Well shoot. What to do now? And why should he do anything? Walter had made it plain he didn't want his son's help. Dammit. He resented this feeling, where the hell had it come from? He could only think of the corny old proverbs. *Blood is thicker than water. Loyallty begins at home.*

And he would hardly describe this feeling as loyalty, more like some kind of awful burden or onus. Still, with or without Walter's help, he had to do something. Sandra Arum was smart and committed and she wasn't going to let up. She would hunt this story down and everybody in it.

He wouldn't be leaving the city just yet.

*   *   *

"You're taking some *leave?*" Ali asked.

"Just a few days," Pete said. "I haven't found any home help yet and I should be around to oversee the repairs to the apartment door." A bit of exaggeration, as he'd come back to find the new lock already installed and a note to visit Jay Gupta to pick up the key.

"Sure, I guess so," Ali said uncertainly. "It's just a bit of a surprise. Did you discuss this with the chief?"

And why didn't you discuss this with me? Usually they would have talked about holiday and leave time together. But she didn't voice the thought. This was not typical Pete Jakes behaviour and she didn't want to over react.

"I'll be calling the chief," he said.

He hesitated, then plowed on. "And it's hard to explain, but I guess I just need some space to think about things."

"Space from *me?*"

He could hear the hurt in her voice and hastened to reassure.

"Not from you honey. From Walter I guess – from the whole Walter and me thing. I figure maybe if I walk around some of the old streets, something will come to me. Whether we can ever fix things or not, one way or another."

"Alright darling," she said into the phone, suppressing all concern from her voice. "Take care and let me know how things are going. I'll miss you."

"You've got Kedi for company," he said lightly.

And she replied in kind. "Kedi doesn't have your animal magnetism."

The telephone call to Walter didn't go as well. It didn't go at all because Walter wouldn't answer the phone. When Pete called the chief, he had gone to the cabin to check.

"He said he was busy," Halstead reported apologetically.

Yeah right. Watching the news no doubt. He thought briefly of asking the chief to go back to the cabin to say that Pete wanted to ask a question about Gary Lucknow, but he'd rather do that himself, face to face.

"I saw Walter take a few steps today without his walker," Halstead added helpfully. "He used the cane."

"Hooray," Pete said flatly. He wished he could confide his growing doubts to the chief but he wasn't sure yet where things were going. He might have to bend the law himself to get Walter out of this. He would try to talk to Gary Lucknow tomorrow. In the meantime, he was facing another long night in the apartment. He picked up the pile of DVDs and wished he'd bought some snack stuff. A search of the kitchen cupboards unearthed some microwave popcorn. Also some lightbulbs. He fetched his mother's lamp, and set it on the table by the couch where the shade spread a soft tangerine glow in the lonely room.

27

"Pete phoned from Ottawa last night," Halstead told Jane. "He's taking a few days leave."

"Oh?" she said, making a vee of her eyebrows. "You can manage with just Jory? I guess you'll be going to that council meeting then, the one about the ATV's."

"I guess I will," he snapped.

She tossed her pen at him, narrowly missing his ear. "Don't you snarl at me, boss. When it's Pete you're mad at."

He sank back in his chair, "Sorry." He handed back her pen. "Of course I'm not mad at him. To tell you the truth, I'm kind of worried. He's taking this business with his father really hard."

Jane crossed her arms and leaned back against the doorway. "It's hard stuff."

Halstead sighed. "Your kids all seem to like their dad."

She chuckled. "Maybe because he was on the road all the time, driving that truck back and forth across the country. Mean old mom had to do all the disciplining at home. Then Tom could come home and be the fun dad."

Halstead smiled. He knew the Carrells were a boisterous, close-knit family.

"However you two divided up the work, you raised a great bunch."

"Thank you sir," she extended her hand in a queenly gesture. "Now what can we do for Pete?"

Halstead shook his head. "I'm glad enough to cut him some slack, but I hope he comes back O.K. This is beginning to affect his work."

"I'm pretty sure some counselling is offered in our municipal health plan," Jane said. "I'll look it up."

Halstead scowled. "Maybe you should ask for a group rate. This could be infectious. Lately Stutke seems to have his head off in some kind of cloud too. I never know what he's thinking about."

Jane nodded. "Some tiff with his girlfriend, I think."

Halstead rolled his eyes. "You can handle that one. I'll keep trying to crack some feeling out of Pete's pop. We should hang a 'Free Therapy' sign out front."

Joking apart, though, Halstead was concerned for his second-in-command. He hoped the lad would get things worked out sometime soon. He liked Pete and liked his family. The Jakes were good new blood for the Island, where the residents could get too set in their ways. They had come seeking peace from their war-time experiences and over the past few years, he'd watched Pete gradually grow more relaxed. He'd found his base – a wife, a home, then a daughter.

But now Pete had been thrown a tough curve and a reminder of a difficult past. This business with his father had hit him hard. Halstead knew that Pete had been injured in Afghanistan and wondered whether he might be experiencing a bout of delayed PTSS, post-traumatic stress syndrome.

The big question was whether he would be able to handle it?

Meanwhile, Halstead was having to deal with the enigma that was Jakes senior.

"Hi darlin'," Steph had asked this morning on the six a.m. Skype call. "How are things going with our new tenant?"

"Slow going," he sighed. "I've never seen anyone so determined not to join the human race. I don't know what his problem is."

"And is he getting along any better with Pete?"

"Not that I can see, those two just rub each other the wrong way. I feel bad for Pete."

"Take Walter fishing," Steph said decisively. "We women know it's impossible to drag you neanderthals to counselling. So fishing is the next best bet. If you're ever going to "talk", it's likely to happen out there on the lake with the fish."

Halstead laughed drily. "I can't get him to come for a cup of coffee, let alone venture down to the lake."

"I bet you're going out there though."

"Oh yes, the fish will be looking for their breakfasts."

"Enjoy yourself. Miss you."

He signed off, musing anew at the wonders of the modern world. Such as this video telephone that had merely been a sci-fi gimmick in the movies of his youth. Fortunately, some things had stayed reassuringly the same. Such as a man, a lake, and a fishing pole. Mornings like this, it was worth getting up to greet the dawn.

He noticed movement by the cabins. Walter Jakes was awake too and already out on the path. He had his cane again and was trying out some steps.

Maybe Steph was right, a fishing jaunt might prompt some conversation. He had time before going into the station, not that he ever needed an excuse to do some fishing. He grabbed up some gear and headed toward the cabins. As he neared Jakes, he stopped and gave a brief round of applause. "Looking good!".

Walter looked around embarrassed. He likely hadn't been expecting to see Halstead about so early. "It's coming," he allowed, perhaps moved to speech simply through the relief of being able to walk again.

Halstead pressed this slight advantage. "I've got an extra fishing line here, want to try it out?"

Walter began his automatic refusal but Halstead persisted. "Just off the dock," he explained. "A few more steps. It will be good practice." And he started to walk without looking back.

Walter, left with the choice of looking utterly foolish or following, set after him. Halstead smiled to himself, hearing the tap of the cane on the path. Once on the dock, he set up a couple of deck chairs and waited for Jakes, who was venturing gingerly out onto the boards. But he got to the chair safely and sank into it.

Halstead tossed him a rod, without comment and noted that Jakes handled it well.

Time passed with no bites, either from the fish or from Walter Jakes. Halstead was uncomfortably aware of the stiff presence in the other chair. The morning mist was lifting and sounds of bird life and other splashing echoed from miniature coves along the shore. He sensed movement and turned to see Walter Jakes looking at *The Lazy Loon*. She was a nice-looking boat, if Halstead said so himself. A sixteen footer, furnished with a tiny galley and beer fridge.

"The fishing's likely better out there," Halstead said laconically. "Do you think you could get into the boat?"

He could see the struggle in the man's face. Halstead might almost have called it yearning.

"Yes, I think I can," Walter said quietly "If you give me a hand.".

Halstead helped him into the *Loon*. Then left him alone while he started up the engine. When he glanced back from the prow, he could see Walter at the rail with his face raised to catch the water spray. He looked like a man communing with his soul. A man who hadn't done that for a very long time.

And Steph was right. Once they got to the fishing spot and Halstead had anchored the *Loon*, Walter Jakes talked.

Not a lot, not a torrent or a spate but some.

Though Walter was ten years older, the two men had things in common, that helped. Both had been widowed in their fifties. The difference was that Halstead hadn't locked himself away, and now he was happily married to Steph. Of course he didn't point that out. Instead asked the other man casually whether he hadn't ever met anyone else.

"Actually I did try dating a bit," Walter said, his expression shaded by a ballcap borrowed from Halstead. "And there was one time the lady and I had quite serious feelings for each other. But I was reluctant to marry again and she moved on."

He re-cast his line and said gruffly. "I was probably wrong about that."

He also talked a bit about his background. His folks had owned a camping supply store up near Algonquin Park. He'd met his wife Jean at university. She was a prairie girl but after graduation, they were married and both found work in the government offices in the city. They shared a love of the outdoors and hikes and camped on holidays. When the boys came along, they just took them along too. The dream had been to buy a little fishing resort and leave the city. They had actually found a place and begun negotiations.

"Then Jean got sick," Walter said, his voice going flat. "Then she died. I lost the deposit but I didn't care. Then Josh went into the army and was killed. There was just me and Pete left. We weren't much good to each other."

For a while, he didn't say any more, just gazed somberly out at his line bobbing in the water.

"You've got a good lad there in Pete," Halstead risked saying. "And he has a nice family. Life springs anew, you know. That's what life does."

Walter smiled bleakly. "Seems you were probably a good father. I wasn't. With Jean gone, I had nothing to give anyone. I didn't even try. I screwed up."

"We all screw up sometime," Halstead said. "Doesn't mean you don't get a chance to fix it."

But Walter was reeling in his line. Winding up the conversation. Winding up the day. "Sometimes it's just too late. Too much water under the bridge."

Halstead said nothing. Fishing was like that. Sometimes there was talk and sometimes it was best just to send another cast out across the water.

In this case metaphorically as well, into the dark waters of Walter Jakes' life.

28

Pete checked his GPS again. Once away from the historic charm and parkland of the inner city, Ottawa was a city like any other. A grid of endless traffic lanes that criss-crossed an ugly industrial landscape. Out here, there wasn't even the tawdry liveliness of the fast food strips in cheap little plazas, just an endless reel of utilitarian industrial buildings, marked apart only by their various corporate logos. A treeless, glaring vista, no autumn colours here.

He stopped at the next traffic light. According to the GPS, GL Solar Industries should be coming up on his right pretty soon now. Though he hardly knew what he was expecting to find or what he was planning to do. Here the place was anyway, he could see a billboard type sign featuring a logo of a stylized solar panel and the slogan, *Take a Step into the Future with GL Solar Panels.*

He turned into the the roadway leading to a half dozen hangar-type metal buildings and followed the arrow directions to the office. The parking lot was near-empty, the place was hardly bustling. It didn't look as if GL Solar Industries was traveling into the future anytime soon. The office was a separate one-story bunker type building, its sole resident currently talking on the phone. *Angela Burke, Executive Assistant* said the nameplate on her desk. She looked up briefly when Pete came in, but seemed in no rush to greet him.

He idled the time, looking at framed photos on the wall, pictures of men shaking hands. Lucknow, who he knew from the photo in Sandra Arum's files, was in most of the photos. Some of the other hand-shaking men were public officials, he read from the names under the photo. The Mayor of the City, cutting the ribbon on plant opening day and the local Member of Parliament. Another picture showed Lucknow with about twenty workers in the company parking lot. Some sort of presentation occasion.

There was also a glossy company brochure. He had plenty of time to read it.

SOLAR POWER – THE NEW BLACK GOLD!

According to the folks at GL Solar, solar power was poised to replace oil as a world energy source. Difficulties to date had centred around storing the power that could only be collected during sunlit daylight hours. Huge batteries were required, expensive batteries running around $3500 dollars each, or$15,000 a household.

But now the GL Solar team had apparently come up with an innovation in battery technology, that would appreciably reduce the cost

CHEAP EFFICIENT HEAT FOR ALL.

Sounded great. But if the product was so good, what had Mr. Lucknow done to mess things up?

Ms. Burke finished her conversation. She was about the same age as Sandra Arum, but rounder everywhere. A bit too old for her gamin haircut, but not unattractive in a bisque coloured pantsuit.

"Mr. Lucknow isn't here," she said crisply, not wasting time on any pleasantries. "He's out of the country."

Yeah I bet he is, Pete thought cynically. And he's likely planning to make it a permanent visit.

Still, he asked. "When's he expected back?"

"Who's asking?" she said tiredly.

He showed her his badge. She barely glanced at it, and didn't seem particularly surprised. Though there'd been no invitation, he drew up a chair before the desk and sat down.

"What he's like?" he asked.

"What's who like?"

"Your boss, Mr. Lucknow."

She frowned quizzically "Really? That's what you're asking me?"

"Sure, I value your opinion. I can get other information from the television or the newspapers."

She nodded. "He's a nice guy to us, his employees. He's a good salesman, or was, I guess. But it's tough out there, with the world economy tanking."

He waited.

She shrugged, "If you're asking whether he'd bribe that government official, I really don't know why there's such a fuss. In case you don't know, the world of business is pretty cutthroat. If bribery is the name of the game and everybody's doing it, then you've gotta play."

She tapped a photo on her desk. "My daughter's only fourteen. Frankly I don't care if Gary has to bribe some Finnish or French guy to keep the plant going. If it keeps me my job, then it's O.K. with me."

Pete was sympathetic to her plight but refrained from pointing out that a Lucknow conviction of bribery wasn't going to do the firm or her any good either.

"Sorry," she added. "I hope I haven't disillusioned you. It's different for policemen. There's always plenty of work for you guys."

"Too true," he said.

She crossed her arms, leaned back in her chair and took a better look at him. "So are the cops getting in on this now? I just figured you were another anxious creditor looking to see if your bill was going to be paid."

"Are you getting a lot of them coming through?"

"A trickle, could become a stream any day now." She smiled and gestured behind her. "Mr. Lucknow isn't crouching behind my desk or in the john, you know. There's no point in you waiting."

"I'm just making inquiries," Pete said. "What's his schedule?"

She made a face and threw up her hands, "We don't know his date with the ethics committee yet, they keep changing it. Governments!" she said disgustedly. "And it's not as if those people aren't as corrupt as anybody else. It takes two to tango."

"Maybe you can help me," he asked. "Who does the firm's accounting?"

Her expression changed, became wary. "That doesn't sound like a friendly question."

"It shouldn't be a secret. You must have a list of employees."

She sighed. "It's not an in-house job. For the last couple of years, it was this semi-retired guy who came in here a couple of times a month. But we just switched accountants last May. We needed a bigger firm." She looked pained. "Or thought we did."

A semi-retired guy. No doubt who that was. One Walter Jakes.

"So who are the new firm?" Pete asked.

Her friendly manner was definitely fading now. "You should probably talk to Gary about that stuff."

He nodded. "If I leave my cell number will you let me know when he gets back?"

She shrugged and reluctantly picked up a pen.

On leaving, he took another quick look at the photos. Now he knew a bit more about Gary Lucknow, that his secretary was one forgiving fan at least. The other employees looked pretty happy too. At least in the exuberant flush of the plant's early days of operation.

"What's happening in this picture?" he asked, pointing to a shot of Lucknow and another man standing in front of a car with a big red ribbon stuck on the windshield.

"That was a great day," Angela said, her tone nostalgic. "We'd just won the contract and Gary was giving Eric a special present. He's the designer of the new solar panels."

Pete whistled. "Nice going. And that Porsche is a very nice car."

Angela looked morosely at her empty desk, the silent hangar buildings across the way. "Yes, well now the contract could be cancelled. Forget new cars, we'll be lucky to get our last paychecks."

* * *

Pete returned to the car. What had he learned? Sandra Arum was right. Gary Lucknow had a lot riding on this contract and he had risked a lot to get it. Maybe everything. Even his executive

166

assistant acknowledged the possibility that Lucknow had bribed someone to ease the acceptance of the contract. Not that she thought there was anything wrong in that.

Was that why Lucknow had changed accountants, to get someone more adaptable to his purpose? But that would mean that Walter had refused to be adaptable and wasn't that a point in his favour? Maybe, but that wouldn't have endeared him to Gary Lucknow. Especially if the financial finagling was done before he dismissed Walter.

Pete cudgelled up what little he knew about accounting procedures. Double books? He'd heard that phrase in movies. Spreadsheets, accounts payable, accounts receivable. He knew about bribes of course, he thought grimly. He knew that much.

But how to find out had actually gone on? Walter wasn't likely to tell.

Deep in thought, he waited at the corner of the access road for a break in the highway traffic. He noticed vaguely that another vehicle, a green van with the Lucknow company logo was waiting behind him. When the stoplight at the intersection turned red, both vehicles took advantage of the opening and pulled into the access lane. Pete only started to pay attention when he stopped at another intersection about a half mile distant. The company van was still behind him. The sun was glinting off the windshield and he couldn't make out the driver's face distinctly.

Was he being tailed? That was a first. He laughed aloud, feeling like a private eye in a television detective show. But he should test his assumption. Yes, the green van followed him faithfully through the next four stoplights. He wondered who could be doing the tail. A Lucknow worker, a Lucknow creditor, maybe even a government investigator?

Now if he was the gumshoe, he'd lead the other driver to a deserted area, then leap out of the car, accost him and demand to know who had sent him. Instead, despite Pete's efforts to keep the van in sight, the driver got marooned behind a transport truck at the next intersection. Pete even thoughtfully parked and waited a bit but didn't see the vehicle again.

Jory drove the cruiser into the Lodge lot and turned off the ignition. Barely two weeks since the explosion and the new kitchen was going up fast, the exterior now completed and the drywallers already working inside. He could see the contractor's van out front. He wished his task was that straightforward and certain of a result.

Because he wasn't sure at all what he was doing here. Or what he hoped to find. Zak had gone back to school for the week. Unfortunately, though he had been grateful of the offer to help, he hadn't anything useful to tell. Except maybe to narrow down the time frame. And was that going to be any help?

Jory left the car and moved aimlessly towards the new building. Sounds of a power drill came from within. He walked around to the side, stopping by the notorious gas valve. The two foot length of green metal pipe with cap on top looked innocuous in the sunny morning. There was nothing to implicate it as the cause of a blast that had destroyed a building and direly injured an employee.

The pipe was almost flush against the building and there were no windows on this side of the kitchen, not on this new construction anyway. But Jory thought there had been a window before, he would check. As for the surrounding terrain, there was no cover on the side lawn, the nearest tree was at least fifty feet away. He wondered how a stranger or anyone else could approach the building, slink close under the window and pull out a wrench to turn that valve handle. It would take a hell of a lot of nerve, that's for sure.

Unless the person was wearing a fake uniform. He'd seen that enough on tv. It seemed that people would let anyone in their door if the person was wearing some kind of maintenance uniform. According to those plots, any house, top secret weapons factory or even a president's office, was accessible. And maybe the Lodge staff, like people anywhere, even if they did see the guy out the window or on the lawn, wouldn't even take a second look. It would just seem routine.

Pete Jakes had checked with the real gas inspection guy and found he'd been there a week earlier, but Jory doubted that Zak or Kristy kept track. That would be one of Pat's jobs in the office. If it ever happened at all, he thought glumly. He scanned the lawn frustratedly, as if trying by sheer force of will to make the events of the day of the explosion magically re-appear, with suspect handily revealed.

"Can I help you, officer?" came a voice, making him jump.

Kristy Chambers, looking as good as she did in high school, he noticed. Like every other red-blooded male in the school, he'd had a crush on the pretty blonde, but he was a couple of years younger and she just thought of him as a kid. Then she and Zak broke up and she went away to college. The school corridors echoed hollowly for Jory for a couple of weeks and then he noticed that one of the new grade niners was looking pretty cute and life brightened up again.

"Oh, it's you," Kristy said, a grin in her voice. Stripping away the years, not to mention his cop's uniform. He felt sixteen years old again, in baggy gym shorts. At least he didn't stammer when he answered her.

"Just having a look around." he said. "The boys have got a lot done."

"Thank goodness, it was a horrible sight!" She gave a little shiver and pulled her hoodie more tightly round her shoulders. Under the hoodie, she was wearing a white chef's jacket.

"So, how's it going?" he asked. "Things pretty well back to normal?"

She shrugged. "I guess so. Though sometimes I'm not so sure I know what normal is anymore."

"I know what you mean," he said. "I guess that's just part of growing up."

She smiled and patted his arm. "You could be right."

He could see now that she wasn't that unreachable high school princess any more but it was a good change. He could feel that change in himself.

"I heard that they're going to operate on Cameron's eyes," he said. "I guess that's good?"

Kristy held up crossed fingers. "We all hope so. The right eye got hurt the worst. It's really bad."

He made the crossed finger gesture too.

"Do you want some coffee?" she asked. "I just made some fresh."

He followed her through the back door into the temporary kitchen. They had company, Trudy Carter a nurse who worked at the Taylors. She knew Jory of course, was a friend of his mother's.

"Trudy's just back from Whitehorse," Kirsty said as she fetched mugs. "She's been visiting her new grandchild."

"My cousin is up there working on some mine construction," Jory said. "He says there's great snowmobiling in the winter."

Trudy laughed. "I think I prefer to visit in summer. And I was doubly lucky, I flew the day of the explosion here, missed it by just a few hours."

She shook her head, marvelling again at the timing.

"I heard about it on the news at Whitehorse when I got there. It gave me an awful shock, expecially as we didn't get any details about Kristy and the others till later on in the evening."

Kristy nodded soberly. "It was terrible. The old follks were really upset. Some of them haven't settled down yet."

A buzzer sounded. "That's me," Kristy said. "Got to go help Pat. Finish your coffee," she motioned to the others.

Trudy stifled a yawn, then apologized. "I shouldn't be sleepy now I'm working days again. Before I went on holiday I was on nights for the whole month, subbing for a workmate."

She sighed. "I don't know how the woman can take that shift all the time. Your inner clock gets completely turned around. And it's lonely - you leave work at 6:30 in the morning and go home to bed just when the rest of the world is waking up."

Six-thirty a.m. Jory was thinking. *No one around. No one awake.*

No one but the night nurse going home.

A good, quiet time to go prowling around, unobserved say if you wanted to apply a wrench to a gas valve handle. Would fit the time frame right, too.

Say wouldn't it be something if he, Jory Stutke, found a witness all by himself. Wouldn't that impress the heck out of the chief and Pete.

"So did you never see anyone else around?" he asked Trudy. "No workmen even?"

She laughed. "Nobody but little old me. I bet you're not up and out then, what time do you police fellers start work?"

"Eight-thirty," he had to admit.

He watched glumly as Trudy rinsed their cups. So much for his promising lead.

But just as he was leaving, Trudy hailed him from the doorway. "Jory – hang on a minute. There was a man here that morning. I just remembered him. Sorry, but I had so much on my mind, I had to sign out from my shift, and my husband was picking me up to take me to the airport...."

"So there was a man....." Jory prompted, trying to stifle his impatience.

Trudy giggled. "Sorry .... Yes he had quite a snazzy-looking car and he had a beard."

"A beard? You mean he was old?"

She shook her head. "Not old. It was one of those little, shaped beards. Both the guy and the car looked sort of foreign, like one of those ads for fancy European cars."

Jory was puzzled. "Doesn't sound like any kind of workman."

Trudy agreed. "He was likely visiting one of the residents."

"That early?"

She laughed her hearty laugh. "Maybe he was still on European time!"

Still, it was something. Something to take to Zak.

He wished that Pete Jakes was around to talk to. The chief would never pay attention to anything that Jory Stutke said.

Pete microwaved a chicken pot pie and settled on the couch before the television. Home Sweet Home. Yeah, sure. No game tonight, the Jays were resting up for the next round. There was nothing new on *News from the Hill* either, just cobbled together bits from the past few days.

So, no handy diversion, justifiable or otherwise. Time to think.

It seemed that Gary Lucknow wasn't out of the country at all. In fact he'd been somewhere on the GL Solar premises that very afternoon. He wouldn't have been expecting a visit from Pete of course, but had likely instructed Angela Burke to screen all visitors. Angela had said that there were uneasy creditors starting to show up at the office.

So she must have told Lucknow about Pete's enquiries, and unless Pete was having delusions, the man had followed him. Why? Someone had also tried to break into Walter's apartment. Pete rejected the idea that the break-in had been random. That would be far too much coincidence. It would also be too much of a coincidence if the intruder had been anybody but Gary Lucknow.

He must think there was something important in the apartment. Something like Walter Jakes' accounting records for GL Solar Industries. Such as Walter's laptop computer. Well good luck with that hunt, buddy. If we're all lucky, maybe Walter already tossed the thing in the canal.

Still, Walter was a methodical man, both by temperament and by profession. His home files wouldn't have been the only copy of his work, he would have backed the files up. And despite his one determined attempt to escape Middle Island in a taxi, he'd had no chance to get back to the apartment since his accident.

So the back-up files, likely on a memory stick, must still be here in the apartment. The question was where?.

Pete tried to view the bland surroundings with a fresh eye. He had already sorted through everything in the office twice over, but he went through the room again. Still coming up empty, he began a thorough search of the rest of the apartment. Every closet, shelf, cupboard, the toilet reservoir. There was that police training, finally proving useful. But he found nothing except a few dustballs. Walter's cleaner hadn't been by for a few weeks.

He carried his coffee out to the balcony. "You've got keen eyes," he addressed the falcon, or at least the night air where he assumed she was. "Got any suggestions?"

He searched the balcony too, but found only some plastic shards of an unused window box. Back in the apartment, he just sat and let his gaze rove discouragedly around the room.

Wait a minute, what was the only anomaly in the entire apartment? The only beautiful thing. His mother's colourful Mexican lamp. Excitedly, he pulled the cord out of the socket, held up the lamp and carefully shook it. There was a soft thunk. He removed the shade and bulb attachment. There was just room for his hand to reach down into the ceramic base.

Inside he found a sheaf of bills. Money. A quick guess, about five thousand dollars. And a passport, Walter's.

And something else. The key to a safety deposit box.

* * *

Next morning he left the apartment to the excited yipping of Mrs. Verga's little dog. The neighbours were back. Mrs. Verga opened the door to greet him and Pepper came out for a sniff. By now, they were old friends.

"How is your father?" Mrs. Verga asked brightly. "Please tell him I said hello."

He smiled wanly. "I'll do that."

The morning was sunny, in the sky a vee of geese from a nearby pond were honking noisily over the grey buildings. The drive downtown was agonizingly slow as wild speculations flitted through his thoughts. What the hell had Walter got himself into? Then he had to search for a parking space.

He walked to the bank, an old three story building with a modern glass-fronted entrance. Once inside, he was directed to the manager who led him to the room that housed the safety deposit boxes. He had the key so she didn't question his right to be there. She brought the slim metal container to the table, inserted the bank key, then left, shutting the door behind her.

Pete looked at the box, struggling briefly with his conscience.

What the heck. He was next of kin. Practically the man's executor.

He turned the key, opened the lid and began to sort through the contents. Two envelopes, one marked Photos. He'd look at that later. The second envelope had nothing written on the outside. No handy note, as in the movies,

Open only in the event of my decease, signed Walter Jakes.

He opened the envelope. A couple of pages of computer print-out, that seemed to be a record of stock investments. There weren't that many but they were for appreciable amounts. About $50,000 in all.

The amount wasn't particularly incriminating as the savings of a single man who'd worked for years at a good job. It was about ten times more than was in the current Pete and Ali Jakes bank account but that wasn't surprising.

What else? Aha this was more like it. His fingers closed in on the small compact tube of a memory stick.

He was so excited, he almost dropped the thing. But he stowed it away safely in his pocket and forced himself to finish looking through the box. The last item was a will, from the date on the folder, made a little over a month ago. Around the time the government financial scandal had begun to bubble up.

He realized that he was delaying reading the actual contents. That under normal circumstances, he would only be receiving the information in a letter from a lawyer, along with the information that his sole parent was deceased. Still, he felt he had to look, to see if there was anything relevant to the memory stick or what should be done with it.

There was the familiar introduction, *I Walter Jakes, being of sound mind…..*

And not much else. The short document finished with *Leave all my worldly goods to my son Peter James Jakes.*

The only other bequest was to a local children's summer camp.

There was no mention of any memory stick or other reference to his accounting business. No last-ditch confession either.

Conflicting emotions. Pete had read the phrase in books. Well, his were a virtual battlefield right now. He sat perfectly still for a long moment, in that room full of symmetrical metal boxes. Boxes that contained what people held to be valuable, their money, their documents and their secrets.

There hadn't been a personal word in Walter's scant final instructions. Not one personal word in the damn document, just straight legalese. As if he couldn't think of anything else to do with his worldly goods.

Likely his ill-gotten goods as well.

Thanks for nothing, dad.

He packed everything except the photos back in the box, locked it and knocked to be let out of the room.

* * *

Half an hour later, he had parked in a lay-by near the canal, and was firing up his laptop. On the canal path, a few seagulls quarreled over a spilled paper cup of french fries.

"Here goes nothing," he said and installed the memory stick.

There was a list of files, including several for GL Solar Industries. A file for each month of the year and a half that Walter had worked there. Pete clicked on a month at random. There was a spreadsheet, a record of disbursements, of payroll to staff. Other months were the same.

He sighed and leaned back against the seat, the sun warm on his face. He wished it was just an ordinary uncomplicated September day. A day when he wasn't wondering whether his father was a crook.

What was he looking for? or? Some neatly logged reference to a bribe? PAID to Andre Lariviere, by Gary Lucknow, $500,000.

Oh sure.

He scanned the screen again, the rows of entries. He wasn't an accountant, he didn't even know what he was looking for. But Sandra Arum would have someone on staff or know someone who could make sense of it. Big question though, was he sure that he wanted to let them look?

Then there was the elusive Gary Lucknow himself. Even if Pete ever did meet the man face-to-face, he had no jurisdiction here in the city. And what did he hope to say?

Did you try to break into my father's apartment? Are you planning to drag an innocent man down with you?

Lucknow might just turn the tables on him, say that Walter was mired in the mess just as deeply. That he had taken a bribe, hush money.

Would Pete then still be able to help Walter? Would he want to?

He stopped at a supermarket for sandwich fixings and headed back to his temporary quarters.

In the apartment, he slapped together a sandwich and settled in front of the television. At least there was a baseball game on tonight. But a couple of pitches in, he couldn't even pretend to concentrate and he pushed the plate aside. He could feel the damned memory stick burning like a hot coal in his brain. Would he take it to Sandra Arum and her investigatative crew, or not?

Speaking of memories. He fetched the envelope of photos from his jacket, handling it as cautiously as if it too, was a hot coal. There must be *some* good memory, there must be! Some good times before the bad times came. But it was hard to think past those years of antagonistic encounters with Walter. A half dozen photos drifted into his lap. They were summer pictures, he and Josh in bathing suits, Walter in shorts carrying a fishing pole, Mom sunning in a deck chair, waving at the camera. The cabin, yes, there had been the summer weekends at the cabin.

Those had been good times. The place was just a modest wooden structure, perched on a rocky outcrop on the lake. A main room and two curtained off bedrooms, a privy out back. Most summer weekends the family travelled the short distance to the lake, but during Walter's vacation they could stay there for a magical entire two weeks without going back to the city. It was at the cabin that Pete had learned to canoe and swim and developed his love of the natural world. He supposed that Walter must have anticipated those trips too, through the long winter months at work in his government office.

He looked at the picture of his mother again. He barely remembered her, just felt at times a soft, enveloping warmth, the memory of an embrace, a goodnight kiss. But he knew with a certainty that she would want him to help Walter, no matter what he had done.

He watched the game, then a crummy movie. Then he fell into a restless doze on the couch.

It's summer, he is in the lake at the cabin.

Walter is treading water a few feet out from the dock and calling.

"Come on Petey. You can reach me, just start paddling and go."

Pete's O.K. for the first few strokes, then the water starts to close over his face.

It's frightening, a terrible feeling. Pete struggles but he's losing the battle. There's water in his mouth, in his eyes, in his nose. He's being pulled under.

Then, miraculously the process reverses. He's rising, he's going back up! There's the blue sky and the sun-warmed boards of the dock under his chest.

And Walter is saying it's O.K. Petey. You're alright now.

He lies there for awhile on the warm dock, he's never been so conscious before of how wonderful a thing it is just to be able to breathe. How delicious a thing is air.

Time passes. He sleeps a long time, then wakes to hear someone calling.

'Help me, Petey. Help!'

Far out on the water he sees an overturned boat. Someone flailing in the waves. It's Walter.

Pete is scared. He's only a kid, a kid who can't swim yet. How can he help?

But Walter is disappearing under the waves. Pete knows what that feels like. He has to try to save Walter. He takes a deep breath and jumps in the water.

Amazingly he can swim! Somehow he's become big and strong and grown up. The strokes of his arm are pulling him through the water at an astonishing great speed.

'I'm coming, Dad. I'm coming."

But Walter and the boat just keep moving farther away. Finally, they disappear beneath the waves and the lake is empty and silent.

Pete woke up, sweating.

Enough! What good was this trip into the past? He wanted to go home, to his real home. To get on with his life, with Ali and Nevra.

31

Ali gratefully watched the unruly exit of seventeen Grade Three and Four students, from her classroom. It had been a long afternoon. A thin rain had started at lunchtime and the kids had to stay in at recess. She and the other teachers who took turns supervising the playground recess ventured out in most weathers, including snow in all its aspects. But rain, with its aftermath of damp sweaters and jackets was just plain miserable.

Now she switched off the smartboard, and packed up a thick file of spelling tests she would take home to mark. In the front lobby, she met Eileen and the two women paused before making the wet dash to their cars. Ali tucked the file of papers under her raincoat.

"And where will Eileen's taxi service be going tonight?" she asked. Eileen had young teenage boys who were involved in some sport or other whatever the season and needed constant ferrying to games.

Eileen groaned. "Basketball practice in Bonville – I can't wait till Jordan gets his driving license! And what about you, supper with your handsome hubby?"

"No unfortunately. Pete's spending a few days in Ottawa. He's trying to speed up the search for some home help for Walter."

"Good luck with that," Eileen said drily. "I hear there are long waiting lists. And with millions of aging baby boomers coming along, it isn't going to get any easier."

Ali felt a little lonely at the prospect of another supper on her own with only a three-year old as a conversational partner. Maybe she would phone Miranda and see what they could cobble together out of their cupboards. But once she got home with a cranky Nevra in tow, she opted for baths for both and an early night. She hoped Nevra wasn't developing a cold. It wasn't till they were eating their soup and grilled cheese sandwiches that she noticed the blinking message light on the phone.

There was a call from a parent who wanted to reschedule the parent/teacher interview meeting. And then not a message from Pete, but a message for him. A woman's voice, asking Pete to call someone called Sandra Arum at her office. At the closing click, Ali stood there with the phone in her hand, watching Nevra chasing noodles around in her soup with her spoon. The strange woman's voice echoed in her head.

She played the message again. The speaker sounded efficient but friendly, probably someone from the home help agency. Pete must have given her his home number by mistake. Even though it was after closing hours, she'd better call the woman back and leave Pete's cell number in case they had found some help for Walter.

"Arclight Television Productions," said the answering machine. "Please leave a message for Sandra, Anthea or Peter after the beep."

Ali was so surprised that she hung up.

A wrong number? No – she checked.

Why would someone from a television production company want to talk to Pete? The woman had a nice voice, and had called him Pete, as if she knew him. Though why shouldn't Pete have all sorts of old friends to look up in the city? He'd already told her about meeting up with Matt Braden who he'd played hockey with in high school.

So why couldn't he look up a woman as well? she chastised herself. Pete had said that he was on a quest through the past. But the unease hovered, as she bathed Nevra, and read the bedroom story. It was just that he had been so *different* lately. So moody and preoccupied. Not like Pete at all. She had thought it was the effect of having to deal with his father. But maybe there was some other reason.

Such as another woman? – of course not. It was those darn television shows. To credit those shows you'd have to believe that every time a policeman opened a door, he was faced with a scantily-clad temptress ready to pour him a martini. Not too likely, from Pete's own accounts!

But after she'd tucked Nevra into bed and had her own bath and was cuddling on the couch with Kedi, she looked up Arclight Television Productions on her laptop. It seemed to be a subsidiary production company to the national television network. Chiefly covering news stories, and supplying content to programs such as *News from the Hill*. Sandra Arum was listed as an award-winning researcher/journalist.

Ali frowned, then shrugged. What the hey, she was curious to learn more about this noted newswoman. And to sneak a look at her photo, she couldn't be that young, not with such an illustrious resume. Feeling slightly ashamed of herself, she googled Sandra Arum.

Hmmm. The woman was younger than she thought, at most a youthful forty. Maybe this was an old photo? No it was dated just the year before. An interesting face with large, intelligent eyes. A great haircut too. So, Sandra Arum was smart and attractive. Obviously not an old schoolfriend either. Someone new. Phooey.

Serves you right Ali, for looking.

The rain had ended but the wind was picking up. She felt a sudden chill and was glad of the company of the big, purring cat. It was good too, to know that Miranda and Emily were across the road. She remembered when she'd first moved to the Island she thought of Miranda as unfriendly and intimidating. So different now. She supposed that Maria Sorda was feeling quite the opposite, as the friends of a lifetime turned against her family. How quickly things could change and the known world be swept away!

"I suppose I could simply ask Pete about the phone message," she said to Kedi. 'By the way," I could say, "Some woman called for you yesterday."

But no. She would trust in the fates, she would trust in the wind, most of all she would trust in her husband. She just hoped that once Pete had finished looking into his past, he still wanted to come back to the present.

*   *   *

"So how did the fishing session go?" Skype Stephanie asked Bud. "Have you successfully re-united the Jakes family and and will you now be hanging a psychiatrists' shingle on the Retreat porch?"

"Afraid not," Halstead said ruefully. "I guess I just don't have the touch."

"Didn't he open up at all?" Steph sounded disappointed. "I was sure that fishing would do the trick."

"It was a good suggestion," he assured her. "Walter Jakes is just a really tough nut to crack. He did talk a bit about his background, but he says it's too late to make it up with Pete."

"It sounds as if you made a beginning anyway. Maybe the next session will go better."

"I doubt it," Halstead said. "He made it sound pretty final and you can only intrude so far into a person's private life."

"Tsh," Steph dismissed this. "I'm more optimistic than *that*. You keep working on him."

"And how are things over there?" he asked, wanting to change the subject.

"Yesterday we took a train to this wonderful park in the mountains to see the snow monkeys."

"Did this Haruto guy come with you?"

"Yes, he took another day off from his classes." She sighed. "They seem pretty close. I hope she doesn't *marry* the fellow. Or I'll be visiting my grandchildren on Skype."

Halstead chuckled. "That's a stretch even for you Steph. The girl goes out for some sushi and you're worrying about where your grandchildren are going to be living."

"These things happen more quickly than you think," Steph said direly. "Love doesn't respect distances or the price of airplane tickets."

"I'll make sure you get to the wedding," he promised.

"Gee thanks." She stretched langourously. "But tonight I'm too tired to worry about it. Here I am in glamorous Tokyo and I'm going to spend the evening blissfully by myself. Put my feet up and rent an American movie. Between you and me and the gatepost, I'll be glad to get home."

"Me too," he said fervently.

"What are you doing tonight?" she asked belatedly.

"A council meeting," he sighed. "Big discussion re ATV's. Pete should be doing this but it seems he's never here these days."

"Pete isn't the type to slack off," Steph said.

"No, he's booked off a few days' holiday time. But even when he's here, he isn't here, if you know what I mean. I hope he and his dad soon get things resolved in one way or another. Then I'll get my right-hand man back."

"What about young Jory? I hope you're being nice to him."

"Actually he seemed to be improving for awhile. He handed in a couple of good reports and wasn't always thinking of places he'd rather be."

"And now?" Steph asked.

"Oh he's off in the clouds half the time too. It's getting where I feel I don't have any staff at all." He told her Jane's comment re charging for therapy sessions.

Then noticed she was looking somewhere off screen.

"Are you listening to me at all?" he asked aggrievedly.

"Sorry," Steph said. "Livy is just on her way out the door. She says hi."

"Wave to her for me," he said grumpily. "I'd better get off to my meeting, though I swear I'm getting too old for this job Steph. I should pack it in."

"Promises, promises," she laughed. "You say that every year."

She reached for something off screen. "These should cheer you up."

She held up what looked like a pair of red silk pyjamas and smiling lasciviously, she stroked the smooth, slippery fabric. "For our reunion."

"Promises, promises", he snorted.

"Stay strong sweetheart. See you in ten days."

32

Jory drove into the hospital parking lot, turned off the car and sat silently looking at the sprawling complex. The Bonville hospital served patients within a hundred kilometer radius and the parking lot was always busy and the meters expensive. But he didn't care if he paid for some extra time. He was nerving himself up to go in and visit Cameron. Because Zak was wrong, there had been one other potential witness on that fateful morning. Cameron had been working out on the lawn, at times with a good view of that gas pipe.

It had been three weeks since the explosion and Cam had been home for part of that time. Now he was back at the hospital though, in preparation for his big operation. It was make or break time and Jory felt for the guy, but he still had to talk to him. He owed it to Zak. In the building he got directions to the third floor in the east wing. Mrs. Parks was there, her eyes widening in surprise when she saw him coming along the corridor in his uniform.

"Howdy Mrs. Parks," he said, removing his hat. "I just dropped by to say hi to Cam and wish him luck. I heard he's going to have an operation soon. Is that O.K.?"

She smiled, "How nice of you. He'd like that. He's not supposed to move his head much and I think he finds the days kind of long at the moment." Then she added nervously, "You're not going to say anything to upset him?"

"No ma'am," he said, crossing his fingers behind his back. He certainly hoped not. He hesitated outside the room, took a deep breath and opened the door.

It was a good-sized private room. Cam was sitting in a chair and watching the baseball game, or the set was on anyway. He was dressed in pants and a buttoned shirt and there was some kind of gauzy bandage wrapped around his head, covering his eyes. They'd shaved his head above his ears to make it fit better, Jory guessed.

"Who's that?" he asked without turning his head. "Mom?"

"Hey Cam, it's me Jory. How are you doing?"

Cam's mouth twisted. "What do you think? Why, were you going to suggest we go out to kick a ball around?"

Jory sat down gingerly on the other chair. On the screen, the Jays player hit the ball out of the park. Two runners came home. There was lots of commentary, so that Cameron could tell what was going on.

"Only a coupla more games to go," Jory said, "and the Jays win their division. They could have a chance at the pennant."

They sat through another inning till the commercial came on. The score was six to three for the Jays. Top of the eighth.

"Good game," Jory said.

Cameron slumped in the chair, then seemed to rouse himself. He waved vaguely towards the wall. "There's some pop in the fridge, if you want. My brother just brought in more last night."

Jory fetched a couple of cans of ginger ale and popped the tops. The game came back on and the Jays wrapped it up in the ninth. It wasn't like being there at the stadium, but he and Cameron did share a shout of triumph. Which made it even harder to start talking about the explosion. It had been three weeks now, three tough weeks for Cameron and more to go. He felt crummy to bring it all up again but on the other hand, there was Zak. They'd been tough weeks for him too.

Unexpectedly, Cameron helped a bit.

"So how's everybody been? All gone back to school I guess."

"Yep." He took the plunge. "Zak, too."

Cameron's mouth twisted. "Good riddance, the lousy bastard."

"Cam," Jory leaned forward. "I know your folks think that Zak set that explosion. But nobody's ever proved it. Did you ever think that maybe Zak didn't do it?"

"No I never think that," Cameron said savagely."Because I know the jerk *did* do it. I can't believe he might get away with it and just walk away. While I'm stuck here with a white cane."

Jory ignored this, hoping fervently it wasn't going to be true.

"Zak feels real bad about what happened to you Cam, but he says he didn't do it. I've been talking to some other people who were working at the Taylors' that morning and it's interesting. There's something fishy about what happened. It looks as if there was some strange guy hanging around there that morning. Somebody who could have tampered with that gas valve."

He paused. "So don't get mad, but I gotta ask if you remember seeing anyone near the gas tank when you were doing the yard work.

"What did I see!" Cameron said bitterly. "How can you ask me that?"

You could see then. Jory thought, but didn't say.

Cameron subsided. "Anyway, why should I help that jerk Zak."

"He used to be a friend of ours," Jory said. "Our hero even."

"Yeah well now he's a crazy arsonist."

"Prove it to me then," Jory challenged. "Maybe your parents and the others are right. If you can't remember anything different, that will just be more proof that Zak did it. But help me figure this out, one way or another. Come on Cam, what about it?"

Cam shook his head disgustedly. "O.K. it's not like I have a million other things to do right now. Like going out and having a good time for instance. So, what do you want to ask me?"

"Just try to go over that morning in your mind."

Cameron tilted his head against the chair back. Jory winced, thinking that Cameron didn't have to close his eyes to think. They were already shut and swathed in bandages.

Cameron gave it a minute, then shook his head. "No, nothing, nobody. And I couldn't have heard anything over the mower anyway. Dad makes me wear ear protection. Maybe you should hypnotize me or something."

"Take your time," Jory said. "Do you remember seeing any strange vehicles. Delivery trucks, anything like that?"

Cam tilted his head back again. He started to talk slowly, remembering that morning maybe for the first time since the explosion.

"It was a nice morning. There's been lots of rain this summer so the grass has been growing good. I always cut the front lawn by the road first. That's where the sun dries up the dew first."

Jory could almost smell the fresh cut green smell of the grass.

Cameron went on. "I do the side bit after coffee break. Then when that's done, I go around to the back. I usually finish up around eleven thirty. Just before lunch."

He broke off, adding bitterly. "Of course I haven't been cutting any grass lately, Dad's been sending my brother. I haven't been driving, or even walking on my own."

"Ah you'll be back at all that in another couple of weeks," Jory said, hoping that he sounded convincing. In the meantime, he had to press on.

"When did you first start to smell the gas?" he asked.

Cameron thought. "I don't think I did notice it. Not in time to know the danger anyway. Or Kristy and I would have got the heck out of there. My dad said it could have been leaking for a couple of hours."

He grimaced and raised a hand to his bandaged temple. "This is making my head hurt. I keep telling you there was nothing different. It was just like any other morning, with the nurse taking the old folks out to sit on the patio like always."

"O.K." Jory said. "Thanks for trying anyway. I'm sorry if it gave you a headache. Do you want me to ring for the nurse?"

Cameron shook his head. "That would just freak my mom out. Just *go*," he said angrily. "Why do you care who else was there anyway, when you know that freak Zak did it?"

But in fact Mrs. Parks, operating on some motherly intuition was already at the door. She glanced at Cam and turned on Jory.

"You said you wouldn't upset him!"

He backed away. "Sorry ma'am. I was just leaving."

She held the door for him, when he realized Cam was saying something.

"Oh yeah maybe one thing. I did notice a real sharp car on the road, just before we turned into the Lodge. I guess I thought he'd been staying somewhere up the road."

"What time was this?" Jory asked, aware of Mrs. Parks hovering like an anxious sparrow at his elbow.

"When I was coming into work," Cam said tiredly. "Dad dropped me off early. About seven."

"What kind of car?"

"Some kind of foreign job," Cam said. "Silver colour, expensive. Coulda even been a Porsche."

So not likely a local, at least no Islander Jory knew.

"Did you see the driver?" he asked.

Cam shook his head and Mrs. Parks would be ignored no longer.

"Can't you see he's tired?" she said, half-pulling, half- pushing Jory towards the door.

He felt bad as he walked along the corridor. The job was turning out to be tougher than he he had ever imagined. If he kept on making enemies at this rate, he'd have to leave the Island. No bullet-proof vest would help. He wondered if there was an emotion-proof vest for use in these circumstances or at least an insult-proof vest. He envied city policemen their anonymity. Chasing a convenience store robber sounded easy compared to this.

At least he had a lead to follow up. He wasn't exactly sure how he was going to go about it but he'd figure out something.

After supper, he phoned Zak, glad to have some good news to tell the guy.

"This guy in the foreign job would have been long gone before you and Kristy got to work that morning," Jory explained.

But Zak was quiet on the other end of phone. Thinking, Jory guessed.

"That's good news isn't it Zak?" Jory said finally. "I'm going to start making inquiries tomorrow about the guy in the car. Maybe somebody else in the village will remember seeing him."

He heard a long, drawn-out sigh over the line.

"Sure kid," Zak said. "Do what you want, but you can't get around one big hole in this theory. Namely, why the heck would anybody else want to blow up the Lodge's kitchen? Anybody but me that is, which is what everybody thinks. And you'll never change their minds with a story of some phantom foreign guy lurking around the place that morning."

"He won't be a phantom when I find him," Jory said.

But Zak was right of course. Jory switched off the phone and stared unseeingly past the view of his father's corn fields to the serene waters of the bay.

What could be the stranger's motive? Why set up an explosion and the resulting fire? Aside from Cameron, the people most hurt were the Taylors. And their insurance was going to cover the renovation. Was their another target? One of the old codgers staying at the Lodge – some ancient feud?

He grinned and shrugged off the thought.

The 'why' would just have to remain a mystery for now. When he found the phantom, he would ask him.

33

"You're stonewalling me," Pete told Angela Burke. But he said it nicely. "When I called, you said that Mr. Lucknow would be back in the office today."

She answered equally nicely but without repentence.

"Mr. Lucknow was supposed to be here this morning but he was called away." She checked her calendar. "Something to do with the upcoming ethics hearings. He had to deliver some documents downtown."

She smiled, "You could go hang around the Parliament Buildings and maybe catch him there. You could take the tour while you wait, it's very impressive."

"Thanks," Pete said drily. "I took that tour in Grade Eight."

And grade five, and grade six.....

"Have a nice day, Officer Jakes."

But he had no better suggestion as to what to do. So he too headed downtown and found a parking garage only four blocks away from the Parliament Buildings. It was always a bit of a surprise to come upon the sprawling stone complex fronted by green parkland, right in the downtown city core. And yes, they were still impressive, even from an adult point of view.

The seat of the Canadian government since 1860, if he recalled the tour guide's speil rightly. Maybe not hundreds of years old as were many European structures, but still a venerable, solid presence for a new country. Though the buildings had suffered their share of danger, from an early fire soon after they were built, to a rampaging gunman only a year ago. And the old stones had witnessed many more political storms as well, through the decades.

Pete hadn't thought much about the place while growing up, the complex had just been part of the backdrop of the city. Today though, he walked up the path that lead to the iconic Peace Tower in the centre block, a symbol well known to all Canadian school children and the subject of a million tourist photos. And, judging by the crowd gathered there this morning, soon several hundred more.

He felt a stirring in his own heart as well. His feelings about politicians and political parties might have been mixed -- as a soldier, his fate and those of his buddies had at times rested in those not always competent hands. But his feelings for his country had only strengthened in his military tours away.

He checked the address Angela Burke had given him. The committee chamber room was in the plainer western block building, home to government offices and away from the tourist attraction sites. But since the gunman incident a year ago, there was security to go through here as well. As he hadn't got a pass, he was denied access. Ah well it had been a long shot anyway. He was hardly likely to bump into Gary Lucknow by chance. However he did recognize the man caught in the middle of a small media scrum on the steps. Andre Lariviere, the cabinet minister's aide who was at the centre of the growing scandal.

LaRiviere was tight-lipped, staring straight ahead as he doggedly headed down the stairs. Another man, probably his lawyer, warded off a battery of thrusting microphones. "No comment!" he protested. "*Sans Commentaire.*"

*   *   *

"Well if it isn't my friend, the country cop," Sandra Arum greeted Pete. "Been watching the news lately, Officer Jakes"?

He sat down. "I need to know more about this Gary Lucknow and his GL Solar company. How bad a spot is he in?"

She crossed her arms. "Why should I tell you anything? You can wait till the ethics hearing like everybody else."

"I need to know," he said doggedly.

"Hmmph." She thought, then said. "It's got to be a fair trade this time. I don't give info unless you do."

He nodded.

"O.K." she said. "I've heard that the GL Solar panels may be too good to be true. That the company can't supply panels at the price quoted, without sacrificing quality or safety." She sat back in her chair. "So you see, it doesn't look good at all for Lucknow industries. Or for Andre LaRiviere for granting the contract."

Pete was silent, thinking this over.

"I'm waiting," Sandra said finally.

He looked up, said reluctantly. "O.K., but this is off the record."

She shook her head. "You're a policeman. You know that nothing is off the record if it comes to the crunch."

"Do you have any parents?" he asked.

She blinked at the unexpected question. "My dad died a couple of years ago. Mom is still going strong."

"My father is an accountant," Pete said. "I think he might have some information regarding a bribe that Lucknow paid to Mr. Lariviere."

Sandra raised her eyebrows at that.

"You *think?* Why don't you just ask your father?"

"I did. He's not talking. He's still recovering from a bad fall. But he's worried, I can tell. I just can't tell whether he's knowingly involved or not. I'm beginning to think it might be true. He refused my help to try and clear things up."

She nodded sympathetically. "That's tough." Then said briskly. "You'd better get him in here to talk to me."

His laugh was hollow. "My father won't talk to *me.* I hardly think he'll want to be part of a television documentary on parliamentary corruption."

"I'm surprised he hasn't been subpoened already," she frowned. Pete shrugged helplessly. "Maybe he has. I wouldn't know."

She leaned forward across the desk and said seriously, "Then if your father doesn't show up at the hearing, he'll be in pretty big trouble for that offence alone. If he's been part of falsifying financial records or creating dummy books, he doesn't have a lot of choices. But if he fesses up, it might help him with the authorities."

"And," she shrugged. "If you bring him here, I could scare the crap out of him with stories of the charges he might be up against."

"I think he's already scared enough of that." He paused. "But you've been investigating similar cases - what would the charges and penalties be?"

She frowned, considering the question. "For the accountant? He'd lose his business license anyway, expulsion from the accountants association, a fine for sure. Maybe even jail time, if he commits perjury." She sighed. "I'm not a lawyer. If he would consider giving evidence to the committee, that might help."

Changing her tone, she asked. "So are you going to tell me what you've got. Better yet are you going to show me what you've got?"

"So far, I don't have much," he temporized. He wasn't handing over the memory stick yet. "But I'm thinking now that it must be something pretty incriminating, for someone to risk a robbery attempt at my father's apartment." He explained about the incident.

Sandra looked incredulous. "So you think Lucknow might have broken into your father's apartment? Maybe you should be talking to the city police."

She paused. "Unless maybe you think that your father is blackmailing Gary Lucknow. Or has that occurred to you?"

He clenched his jaw. "Nope. Hadn't thought of that one, thanks very much."

"I've got that sort of mind," she apologized. "Must come from constantly researching all this corruption."

And she doesn't even know about the money and the safe deposit box.

"If that's what he's doing, it's taking a terrible toll," Pete said. "He's not cut out for the job, he's too scared."

"Bring him to me," she said crisply. "No matter what's going on, I'm the best chance he's got. I've got contacts with the ethics committee. Maybe I can arrange him to give his testimony privately. That might gain him some clemency too, if he is involved."

"He'll never come," Pete said. "I'll have to drag him here."

Sandra Arum shrugged. "Then that's what you're going to have to do, my friend. I'll be here."

34

Elmer Hicks slammed the door on Jory with a triumphant sally. "And don't you come back here bothering me again till you're old enough to wear that badge. Or tell your daddy to come." Ha ha.

Still there was nothing left but to make yet another undignified exit through the junk-littered yard. Jory resisted looking back, but he kept his shoulders hunched protectively over his neck. On an earlier visit, the old man had thrown a hub cap after him. He felt better when he had an abandoned fridge and several other mud-stained appliances, between him and the pitcher.

He picked his way carefully past the last obstacle, a rusted truck frame propped up on cement blocks. Two mangy cats had taken up residence on the truck seat and snarled at him through the broken window. It was like they were laughing at him for trying to get through to Elmer. Yeah that was all he needed. At the listing gate, he took a big breath of clean air. Shoot, here was another unsuccessful attempt to deliver Hicks' court notice. The Chief was really gonna love this. And he wasn't exactly getting anywhere with his plan to help Zak. It was turning out to be a lousy week all round.

He looked up at the heartlessly cheerful blue sky. This was the type of day when the old high school gang would have cut classes and gone for a last swim at the beach. The water would be cold but that would just make things more fun. He sighed, he would drive down to the shore anyway and try to walk away his blues.

The beach was deserted, he guessed the current high school crowd were better behaved. He watched a solitary gull plunge like an arrow into the surging waves and come up with breakfast. Restless, he got out to walk, his shoes etching a trail of footprints on the soft sand. He couldn't escape his thoughts though. Eventually he sat on one of the big flat rocks and idly breaking bits off a twig, began gloomily going over the 'case'. If he could even call such a slim bunch of info a case.

It was too bad he had no one to talk it over with. He didn't want to risk the chief's scepticism. And he didn't want to go on giving false hope to Zak. It would have been O.K. to talk to Pete Jakes but he was away in Ottawa. He missed Gayle too, he didn't enjoy having her mad at him. Or the rest of their friends, either. In fact, he was pretty close to giving up on the case altogether. Throwing in the towel, whatever you wanted to call it.

He'd quietly asked around the village to find out if anyone had heard or seen a 'foreign' fellow or car. It was a good time to ask too, as the Island Main Street wasn't busy with day visitors, boaters and tourists, like it was in the summer. At that time of year, there were lots of strangers on the Island roads and it would have been easy for a stanger to go unnoticed.

But he'd got nothing. It seemed his phantom visitor was becoming exactly that. Might as well be a ghost, a kid's bogeyman that he'd just made up. But dammit he'd really wanted to help Zak. O.K, he also wouldn't have minded dazzling the Chief with his amazing detective powers either. But now it looked as if he was going to come up bust on both counts. At least he'd caught out those jerks Curtis and Brad for vandalizing the Sordas' chip truck. Even if he hadn't figured out what to do about that yet. Maybe he'd just give them a warning and collect an anonymous donation to leave at the chip truck.

His steps had carried him back to the cruiser but even after he'd got back in, he continued to stare out at the water. The sound of the waves was hypnotic. Questions floated into his mind, teasing, unsolvable.

Where did the stranger go? Where was he now?

Why had he come here in the first place?

Had he finished his task?

And ominously - would the stranger be coming back?

He jumped, as a vehicle drove up beside him on the sand and the driver hit the horn.

Hi there.

"Jeez, Gayle," he gasped. "You surprised me."

"You didn't hear me coming along the road?" she laughed from her rolled-down window. "That must have been some good dream you were having."

"What are you doing here?" he asked.

She shrugged, tossing her shiny dark blonde hair back over her shoulder. "Used to be one of our favourite spots."

She was blushing, which made her creamy skin pink.

"Can I come over there?" she asked.

"I'd better come to you," he grinned. "The cruiser cage isn't very romantic."

They snuggled pleasantly for a few minutes. Reunion was sweet.

"So what have you been up to?" Gayle asked belatedly, on coming up for air.

"Oh you don't want to know," he said, loath to wreck the mood.

"Yes, I do," she nodded. "Really. Have you found out anything to help clear Zak?"

He sighed. "Nothing definite. You sure you want to hear this?"

She nodded again, so he told her about the stranger. "I call him the phantom, even though both Trudy and Cameron saw him. And here's the really crazy part, I think the phantom might have set the explosion to kill one of the old geezers in the Lodge."

Gayle's eyes lit up with curiosity.

"No kidding! You mean like maybe the phantom and some old guy were once partners in a robbery or something. And he ripped off the phantom and the phantom has finally tracked him down and wanted to get his revenge. Or wait - maybe it's an old woman he wanted to kill. An old lover who left him for somebody else".

"Jeez, Gayle," Jory tried to stop this imaginative flow. "Yeah sure, something like that. Whatever."

"Or it's a sister or a brother who cheated him out of his inheritance. Or it's an old Nazi guy who's been hiding out!".

He had to kiss her again to stop her talking.

"Can I help?" she asked later. "I could be your girl detective."

"Thanks, but if the phantom ever really was on the Island he's long gone now."

"Well at least you tried," she smiled. "I think it's neat what you said about keeping an open mind and looking for the truth. You were right."

She drove off, with a happy wave and the promise to meet later that evening.

But she'd given him more than one thing to think about.

35

BELEAGUERED MINISTER'S DAY IN COURT LOOMS
PARLIAMENT HILL 'BUZZING' AS CABINET
AIDE'S TESTIMONY NEARS

Miranda set her omelet on the coffee table and poured herself a generous glass of plonk. Emily Dickenson, though already fed, curled at her feet, awaiting toast.

"Ahh!" Miranda sipped the red stuff with deep appreciation. Nothing better to drive away the frustrations of a long day dealing with a computer problem at the library. Sometimes it all made her long for the file card system of days of yore.

She switched on the television remote to watch *News From the Hill*. This could be extremely frustrating too, however tonight promised some rare entertainment. Yes indeed, she grinned with anticipation as the familiar view of the national Parliament buildings appeared on the screen, the Canadian flag topping the graceful central Peace Tower.

She tossed Emily a piece of toast. "This should be good, " she said gleefully. "Watch and enjoy the folly of humans.""

As an English teacher of over forty years, Miranda had a deep respect for the printed word. As a librarian, she was concerned about the future of books in a computerized world. However, she had to admit that there were occasions when the maxim 'A picture is worth a thousand words' was wonderfully true.

Such as the sight on her television screen of Andre Lariviere and his lawyer emerging from his office in the city, surrounded by a media frenzy of reporters stretching out their microphones for a word. As the pair scrambled into a waiting car, the network announcer commented in a voice-over.

"Three weeks have been set aside for the hearings which will involve testimony from many witnesses. The Minister's aide has been charged with twenty counts in all, including fraud, breach of trust and bribery. The arguments are expected to be complicated, based on differing interpretations of rules and legislation regarding anti-bribery controls. In a statement issued yesterday through his lawyer, Mr. Lariviere says he has no doubt the evidence will completely clear him of these false charges."

"No doubt!" Miranda snorted, pouring out a second glass of plonk. "Yes and we've no doubt Emily that the Minister himself is mired as deeply in the muck as can be. And he won't be the only one. Ah, but it's an old game that one,

Direly, she quoted Hamlet. "*The wicked prize buys out the law.*"

Then added, "But only for so long Emily. Only for so long."

*   *   *

At the Island Grill, Gus Jones poured himself a cup of coffee and sat at the table overlooking the bay. Though he ran a licensed restaurant, he hadn't touched booze himself for a couple of decades. Some could handle the stuff, but it had brought him a lot of trouble. Luckily he'd pulled himself up in time and got his business going. The Island Grill and the small motel behind, suited him to a tee. He had his own boat too. He'd be hauling it up into dry-dock soon, along with a half dozen other boats whose owners rented over-wintering space. But there were still a couple of nice weeks of boating left before the cold weather settled in.

Bud hadn't been in tonight, maybe he was having supper with his temporary tenant, Walter Jakes. A testy character, so Bud said, explaining the situation between Walter and Pete. Fathers and sons, Gus shook his head. He'd fathered a son himself once, back in those drinking decades. The kid's mother had remarried and done a good job with him, he'd heard. Gus had dismissed any fleeting guilt long ago. He wished the kid well in an ever-changing universe. But Bud was a good father, so was young Jakes.

His own advice to Pete, though he hadn't been asked for it, would be not to bother too much with the old man. Do what you can, give it a good try and then move on. That was his own motto regarding human relationships or any circumstance, come to think of it. Which may be why he had ended up single at sixty. His customers were friends though, who were badgering him now to switch the television channel from the news to the ball game.

Ah they were likely right. Lately, the only story seemed to be about corrupt politicians. Nothing new in that.

*　*　*

Ali shut her daughter's door and tiptoed down the stairs. She'd almost dozed off herself over the bedtime story. Luckily, after umpteen readings, she could read the tale in her sleep. She yawned, but there were still lunches to make for tomorrow. Some nights she wished she could just twitch her nose like Samantha the television witch and finish her chores in a magical minute. Instead she stood in the kitchen, cutting fruit and cheese, and wrapping muffins, paying only half attention to the voice of the televison in the living room.

It was just *News From the Hill* with more coverage of that financial scandal in Ottawa. Honestly, some people never grew up! She thought of a recent incident in the kindergarten class at the school. A little fellow had coveted another student's toy car and had taken it from his jacket pocket. A small theft. The teacher had made it right, using the approved procedure. Get the little thief to fess up, to apologize and then return the item. Maybe no one had ever taken these politicians through the process. Or maybe the lesson just didn't take with some people.

She supposed Pete was watching the show too. She heard the name Sandra Arum and, despite herself, she carried a half-made sandwich into the living room to have a look at the journalistic wonder at work. She looked as attractive as her picture and sounded smart and authoritative, as she outlined the schedule the committee would be following.

Ali wondered if Pete had met up with Ms. Arum yet and what they had talked about. She wished Pete would call. Intellectually she could appreciate that he needed his space to work out the problems with Walter. But emotionally she was devastated at the huge gulf of non-communication that had opened between them. Why couldn't he let her help him?

She was beginning to wonder if Pete would survive this emotional tailspin. After the bombing incident in Afghanistan, he had undergone all the physical therapy needed to heal his body but he had avoided the psychological treatment.

That's the army, he said. I was injured, some of my friends were killed. Some of us lived to fight another day. End of story.

Then he had kissed her and said, *You are the only therapy I need.*

Romantic yes, wonderfully romantic.

But now she wondered if love was actually enough. She'd read recently that post-traumatic stress syndrome could show up years after the actual traumatic event.

Was that happening to Pete now?

Oh, she needed to talk to someone! She missed Steph, and wished she was back. Miranda was a sweetie and a mentor in so many ways, but she wasn't married. Never had been. Miranda would likely say and quite rightly, that her unease was ridiculous.

But that wouldn't be much comfort in the circumstances.

Not when what Ali really wanted was a really good schoolgirl natter about men and their at times utterly maddening obtuseness.

* * *

Dusk was settling over the lake. Halstead had barbequed some burgers and invited Walter Jakes to supper. Later he built a fire in the pit.

"One of the many pleasures of living by the lake," he said, lighting the kindling.

They sat, watching the flames flicker in the night. It was cool enough for jackets, so Halstead had found an extra in the closet for Walter. Over the burgers, they had talked about fishing and now Halstead moved on to a favourite subject, the changing nature of crime. As Steph was wont to say indulgently, Bud always enjoyed talking to a new audience. Especially when he had a beer in his hand.

Still it was a pleasant way to pass an evening and Walter Jakes seemed content to let someone else do the talking.

"So a hundred years ago," Halstead said. "Police work was all about maintaining public morality. Ninety percent of arrests were to do with drinking, the rest for prostitution or vagrancy, mostly because there was a lot of poverty."

He paused for dramatic effect. "What do you think occupies ninety percent of police work nowadays?"

"Car stuff?" Walter ventured.

"That's right! Traffic offenses and enforcement. Most of our work revolves around incidents involved with the almighty car. And the highways we drive on, of course."

He paused to stoke the fire. "Mind you there's still lots of booze offenses. And drug offenses, that's a problem they didn't have a hundred years ago. Robbery too, there's a field which was actually improved by the coming of the car. Thieves could go farther to fence their stolen goods."

"I suppose they could," Walter said.

Halstead took another beer from the cooler at his side. "And now we've got this so-called white collar crime. *White collar*," he scoffed. "as if it's somehow a cleaner kind of crime because it's carried out in an office instead of a back alley. It's still just low-down theft, still about cheating, robbing, taking someone else's money. It's still *criminal,* whether it's a smash and grab at a convenience store or fixing a bid on a contract in Ottawa."

Whoops, he was losing his audience. Walter had gone silent. That was what happened when he didn't have Steph here to rein him in.

"Sorry," he apologized. "My wife would have shut me up and stopped me going on about my hobbyhorse."

"No it was all interesting," Walter said. "I'm just tired, still not completely up to scratch I guess." He looked across the fire. "I want to thank you, for providing me with this haven. I've needed this."

Halstead raised his beer. "Glad to have been some help."

Emboldened, he went on. "Now that you're feeling a bit better, isn't it about time that you met your daughter-in-law and that sweet little granddaughter of yours?"

Walter shifted uncomfortably, his face difficult to read in the firelight. He sighed.

"Look I don't want to be rude, especially when you've been so hospitable to me but I don't want to talk about my son and his family. I appreciate that you want to help but you can't."

"I could just arrange the meeting, " Halstead promised. "Ali could drive out here some afternoon. I'd stay in town at the station and leave you to it."

"I don't know," Walter hesitated. "Sometime, maybe. I'm not ready."

Halstead watched him walk up the path to the cabin. A shadow shape, a shadow man, flickering past the solar lights. *I wonder if he ever will be ready.*

Then he stayed on by the fire till it went out.

The female falcon shifted as the wind rose. A thin chill in the wind was stirring up more than her feathers. It had awakened in her an ancient restlessness, the annual migrating urge emerging.

But the urge wasn't full force yet, it wasn't yet time to leave the city.

On the ledge, she shifted from one fearsome clawed talon to another, as she stared out into the night. Feeling, smelling, tasting the wind for signs of prey.

Her sleek head with its fierce hooked beak, swung at the sight of movement far below on the street.

It was only one of the bipeds who lived in the concrete structures and not of any interest to her. The biped set off walking in the night. But over there, darting confusedly in the street light, there was a bat.

37

Pete had switched off the remote, the newscaster's words echoing in his thoughts.

Three weeks have been set aside for the hearings. Mr. Lariviere has no doubt the evidence will completely clear him.....

And exactly how was that going to happen, Mr. Lariviere? Will you be throwing the little fish to the wolves. Little fish like Walter Jakes?

He tossed the remote angrily, watched it skitter across the room and leapt up from the couch. He was getting nowhere fast here in the city. He'd had no success in tracking down Gary Lucknow and unless he came clean to Matt Braden about Walter's involvement, he had no jurisdiction to get tougher in the search. Sandra Arum had made it pretty clear that he had to confront Walter and she was right. He should have left for the Island that evening, instead of hanging around here.

Only nine o'clock. He sighed, jammed his hands in his pockets and paced restlessly around the small, suddenly claustrophobic space. He supposed he could go out for a walk, and try for the hundredth time to draft out his conversation with Walter. Because if it didn't go well, if he couldn't convince Walter to come back with him, he'd just have to wrestle the man into the car and drive away. And wouldn't that create a buzz on the Island grapevine network.

At least the walk might tire him out enough to sleep. He grabbed his jacket and baseball cap and took the stairs, he wasn't in the mood for chit chat with any of the tenants. It was a warm, moist night, likely good hunting for his falcon neighbours who were apparently far better at capturing their quarry than Pete Jakes.

He covered a few blocks, moving moodily along under the dull sodium streetlights. The orange glare was strong enough to blot out the night sky. Not like the wonderful, star-lit canopy that you saw nightly above the Island. He craned his neck, trying to catch a glimpse of the moon's silver disc through the tree branches. He wouldn't want to live in the city again, for sure. Like the country mouse in Nevra's storybook, he just wanted to go home.

This is great, I thought you were trying to cheer yourself up.

He moved on, feeling marooned in the cityscape of apartment blocks, he might as well have been in a foreign country. An occasional car passed, leaving behind snatches of light and sound. There were streets he knew farther north in the old neighbourhood. There were landmarks too such as the high school and the house where he'd lived, but he couldn't face the prospect of dealing with old ghosts tonight.

Instead, he ducked into a well-lit donut shop, preferring even that limited companionship. The place was sparsely populated with a few lonely city dwellers but when he was ordering his coffee a burst of noise erupted at the entrance. Some junior sports team coming in for a box of donuts after practice. The sight of the excited young faces, merely emphasized his loneness. He missed his own team of hockey kids back on the Island. Quickly finishing his coffee, he escaped back out into the night. Now he wanted only to get back to the apartment and sleep. Tomorrow he would go home.

It was later now. The sidewalk was empty of pedestrians. No one waited at the bus shelters. Pete walked along like a kid, looking down at the pavement and idly kicking fallen leaves towards the gutter. He turned down Walter's road automatically, without glancing at the street sign. A few feet in, his dulled senses prickled, awakening slowly. He became aware of the dark shape of a car moving slowly alongside of him. Quietly, like a big, silent shark. Some kind of sedan.

The driver's window was up, not someone looking for directions then. He stiffened but kept moving at the same unhurried pace, meanwhile checking out his immediate surroundings. He was just now nearing the apartment visitors' parking area. The lot was fairly well lit but he could see at a glance that none of the few cars parked there was occupied. And the apartment entrance door with its brightly-lit lobby was still several hundred feet away. A good long sprint that he wasn't likely to win.

Best to go on the attack then. And quickly.

He turned to face the car. There was no streetlight at this spot and behind the dark window, he saw little of the driver's features. Just enough to see that it was a man.

He rapped hard on the window with his knuckles. "Looking for somebody, buddy?"

The car kept moving, he had to walk quickly to keep up. He made a grab for the door handle but it was locked. The car began moving faster and Pete had to let go as it sped off.

"Damn!" He grabbed his smarting hand.

The driver was probably a mugger who had moved on to look for an easier mark. Or worse, some cruising predator, though he hoped not. It would have been better and more useful to get the license plate. Cursing himself again, he headed across the parking lot towards the apartment building. He would call in the incident to the police station anyway. Then patrol cars could keep a lookout.

He only heard the car at the last minute. Even then, it was more like a disturbance in the air behind him, as if the car was breathing down on his back. Like the hot breath of a dragon. With no time to look back, he could only dive for safety on instinct. Luckily he chose to go left, as the car whistled past him, grazing his hip as he fell to the pavement. It careered away, the driver using no lights. For a long moment, Pete lay on the dark pavement, breathing heavily. Then he rose shakily, first to his knees then to his feet.

Jay Gupta was running to him from the lobby. "Officer Jakes! Are you alright? That car tried to run you over!"

"I'm O.K." Pete gasped.

"Let me help you."

Jay helped Pete limp to the lobby door, then looked him over in the bright light. "Your head is bleeding," he said. "Come to my office and I'll call a doctor."

Pete raised his hand to his forehead, brought away a streak of blood.

"No doctor," he said. "Just a wet cloth thanks."

"I'll call the police," Jay said.

"I'll do that," Pete said. "I know just the policeman I want to talk to." It was time to ask for some help.

* * *

Matt Braden had driven in from his home in the Gatineau Hills, north of the city. A friend indeed.

"That's O.K.," he said when he arrived at the apartment. "The kids were in bed and Carol and I were enjoying our first evening together in two weeks, but what the hell."

"You're sure the guy tailed you here? " he asked now. "He wasn't just a mugger waiting for whoever would show up?"

"I'm sure," Pete said, wincing as he applied a wadded up washcloth to his forehead. A good-sized lump was forming there already. "If he'd just been a thief, he would have left after I asked him what the hell he was doing."

"Maybe you didn't ask nicely," Braden said.

"Ha, ha,.... *ouch*," Pete yelped.

Braden sighed. "Sorry about your goose-egg, buddy but I can't do much, when you're tying my hands. You know about evasive witnesses as well as I do, and you're proving to be a textbook case. You say this guy tailed you, but you won't tell me why."

Braden had made coffee, strong and hot. Pete took a reviving swig, and wiped his mouth. "It's complicated."

"Try me," Braden said. "There may be various crimes going on in our nation's government but the streets of our capital city are usually fairly safe. You'd better give me what you've got."

"O.K." Pete took the plunge. "There's a man called Gary Lucknow, owner of GL Solar industries, who's connected to the Lariviere hearings. I think he tried to break into Walter's apartment the other night."

"You mean that attempted robbery that Price and I were investigating?"

"Yes, but I think Dad's apartment was the actual target."

Braden grimaced. "And you're going to tell me why?"

"Walter did some accounting work for him. Now Lucknow thinks that my father is going to incriminate him at the ethics trials next week. I'm guessing he's looking for dad's records."

Braden gave a low whistle.

"And you haven't told me any of this because….."

Pete took a breath. "I m not sure how deeply Walter is involved. Whether he was happy to go along with things, at least until this ethics committee came along and he found he was facing the possibility of a jail sentence."

He paused, "And there's more." He told Braden of the money he'd found in the safety deposit box.

Braden thought a moment, then echoed Sandra Arum's sentiment of a few days ago. "What does Walter say about this?"

"Not a damn thing." Pete filled him in on that situation. "He wouldn't give me the time of day."

Braden sipped coffee, thinking. "I can see it's been tough for you. Walter being your father."

Pete laughed hollowly. "I'm not so sure. He's just as hard-headed as I remember. He doesn't want to meet my family and I guess part of me doesn't really care what happens to him."

Braden shook his head and returned to the less complicated behaviour of criminals. "It seems that Lucknow hasn't been successful yet. He hasn't found whatever he was looking for."

"That was in Walter's safety deposit box too." Pete explained about the memory stick.

"And where is this interesting, possibly incriminating bit of evidence now?" Braden said, then waved his hand dismissively. "No, forget I asked that. In a safe place though, I assume."

Pete nodded. The stick was locked in the car glove compartment. He'd considered stowing it in the Mexican lamp for old times' sake, but decided that was risky, and foolish.

Braden frowned, "Of course there's still the prime source where Mr. Lucknow could look."

Pete unwrapped the washcloth, reaching into the bowl for some fresh ice cubes.

"Where's that?"

Braden poured out more coffee. "Walter himself," he said.

"That's looked after," Pete assured him. "Lucknow doesn't know where he is. Plus Walter is staying with my boss, the local chief of police."

He explained about the Retreat. "I'm on my way there in the morning."

"So what do you want me to do?" Braden asked. "What's the plan?""

Pete realized how much he had missed talking over his concerns with the chief. It was a relief just to go through the process with someone else. Helpful too, to have a fresh perspective on the case. Because case it seemed to be.

Holding the cloth against his forehead, he told Braden of his talk with Sandra.

"I'm going to pick dad up and bring him here. Sandra says that if he turns evidence against Lucknow, he might not face any charges himself. In the meantime, you could check what kind of car Lucknow drives and where he was tonight."

"With what you got of the license plate, you mean, " Braden said drily.

"Sorry. Half of it was all I could see with my face plastered to the pavement."

Pete hesitated, then asked. "Could you also see if Lucknow was in the country the night of September second?"

"What happened then?"

"Walter fell down the stairs here. Broke a hip and several ribs. That's why he's on the Island now, Ali and I came to fetch him."

Braden whistled again. "You think Walter was pushed? That would mean we're dealing with a pretty nasty customer indeed."

"Nastier than trying to run me over?"

"Oh yeah, I guess that was pretty bad, too."

Braden's expression turned serious. "You sure you don't want some more help?"

"Thanks, but I think I've got a better chance of getting Walter back here myself, rather than raising some big fuss. As it is, I'll likely have to lock him in the car."

Braden nodded. "You could be right. But stay in touch. There's no worry about Lucknow for the next few days – he'll be on the hot seat at the ethics hearing, in full view of the committee members and the ladies and gentlemen of the press."

38

"Thanks, Gus." Jane Carell paid for the take-out burger and fries, a payday treat and small dietary sin. Other days she brought her lunch to work, neat little plastic containers filled with healthy slimming carrot sticks, fruit cups and yoghurts. She was finding that middle age brought extra pounds as well as crowsfeet. Very unfair! And she did want to fit into that new dress for her neice's wedding next month.

"When's Steph coming back?" Gus asked. "Bud's starting to look a little woebegone."

Jane tutted unsympathetically. "He's coping just fine. Steph deserves a holiday. Anyway," she teased, "won't you miss the extra business now he's eating at your counter regularly again."

Gus flicked the bar towel at her. "I like to see happy people. Guess I'm just a romantic at heart."

She smiled, "So's Bud. Steph will be back late next week -- he's got a big heart drawn on the calendar."

She picked up her greasy treat bag and a couple of napkins. "Sorry," she said as she bumped into a man who was coming up to the counter. The man paid her no attention. Jane raised her eyebrows at Gus. *Rude!*

Once outside the Grill, she noticed an expensive silver-coloured car parked among the pick-ups and SUVs. A *very* expensive car – one of her son-in-laws was a buff and frequently briefed her on the subject at family dinners. Not that it lessened the man's rudeness. Oh well, it took all kinds. She headed off briskly for the station, anticipating her lunch.

In the Grill, the man ordered a beer, a foreign brand that Gus didn't carry.

One of *those*, Gus thought, anticipating a snotty remark. But the man just raised his hand vaguely and said "Beer – just a beer. Any beer."

He sounded a bit foreign too, and looked it in his slacks, belted leather jacket and expensive shoes. Definitely not the outfit of any of the regular lunchtime patrons of the Grill, who generally wore a farmer's overall or maintenance worker's jumpsuit and construction-style safety boots that they bought at the co-op store. The businessmen or council members weren't a lot more fashionable. They lunched in short-sleeved shirts in the summer and when they did wear suit jackets, they were off the rack of some mall store in Bonville.

Still, this guy's hair was sticking up like a paint brush and he had a sort of zonked look, which kind of ruined the overall effect. Gus drew the brew and pushed it across the counter. The stranger didn't carry the glass to a table but stayed on the bar stool, not to talk like some, just staring absently into his glass.

Gus turned his attention back to the sports news. There was a cheer in the room at the announcement that the Jays had officially reached the playoffs. He realized that his customer was asking for another beer. He'd downed the first one fast enough. The drink seemed to have done him some good though. He actually asked a question.

"This place, this Middle Island. It is not very big to travel?"

Gus nodded. "About twenty square miles." Just the right size he thought, but didn't add the comment.

"And how many people live here?"

Gus thought. "About forty-five hundred, last count."

The guy didn't look like a tourist, or someone on a holiday. Boating was over for the year, and he couldn't picture this fellow pedalling along a country road for the pleasure of the scenery.

Maybe he was a businessman. The Island didn't get many people looking to start a business, though more than they used to. But those people typically tended to have dreams of owning a Bed and Breakfast place, or setting up an artist's studio, or a shop that sold handmade soaps and candles. And this fellow didn't have that look about him. He was too tensely wound to spend a day standing in a shop. Instead, he asked Gus for a telephone directory.

Gus frowned, "I guess I've got one around here somewhere, the Island is included in the Bonville book. Hardly ever use it though, we mostly all know each other's numbers."

The man waited, while Gus made a sketchy search in the shelves under the bar.

"Who are you looking for?" he asked finally.

"Peter Jakes. Actually I am wanting to see his father Walter."

Gus brightened. "Oh Pete, sure. Know his father do you?" He wrote out directions to the Jakes place on a scrap of paper. The man didn't thank him, just grabbed up the paper and tossed a twenty on the counter. He didn't wait for change.

"Who was that?" Asked a curious regular, who had come up to pay at the cash register.

Gus shook his head. "I don't know. But he's driving a Porsche."

The customer whistled. "Musta robbed a bank. Some of those cars go for $100,000 used."

* * *

"My favourite hen hasn't laid an egg for nearly three weeks. What could be wrong with her?

Miranda tsked impatiently and typed. *Check the feed for mould.*

She looked up from her laptop as Emily Dickenson wuffed from her perch on the living room couch.

"What's up Emily?" she asked. "Getting impatient for our walk?"

It had been chilly this morning, one of those days when you realized that despite all the beauty of fall, winter was just around the corner. She'd preferred to stay at her computer with tea. But Emily wuffed again and stood up, paws on the back of the couch.

Curious now, Miranda put down her cup and went to look. There was a car stopped in front of the Jakes' house. She didn't recognize it or the man who was walking up the driveway. He didn't look like a local, not in that topcoat and expensive shoes. Maybe he was some kind of salesman, though they didn't get many of those out this way. Not like the old days when people came peddling magazines and vacuum cleaners. An insurance salesman? But you didn't see much of them these days either, and he wasn't carrying a briefcase.

"Shush," she said to Emily but she kept on looking. Some might call it snooping, country people just thought of it as looking out for the neighbours. And with Pete away, she felt a responsibility to keep an eye on Ali and Nevra. She supposed she could go holler to the fellow that the Jakes were out, but he would find out soon enough.

The man had reached the house and was headed for the front door. Another giveaway that revealed him as a stranger to country ways. No local folk ever used the front door. He knocked a couple of times, then realized his mistake and began to walk around the house. Miranda couldn't see him at the back but presumably he found the door to the kitchen porch.

He was taking his time, she thought uneasily. More than enough time to realize that there was no one at home. She hoped Ali had left the door locked. In another minute, she'd go over there herself and see where the heck he'd gone. But then the man rounded the corner of the house and appeared at the top of the driveway. Back at his car, he stopped and looked at the empty stretching road, the stubbled fall fields, then turned his gaze towards her house. She ducked behind the curtain, then felt ridiculous, as the man started to walk across the road. Taking the initiative, she opened the door and stepped out on to the porch.

Emily growled obligingly and Miranda didn't attempt to quell her.

"Please don't open the gate," she called. "The chickens might get out."

He looked askance at the birds but obeyed. As she neared him, she was absurdly glad of the barrier of the gate. He was only a thin wiry fellow but there was a feverish look about him altogether. Like Emily, her hackles rose. For some reason she thought of a salesman from her childhood who Father had invited into the kitchen. That man had opened before their wondering eyes, a case full of gleaming butcher's knives.

This man sent the same kind of shiver up her back.

"Does Peter Jakes lives in that house across the road?" he asked with no pretense at a polite preamble.

"Presumably you read the name on the mailbox," she answered tartly. "I saw you looking it over."

He didn't seem to notice her tone. Or didn't care. His face was shockingly pale under a dark brush of hair. He just pressed on with the next question.

"I am wanting to see his father, Walter Jakes. I believe that he lives here too." he asked.

His tone was so intense that Miranda backed up a pace and felt for the comfort of Emily's collar. "I think you'd better come back some time when the Jakes are home," she said. "You can ask your questions then."

He looked confused for a moment, obviously agitated at hitting an obstacle in his quest. Then he just turned and headed back to his car.

Creepy!

She was glad that Ali and Nevra had been away and resolved to keep an eye out for their return.

*   *   *

Aleta Howard, rural postal delivery clerk, drew her little blue Echo up before another mailbox. She'd almost finished her rounds for the morning. Only seven more mailboxes on the way back into town. Her route covered a circuitous distance of about twenty kilometers, all the way down Hawks Nest Point and back.

This morning she had stuffed the mailboxes with Friday's usual thick packet of advertising flyers, mostly for the mall stores and big grocery chains in Bonville. There were some letters and bills but fewer of these every year as more people corresponded and paid bills on line. She supposed her job and a way of life would eventually disappear. She didn't mind so much, she was coming up to retirement anyway and so was the car. But there were old folks on the route who would miss the daily routine of walking out to the mailbox.

A fancy silver car pulled up beside the Echo, making it appear particularly shabby. A lost tourist, no doubt. Though he was a little out of season, most of the visitors having gone home more than a month ago. The man leaned out the window. He sounded a little funny, maybe foreign, and asked if she delivered mail to the Jakes.

"Sure thing," Aleta smiled. "But they live a bit back that way, where you've come from."

Then he wanted to know if she ever delivered mail there to Walter Jakes.

"Oh you mean Pete's dad," Aleta said. "The one who had a stroke or something."

The foreign man nodded eagerly. "Yes, that is the man. I am a friend of his from the city. I would like to surprise Walter with a visit."

Aleta was always happy to be helpful. "He was living at the Taylors' Lodge but I heard he's staying down the road at the Retreat now."

"The Retreat? Where is that please?"

She turned. "Thataway, last place before the point. I was just there, didn't deliver any letters though. Just another wad of these darn flyers….."

But the foreigner didn't seem interested in any further chat. He was already turning the car. Downright rude really, when she'd helped him out.

*   *   *

At last! I am nearing the end of the chase for the traitor accountant. It was fine for Gary Lucknow, what did he care? He was just losing some money. Just another bad investment to write off. He wasn't losing his dream, his reputation and long-deserved world-wide recognition. Lucknow cared nothing for any of that. Nor that he, Ritter had laboured for a decade to achieve it. Then had the unfortunate necessity to deal with a businessman like Lucknow to develop the idea. His idea!

Now the man whose testimony at the hearing could bring everything crashing down, would be stopped forever. Walter Jakes had destroyed Erich Ritter's life, now he would pay with his own.

"There you go, sir. That new exhaust pipe will get you home. The muffler was pretty well shot."

Pete ran his debit card through the machine. He was grateful that the shop had been able to take him in without an appointment. Even so, it was nearly eleven a.m. and he'd meant to be half-way to the Island by then. Not a good day for a muffler to blow.

Twenty minutes later, he left the last major city traffic artery with a sigh of relief. The goosebump on his forehead had subsided, leaving a hell of a bruise, but at least his headache had gone. As he turned onto the highway he started to plan his talk with Walter. He had three hours driving ahead, might as well rehearse. He'd take no nonsense this time, strictly hardball.

"You're coming back to Ottawa with me, Dad. No fooling this time."

Yeah sure.

He'd probably have to threaten to report Walter himself, whatever worked. Their father-son relationship was pretty well in the toilet already, and he doubted this would bring any improvement. He could only hope that Sandra Arum was right, that Walter could make some kind of deal for turning evidence into the committee.

Looking for any diversion from his thoughts, he turned on the radio. Unfortunate choice, he got the hourly news, reporting that the ethics hearings had begun. There was little more though, there would be no startling announcements for days yet. He waited for the sports report, as another stretch of highway rolled by. There were prettier routes past lakes and rocky outcrops of the Canadian Shield but he was trying to make some time. And even along the main highway the tree colours were spectacular, great rolling swaths of stoplight- bright oranges and reds.

His cell phone beeped.

Pete recognized the number. "Hi Matt, What's up? I'm just on my way to the Island now." He explained about the muffler repair.

"I've got that report on Lucknow's movements," Matt said. "Thought you might be interested."

"You bet. Go ahead."

"He was in town last night and due at the hearings today. And he was also here the night of the apartment break-in. But he was definitely out of the country from August 28th to September 4th. So apparently not shoving Walter Jakes downstairs at that time."

"Are you sure?" Pete asked

"Yep. Seems he was on a last ditch sales trip, making stops in Finland, France and Germany."

Pete was puzzled. "You got this information from Angela Burke, the secretary?"

"Yes, I talked to her just a few minutes ago."

"Well damn, I was so sure."

He could hear the shrug in Braden's voice. "You win some, you lose some. The policeman's credo."

"What about my hit and run?""

"Lucknow's license plate doesn't have any of those numbers. But we're working on it. Take care."

Forty kilometers later, Braden called again.

He sounded oddly hesitant. "Look Pete, I don't know if this means anything but I've been going back over the record on Lucknow's movements in September...."

"And?"

"It's all kosher, he was out of the country then for that conference. But his business partner was here. Name of Erich Ritter."

"Ritter?"

"He's also the inventor of some new gizmo in the solar panels. I guess he's pretty smart. Kind of nutty too, though."

"How nutty?"

"Nutty enough to show up on police radar. He was booked into some clinic, a sort of ritzy rest home I guess. Anyway, they called us when he went AWOL. Well not really AWOL, he had signed in on his own recognizance. It's just that he didn't follow the protocol to check out. He was gone for a couple of days."

Pete was remembering the photos at the GL Solar works. The man being presented with the new Porsche. "Angela Burke told me about that guy. He was upset like the others at the thought that contract could be cancelled. Maybe more upset. So he could have vandalized the apartment on the twenty-fifth."

"I don't know where he was that night," Braden said. "He could well have been tearing up your Dad's place. But this incident report I'm talking about is for September fourteenth and fifteenth."

"What?" Pete was puzzled. "Just a second, I'm pulling the car over."

He stopped on the verge, automatically registering the highway sign that said he was still 30 kms from Bonville.

"Are you O.K. buddy?" Matt was asking.

But Pete barely heard the words. *September fifteenth,* the date was resonating like a bell in his mind. A warning bell. Then realization came bursting through.

"That's the day of the explosion at the retirement home," he said slowly. "The explosion at the place where my father was staying."

Braden was quiet but the connection hummed with their mutual thoughts.

"Holy crap," Braden said finally.

Pete thumped the wheel with the heel of his fist. "God damn it! All this time, I've been barking up the wrong tree. What else has this lunatic been up to?"

"Ritter could have been anywhere on those two days," Braden cautioned. "Or just where he said he was, at a friend's cottage. I've got someone checking on that. And how could he find out where Walter was staying?"

But Pete's thoughts were racing. "None of that matters," he said impatiently, "the question is, Matt, where the heck is Erich Ritter right now?"

Braden agreed. "I'm on it. I'll get back to you as soon as I can."

But Pete hardly needed any confirmation. He knew with a terrible certainty exactly where Ritter was headed. Right for Middle Island.

"I'm leaving the radio on," he said. "Keep me in the loop."

He sped unseeingly past golden strips of fields, his gaze fixed on the road ahead, his thoughts whirling in confusion. He should stop again, he knew. His was a careful, methodical sort of mind that needed time for ideas to gel, time to follow threads, time to make connections.

But today the thoughts wouldn't wait patiently for an invitation, they came bursting through relentlessly. Like an explosion in his own head.

It wasn t Zak Sorda who had loosened that gas valve.

Zak had been innocent all along.

But how had Ritter, a stranger, managed to get at that valve without being seen by the kids in the kitchen?'

With sheer crazy nerve. The worst kind. But never mind, he did it. And there was no time to think about that now.

What did it all mean? One thing was for certain, the worst thing. Ritter knew that Walter Jakes was on the Island. Had somehow found and followed him to the Taylors. Probably through Jay Gupta. Pete had given him the forwarding address to the Taylors' Lodge, so that he could send on bills and any other of Walter's correspondence. Jay would have given the address out freely, but there was no time to check that now.

Though Walter had survived the explosion, Ritter must have thought the experience was enough of a warning to scare the hell out of him. To stop Walter from giving evidence and causing the contract to be cancelled and the factory shut down. But then Pete appeared, sniffing around the GL Solar works. Angela Burke would have told Ritter of his visit and once he heard the name Jakes, Ritter must have panicked anew. He would figure that Walter had confided in his son and therefore Pete was also a danger. Hence the attempted hit and run.

Ritter was obviously getting more wired up as the hearing neared. More crazy. More dangerous. He wouldn't be content with just warning Walter Jakes this time.

At least he couldn't find him too easily, out at the Retreat. Pete checked the time. Another half hour to the causeway. Too long.

He dialed the station number on the speaker phone.

"Jane? Get me the chief. Right away."

*   *   *

Ali drove along the maple-lined road, her spirit singing with the symphony of fall colors. Crimson, golden, claret, flame, magenta. A sumptuous feast for the eyes, for the soul. She had once read that a person would have to be made of stone to drive through the Ontario autumn landscape and not be touched. Mind you, her father-in-law, the man she'd yet to meet, might just be that exception.

Nevertheless she was determined in her mission. Pete would be coming home tonight and she couldn't bear to have things continue on in this wretched way. Bud Halstead, sweet man, had arranged a meeting.

I can't promise how it will go, Ali, he'd said. *I just don't know.*

Ali had decided to go anyway. Emissaries could only do so much. She would have it out with Walter Jakes herself and resolve the situation one way or another. Arriving at the Retreat, she turned the motor off to enjoy the peaceful silence of the most beautiful day of the year. No wind, just leaves drifting down from the trees in a soft, weightless stillness. She gathered up the bouquet that she'd put together from the roadside ditches. Purple asters, goldenrod, silver teasel stems.

Rounding the side of the house she saw Walter Jakes sitting in a chair on the lawn outside his cabin. She sensed his stiffness even from this distance and her resolve quailed for a moment. She almost turned around on the spot, but then realized he had seen her. Pasting a smile on her face, she advanced across the grass, flowers held out in front of her. As an offering or a protection, she wasn't sure.

"Hello Walter, " she began. "What a lovely afternoon! Bud mentioned that it might be a good time for me to drop by, so….."

With utter disbelief, she watched as the man actually raised his arms to ward her off.

"Please go," he said. "I'm not well….. maybe some other time….."

But Ali was in a different frame of mind. She was tired of this Greta Garbo 'I vant to be alone' routine. *Who does this guy think he is?* No way was he going to push her away this time. She was going to blast him out of his shell and thrash things out, come hell or high water. If he never saw her again, Walter Jakes would at least remember what Ali Jakes said to him today.

Though Walter Jakes didn't look impermeable at all. He looked frightened, his face a sickly pallor. Appalled that she would have this effect on him, she started to speak. Instead of anger, her words come out as concern.

"Good heavens, are you all right?"

She watched, shocked, as Walter lurched forward off the chair. He came right at her, pushing them both backwards on to the grass, where they fell in an awkward heap.

Breathless, she struggled to writhe away.

"Walter!" she sputtered when she could. "What on earth……?"

Finally she managed to sit up. Still sputtering, she saw a man coming out of Walter's cabin. A thin, dark-haired man in a leather coat.

He had a gun in his hand.

A gun!

He waved the weapon at her. "Get up, both of you."

She helped Walter to his feet. He shook his head and said helplessly, "I'm so sorry."

She sighed. "You tried to warn me off. If I wasn't so pig-headed I would have left." She glared at the man. "What have you done to Walter? You'd better let us go."

But the man was looking about, paying her no attention. When his gaze returned to them, her heart chilled at the blankness she saw there.

He waved the gun again. "Into that shed there, both of you."

It was Bud's garden shed, a place for the lawnmower and tools. A padlock hung loosely on the door hasp. As Ali hung back, Walter tugged at her arm. "Do what he says, I think it's best."

Reluctantly, she followed him into the dark, close interior of the shed. She heard the door close behind them and the sound of the man attaching the padlock to the door. Quickly, she checked out the surroundings for another exit. There was one small window, so overgrown by a lilac bush that little light penetrated into the shed.

Walter, following her look, shook his head. "He's just outside, he'd hear you."

Ali pulled her sweater more tightly around her shoulders. Though only a few minutes had passed, the sunny afternoon already seemed far away. "Who *is* he?" she asked. "Why is this happening?"

"His name is Erich Ritter," Walter said bleakly. "He thinks I am a threat to him."

"And are you?"

Walter grimaced. "Inadvertently. Through my accounting work for his company, I learned certain things."

"Is this to do with those government hearings in Ottawa?" Ali asked. "Something about bribes?"

Walter nodded. "Ritter works for GL Solar Industries. He was the designer of an innovation in solar panels that would greatly cut the production cost. Tragically, I don't think that Ritter knew anything about the bribes. Or that his partner Gary Lucknow put in a false bid that didn't reflect the true cost of the work."

"Couldn't you help this Ritter fellow, and let the authorities know that?" she said excitedly. "Then he'd let us go." She moved, as if to pound on the door.

Walter pulled her back. "It's too late for that," he said. "The company owner will be jailed or fined anyway and the contract for the solar panels will be cancelled. The factory will be closed down."

Ali was trying to absorb all this. "Ritter could take his invention to another company."

"It's too late," Walter said again. "The loss of the contract and the company closing seems to have sent Ritter off the deep end. He's been racking up some criminal charges of his own."

Ali paled as he told her of Ritter' involvement with the explosion at the Taylors' home.

"So this man was actually trying to hurt *you*? And he would have set the whole Lodge on fire to do that? What kind of monster is he?"

Walter nodded. "He's a very disturbed man, that's for sure, and very dangerous. At first I didn't connect him with the explosion. I think I was still in shock. But a few days later, it started to sink in. Then all I could think was to get away, before I put Pete and his family in any danger."

Ali was busily absorbing all this. "That's why you tried to get away in the taxi." She looked at Walter with warmth. "And that's why you didn't want Nevra and me to visit!"

He looked chagrined. "That was partly it, the rest was just foolishness and stubbornness on my part." He patted her on the arm. "It's a pleasure to meet you at last, my dear. Though I could wish for better circumstances."

Ali felt tears stinging her eyes. "It's enough to know that you care."

He reached for his wallet and took out a picture of herself and Nevra.

"You kept it!" She hugged him then drew back.

"Think of what Zak and his family have gone through! But now he'll be cleared. People will know he's innocent."

She subsided at the expression on Walter's face. "If anyone ever hears about it, you mean."

She shivered then said resolutely. "They *will* hear about it, we'll get out of this and we'll tell them." She glanced at the door. "We'll rush him when he comes back – we're two against one."

Only the one had a gun.

"You heard what Pete was saying?" Halstead demanded, as he came out of the office. "That there's a killer on the Island looking for Walter Jakes?"

Jane nodded, her eyes wide with concern. "I was listening. What's the plan?"

He pulled on his jacket, then reached for his gun and cell phone. "Stutke's got the cruiser, I'll have to take my truck."

"Should I get Jory to follow you?"

He cursed. "I can't have him just barging in there. I don't know what I'll find. Just get him back to the station and he can wait till I call. And alert Bonville too, for back-up."

"I will," Jane said. She handed him his cap. "Be careful."

She looked anxiously out at the parking lot, as he headed for his blue Ford pick-up. But before he could get in, the cruiser came careening in beside the truck. Stutke jumped out and ran over to the chief. The lad sure looked excited about something, Jane thought. She hurried out to join them but both men were already getting into the cruiser.

"I'm taking Jory with me," Halstead said. "Make that call to Bonville for back-up."

And the cruiser sped away.

*   *   *

Jory looked a bit bewildered at the sudden change in events.

"But I've got something to tell you, Chief. Something important."

"Just drive," Halstead said, scanning the road ahead. "You can tell me on the way to my place. And drive fast."

Jory took the back road, skirting the village Main Street. "Should I turn on the siren?"

"No, not yet anyway," Halstead said tersely.

"Zak didn't set up the explosion," Jory said urgently, as they sped out onto the roadway. "It was another guy. A foreign guy."

He navigated a tricky turn, the cruiser tires skidding on shallow gravel. "Trudy Carter, the nurse who works at the Taylors, she saw him the morning of the explosion."

He explained how Trudy had then gone away to her nephew's wedding and forgotten all about it. "It was the same when I talked to Cameron. He remembered seeing a stranger and his foreign car around the Lodge that day, too. He's just been going through so much, he never thought about it again till I brought it up."

He turned excitedly to Halstead. "But some fellows at the Grill were talking about the same car today. It was right here in the village this morning! Now all we have to do is find the man and we can clear Zak."

"I've got an idea where he might be," Halstead said grimly. "Watch the road!"

Jory swung the wheel, narrowly avoiding a side trip into the ditch.

"So how long have you known about this character?" Halstead asked curiously, as they straightened out.

"I knew there was a stranger," Jory said. "I didn't know who he was." He eyed the chief. "I *still* don't."

He took the curve so tightly the car shuddered and shook his head disbelievingly. "What the hell is going on here, chief?"

Halstead gripped the dashboard. "Never mind that now. We've got some tricky work ahead of us. This guy may be holding Pete's father at gunpoint, maybe at the Retreat. Worse, he might have Pete's wife too."

"That's not good," Jory said.

No kidding. Talk about your bad timing.

It would have to be this particular morning when Walter Jakes had finally agreed to meet his daughter-in-law. And he, Bud Halstead had arranged it.

Jory drove in earnest now, his face intent with a mixture of nerves and excitement. Halstead hoped the newbie could hold up to whatever shocks were ahead.

*   *   *

Jane stared at her phone. Well if that didn't beat all. Too many shocks for one morning. Now she had the Bonville Public Works department calling and asking her to put out a news bulletin regarding an accident on the causeway. The crew had been paving the left hand lane, while alternating traffic on the right hand lane. Then a transport truck had slid on the fresh gravel shoring on the causeway and was sprawled across the one good lane. All traffic too and from the Island was blocked and would be for some time.

How was she to get help for the Chief? There were calls to make.

But here was Pete Jakes on his cell again. "Has the Chief left yet?"

"Yes they've gone," Jane said. "But there's been a complication on the causeway." She explained. "No injuries thank goodness, except some damage to the truck axle. It will likely be cleared up by the time you get here."

"I hope so," Pete said. "And Jane, if Ali calls, just say I'm O.K and I'll wait over in Bonville till they get that truck out of there. Don't tell her anything about any trouble out at the Retreat. I don't want her to worry."

*   *   *

Ali peered out the small window of the shed but could see nothing but the surrounding pines at the back of the Retreat.

She clucked in frustration. "What do you think he's doing?" she asked Walter.

Then somberly answered her own question. "He's probably figuring out how he's going to kill us."

Walter's face was pale in the dim shed. "When he comes back, I'll offer him myself if he'll let you go."

Ali shook her head, "He'll never agree, now that I know who he is and that I'll know what he's done." She thought a moment. "I guess the chief doesn't usually get back till after work?"

"Sometimes even later. If he stops in at the Island Grill."

"And Colleen your home help?"

"Not her day."

"Thank goodness, for her sake anyway." She looked around the shed, and said practically. "We'll just have to rush him, overpower him, then make a run for it."

"He's got a gun," Walter reminded her.

She shrugged. "We'll figure this out."

"I like your confidence," Walter smiled, the first real smile he'd ever given her.

She gave him a quick hug. "Let's see what weapons we can round up."

They worked speedily, searching the garage and silently holding up or pointing to their discoveries. A coil of rope, a shovel, rake and other gardening tooks. Half-full paint cans. A bag of grass seed, a spray can of wasp repellent.

Through gestures and whispers, they concocted their ad hoc desperate plan. This consisted simply of piling a barricade at the door to slow Ritter down. Then Walter would spray him with the insect repellent while Ali tried to land a blow with the shovel. Hopefully if they were successful in putting Ritter at least briefly out of commission, Ali and Walter would run out of the shed. Then Ali would hastily padlock the door.

All this to gain a head start in a sprint toward the house.

They had debated the possibilities. Ali said there was no point in heading for the woodlot where the tree cover would offer only a brief respite. Their only real hope was to reach the world of technology. A cell phone, a car. As quietly as possible, she piled the paint cans, rope and gardening tools in a rough heap by the door.

"Ready?" she whispered, on hearing Ritter's returning footsteps.

"Stay back in the shadows," Walter said. "Make him come in the door after us. He won't be able to see as well as us, his eyes will have to adjust to the light."

Ali smiled and raised her thumb.

"Here's to luck."

41

What a mess! Pete looked despairingly at the line of waiting vehicles. Further ahead, on the causeway itself, a red and white transport truck sprawled across the fresh gravel, helpless as a giant upended beetle.

He called Jane again. "I'm at the causeway. Not on it, unfortunately. When's the tow-truck coming to move this monster out of the way?"

"Public Works says the truck is on the way," Jane said. "Sounds like a big job though."

"No kidding. Can you patch me through to the chief, thanks."

Hastead answered. "Where are you?"

Pete explained about the causeway delay. "But I'll get there," he assured. "I'll walk on water if I have to."

"We're on our way lad, don't worry."

"Be careful Chief-- this guy is unbalanced and seriously dangerous. He may have already finished off Walter."

"Don't think like that," Halstead said.

"Ali might never going to get to know him now," Pete said.

There was a silence that throbbed along the airwaves.

"What?" Pete asked with dread.

"Ali's likely out at the Retreat too," Halstead said. He explained how he'd finally convinced Walter to meet his daughter-in-law.

"Today was the day," he said bluntly, aware that Stutke was looking at him open-mouthed. But there was no way to sugar-coat such news and Pete was a police officer. He'd want to know the facts of the situation.

"What about Nevra?" Pete asked rawly. "Is Nevra with her? Good god, chief, that lunatic is on his way out there. He's already tried to blow Dad up. He may even have pushed him down the stairs at the apartment."

"Ali said she was going to go on her own," Halstead said. "I'm sure she was going alone," he repeated, trying to convince himself.

He looked out grimly at the trees that seemed to flick like red and orange flames past the speeding cruiser "We're on our way," he assured. "We'll stop him, Pete."

"Drive fast."

"We're almost there lad. Don't expect to hear from us for awhile."

Pete thumped the steering wheel with frustration. And anger at Walter. If he hadn't been so damned secretive, if only he'd told Pete what was going on. If only he'd opened up to his son just *once* in his life, none of this would have happened. And Ali wouldn't be in the hands of a murderous lunatic.

He looked again at the line of waiting vehicles. There'd be nothing moving here for awhile yet. Time for some action. He got out of the car, leaving the keys in the ignition and started running. When he reached the barrier across the causeway entrance, he vaulted over it.

"Hey!" yelled a works guy in his yellow safety vest. "Get back! Nobody's allowed on the causeway till we move that thing."

Pete kept running. "It's an emergency," he shouted back over his shoulder.

He skirted the downed truck and when he reached the other end of the causeway, pushed his way past another startled works employee. He ran gasping into the Island Grill.

"Keys, Gus, I need a vehicle. Right now! No questions."

Gus reached into his cash drawer and tossed Pete the keys.

*　　*　　*

"We're nearly there son," Halstead said. "Stop before we get to the Retreat driveway. Cut the engine and just coast onto the shoulder."

The two policeman got silently out of the cruiser, and softly closed the doors. They moved cautiously forward, weapons in hand. Jory turned nervously to Halstead and hissed. "There's his car." The silver Porsche. Parked beside the Jakes' SUV.

There was no welcoming party. Halstead didn't know if that was good or bad. The silence was unnerving. He nodded tightly to Stutke. "He's probably got a weapon. Walter's cabin is around the back. You go to the right around the house, I'll go left."

"Stay low," he warned as they parted. "Move fast, but quiet. And be careful, lad."

Stutke nodded and started off in a crouching run.

*　　*　　*

The door opened with a crashing sound as the barricade gave way. Ali froze for a moment, blinking at the sight of Ritter silhouetted against the sudden dazzling sunlight. Then as he moved forward, he stumbled against the pile of paint cans. He staggered awkwardly, trying to keep his balance. Taking her chance, Ali brought the shovel down as heavily as she could on Ritter's shoulder.

He raised his arms ineffectually after the fact and gave an angry shout as he tumbled entirely down into the barricade heap. Walter wielded the spray can wildly and the choking smell of insecticide spread in the shed.

Ali didn't wait to hear more. She grabbed at Walter's arm and pulled him through the door. Then, using precious seconds, she clipped the padlock on the hasp. With this slight lead, they headed for the house. It was soon obvious that Walter, with his bad hip, couldn't keep up. Ali put her arm round his waist, but even with that support, he could only move painfully slowly. Then they heard shots and Ritter's shout as he burst through the shed door.

Walter stopped, gasping for breath. He pushed Ali's arm aside. *"Go!"* he said. *"Run!"*

She hesitated, her face reflecting her torn thoughts.

"Let me do this one thing for my granddaughter," Walter said desperately. "For Nevra, for you."

He pushed her away. *"Now go! Please!"*

"I'll get to the car," she promised, "I'll call for help."

Ali ran for the house with wings on her feet. It seemed so far away!

She heard another gunshot behind her and with an anguished sob, risked a look back. Then bumped with a shriek of alarm into an obstacle. Through barely controllable panic, she recognized young officer Stutke.

She waved her arm, anticipating his concern. "I'm O.K. Back there, by the shed! He's got a gun! Walter can't run…"

Stutke sprinted off, just as Bud Halstead came round the house from the other side. He had his gun out too.

"Ali!" he said. "Thank God."

"I'm O.K.", she said again. "Just go. They're down by the shed."

Then she sank struggling for breath against the side of the house.

*   *   *

Jory topped the slight rise in the Retreat lawn and scanned the scene below. He could see two men struggling a couple of yards from the shed. Walter Jakes lay helpless on the ground while Ritter was kicking him in the side and pulling at him to get up. Ritter was holding a gun. As Jory watched, the older man rose with difficulty to his knees, then to his feet. He tried to take a step, but it was obvious even from this distance that the man couldn't walk. Ritter groaned in frustration, then struck Walter down with the gun. It looked as if he was going to shoot Walter right on the spot!

With no time to lose, Jory started down the hill. He had no cover, no advantage other than simple surprise. Ritter wouldn't be expecting to see him.

"Stop!" he yelled. "Don't shoot!"

Then he hit the dirt himself, rolling in case Ritter tried to take a shot. But when he looked up a second later, he saw that Ritter had dropped Walter and was headed for the dock. Jory scrambled towards Walter and bent to help.

"Go!" Walter gasped. "Get him. He's crazy..... might hurt Ali."

"Get him!" came the chief's voice from the slope. "Stop him. He's heading for the boat!"

Jory started running flat out towards the dock. Ritter didn't have much of a lead and was no doubt torn whether or not to sacrifice the time to take a shot at his pursuer. When he reached the dock, he scrambled awkwardly onto the boards. With Jory practically on his heels, Ritter launched himself into the boat. Jory leapt too, catching at the other man's leg in mid-air. Ritter yelped in pain as his leg twisted, then he fell in a heap to the floor, his gun clattering harmlessly off into the prow of the boat.

"Good lad," gasped Halstead, who had arrived and was now looking down into the boat from the dock. He tossed Jory a pair of handcuffs. "Get these on him."

42

Pete saw the cars in the Retreat driveway, the silver Porsche and his own SUV. He had passed the cruiser a few yards back.

There were people in the driveway too. The chief ...... Walter..... Ali!

He almost fell out of the truck, then rushed to her, his face white. "Honey are you alright. Where's Nevra?"

"She's with Miranda, she's not here." Ali gripped his arm and repeated. "She's not here, Pete. She's O.K."

"Thank god." He hugged her, then still holding her tightly, turned belatedly to Halstead.

"Where's Ritter?" What's happening?"

Halstead was helping Walter into a lawn chair. He nodded towards the lake. "He's down at the dock with a broken leg. Jory's watching him. I've called for the ambulance."

"Jory's O.K.?"

Halstead nodded. "He's a good kid, heckuva runner. He's the one who stopped Ritter."

Pete drew a breath, taking this in. "So you're all O.K."

"Walter's not in great shape," Halstead pointed out mildly, as Jakes senior settled gingerly into the chair.

But Pete had no sympathy for his parent. Anger, augmented by his recent panic for his family, swept over him. He had been spoiling for this confrontation for days, for weeks, he realized. He put Ali aside and loomed over Walter.

"What the hell game have you been playing at?" he demanded. "I'll never forgive you for putting my wife and daughter in danger."

Walter on the verge of collapse, looked dazedly up at his son.

"Pete!" Ali tried to pull him away. "It wasn't his fault. That horrible man was trying to kill him too."

Pete blinked in surprise at her defence of the man who had refused to meet her for the past month. But he wasn't placated.

"I know," he said, "That's why Ritter came here. He was following Walter. And you *knew!*" He pointed at Walter. "You knew you were putting us all in jeopardy and you didn't warn us. Even after the explosion at the Taylors, you accepted the chief's friendship and hospitality…." he shook his head at the enormity of the deceit, as if he could hardly bear to put it into words.

"Pete," Ali protested again. "Walter's been through enough today. He's too tired to defend himself."

"What can he say in his defence?" Pete asked. "What can *I* say in *my* defence? I brought him here, you all gave him the benefit of the doubt because he was my father. *I* gave him the benefit of the doubt, for god's sake. Even though at every turn I was finding evidence that he's a liar and a crook."

"I'm not a crook," Walter said quietly.

"I found the money, Dad," Pete said. "I found the safety deposit box. You were going to run away."

At this, Halstead stepped in.

"Whatever he is, Pete, this is not the time to go into it. Stutke needs help down at the dock. We should get Ritter up to the house. Who knows when the ambulance will be able to get across the causeway. How did you manage by the way, did you walk on water, like you said?"

Pete nodded tiredly, the adrenalin of the past few hours beginning to ebb. "Something like that. I've got Gus' truck. We can all get back to town anyway."

"That's O.K." Halstead said. "You just get Ritter up here to the house. We'll wait for the ambulance and Walter should go to the hospital too, to be checked out."

He looked at Ali. "But first take your wife home. I'll meet you at the station later to hash all this out."

"No," Ali said. "You stay with them Pete. I'll be alright."

Walter spoke up then, in an exhausted but determined voice.

"Take your wife home," he told Pete. "The chief can tell you where I'll be when you want to talk." He turned to Ali. "I'll be back my dear," he assured her, "I've got a granddaughter to meet."

Pete looked in amazement from one to the other. Ali touched his cheek. "We'll talk about it in the car."

"O.K." Pete said. "But I'd better go and help Stutke first."

At the dock, Pete found Jory sitting on the dock, keeping close guard over his prisoner. He seemed no worse for his risky adventure, in fact was flushed with success and grinning hugely. "I didn't tie him up," he pointed to Ritter. "He isn't going anywhere with that broken leg."

Pete looked with curiosity at the man who lay hunched in pain on the deck of the *Lazy Loon*. Ritter didn't look back. He looked shrunken, depleted, absorbed in his own misery.

When they approached to pick him up, he groaned in pain.

"Best to leave him till the ambulance guys get here with a stretcher," Pete said.

"The chief says there's some cold pop in the boat fridge if you get thirsty."

He turned before heading back to the house. "Oh and thanks, Stutke, for saving my wife's life. Much obliged."

*   *   *

Beyond the hospital window, the blue mantle of dusk was settling over the Bay. Pete stood by the bed, looking down at his father, propped up on crisp pillows that were stamped with the Bonville General Hospital logo.

Feels like déjà vu all over again, as a famous baseball catcher once put it.

Had it really been only a few weeks since he'd played out this scene the first time? Walter Jakes was a stanger to him then. Did he know his father any better now?

At least Walter was conscious this time. At least he was talking.

"They're keeping me in for observation overnight," he said. "I seem to have wrenched my hip some."

Pete nodded, "You don't look too bad, for a man who has survived a fall down a flight of stairs, an explosion and being hunted by a killer with a gun."

In fact, Walter looked better than he had since arriving on the Island. That terrible strain had gone from his face and body. Relief from fear, more powerful than any drug, had begun to kick in.

Now he actually smiled. "I'll take that as a compliment." Then his expression sobered. "But how is Ali? I hope she's getting over the shock."

"She's good," Pete said.

"Thank heavens for that." Walter shook his head in admiration. "What an amazing woman you've got there, son. Fearless – and so beautiful. Even though Erich Ritter was holding a gun on me, I couldn't help but notice this exotic butterfly coming towards me across that lawn."

"I know," Pete echoed the sentiment heartfeltedly. "I felt the same way when I first saw her at the school in Afghanistan. " He added, "And our daughter Nevra is just as lovely."

"And they're both fine?" Walter asked anxiously. "Truly?"

"Yes," Pete assured. "Our good neighbour Miranda was coming over to our house to make supper."

"I'll pamper them," she had promised Pete.

Walter looked a trifle misty-eyed for a moment, then grunted as he struggled to pull himself up straighter on the pillows. "I guess I'd better start talking."

Pete gave him a hand. "You're tired Dad, we can do this another time. I just popped in to see how you were feeling."

Walter shook his head. "No. No more delay. God knows, you've waited long enough for an explanation." He grimaced. "I haven't exactly been thinking clearly lately. To put it mildly."

He gestured to the bedside chair. "Have a seat, this might take awhile."

Pete sat, poured two glasses of water from the pitcher. Waited.

Walter took a sip, then began. "I've been such a jerk. When Jean died, I felt betrayed by life. I was angry and bitter. I never dealt with those feelings, so they just got worse, bottled in."

"I know," Pete said. "Losing mom hit us hard."

Walter smiled tiredly. "You can't let me off the hook, much as I appreciate the attempt. I was the adult, I should have reached out to you. Instead you ran off to war. That was easier I guess, for both of us. Certainly for me. I didn't have to do anything, make any decisions.

"After you left, I simply went on. I coped outwardly – sold the house, bought the apartment, stayed in my job which I was good at. But I didn't try for anything more, for promotion or change. I had no interest in getting out of my rut, my hidey hole. I tried a few relationships, I don't blame the women that they didn't last."

He stopped to take another sip from the glass. Pete refilled his own.

"When I had to retire," Walter continued, "I couldn't face the empty hours, the inactivity. So I kept a few clients. Things went along pretty well for awhile. I had managed to create another safe rut for myself."

"I got the GL Solar account, when Gary's accountant got sick. There was nothing particularly difficult about the work. I had no doubts at all, until the newspaper story started to break about this cabinet aide Lariviere and how there was a big financial scandal brewing."

"You recognized Andre Lariviere's name from somewhere in the GL Solar accounts," Pete said.

Walter nodded. "At home that night, I went through the entire year and a half that I'd been working with the company. I didn't catch it at first, the payments were grouped with various other items. But eventually I found them and they were sizeable. They had been recorded by the previous accountant, before I arrived on the scene. When I started the job, I had just accepted the records as they were given to me and gone on from there."

He paused.

"So what did you do?" Pete asked. "Tell me you didn't go straight to Gary Lucknow."

"I didn't know what to do," Walter said ruefully. "I even considered not doing anything, it was no business of mine. Then I realized if the ethics committee ever came calling on GL Solar, they might think it *was* my business."

"So, you did go talk to Gary Lucknow."

"I didn't have to. He called me in for an appointment."

Pete raised his eyebrows. "And how did that go?"

"He said he was sorry but he was ending my employment. That he planned to be doing a lot more international business and he needed someone who was experienced in international trade laws. He'd appreciate if I would deliver all my records and files associated with GL Solar to Angela the secretary. And he reminded me that I had signed a note of confidentiality when I took the job."

"And did you?"

"Yes, I did. But it was just a standard document. It would hardly be binding in a criminal investigation. We both knew that. We both also knew that I couldn't erase what I knew from my mind."

"So what did you say?"

Walter shrugged. "Nothing honourable, I'm afraid. I agreed to what Gary had said and I left. I'm no crusader and I wasn't naïve either. It wouldn't be the first time a bribe passed hands to get a government contract."

He placed his glass on the small bedside table and leaned gingerly back against the pillows. "I think Gary felt good enough after our little chat but then the demand for an ethics investigation started to grow. Every day there were new names mentioned in the paper. I watched the news like everybody else but I figured that GL Solar was no longer any concern of mine. I went about my business in my quiet rut. And then I fell down the stairs and didn't think about much of anything at all."

"And what about that fall?" Pete asked. "I've been wondering whether Mr. Ritter gave you a push."

Walter looked apologetic. "That I can't tell you, I honestly can't remember. I thought I heard the neighbour's dog barking, that it somehow had got out onto the stairs. But it wasn't there, and I could have lost my balance."

No matter, Pete thought. They had enough on Mr. Ritter to put him away in prison for a long time.

Walter continued, "The first few days in the hospital, were just a blur. My injuries, the drugs, I was totally disoriented. Then I woke up and found myself at the Taylors, a completely new and strange place. I hardly knew how I got there.

"At first I actually felt a bit of relief. I was somewhere safe. I didn't have to think about things. I think I half convinced myself that I'd just been having some crazy imaginings." His mouth twisted wryly. "That didn't last long."

"The gas explosion was a message to you, wasn't it Dad? A warning."

Walter nodded. "I didn't see it that way at first. Everyone was saying that the young man who worked in the kitchen must have set it off. And I guess I wanted to believe that too."

He paused. "But my subconscious knew better and it couldn't be silenced. I was appalled to realize just how serious Gary Lucknow was – I thought it was him at the time. That he wouldn't have cared whether the explosion killed everyone else in the building as well. My one thought was to get myself off the Island, to take the danger away from you and your family."

Pete shook his head. "Your taxi ride attempt."

"I was expecting a subpoena any day from the ethics commissioner. I was hoping I could just disappear."

Pete rose and walked towards the window, frustrated all over again. "But what about the Sordas, what that family has been going through? If you'd only confided some of this to me, if you'd only *trusted* me, I could have spared them some of that."

Walter shrugged helplessly. "I do feel badly about the young man and his family. All I can say is that I wasn't thinking clearly for most of that time. I only knew that I didn't want to ask for your help, to involve you. But in the end I just made things worse."

He added gently, "It looks as if you haven't exactly trusted me either, son."

"How could I? You had too many secrets. And then when I got to Ottawa, things started to look really black. Like when I found the money in your safety deposit box. That was not a good moment."

"You thought it was part of a bribe?" Walter asked.

"You bet I did. I thought if it had been legitimate money, why wouldn't you just keep it in your bank account?"

Walter laughed and seemed embarrassed. "It's just a habit I developed, something I've always done. A kind of insurance, maybe against banks failing, against nuclear attack, who knows? I never even told Jean about it." He looked bleak for a moment, "I could have told you that, if you'd bothered to ask me."

"You wouldn't talk to me Dad. I tried."

"You're right, of course." Walter patted the chair. "Please sit down again, you're giving me a crick in my neck. I've been foolish son, criminally foolish. But I thought I could handle this best by myself. At first because I was embarrassed and ashamed at the mess I'd put myself in. And then when I came here, I was terrified that I would bring danger to your wife and daughter."

He said heartfeltedly, encompassing all the lost years. "I'm sorry, son. So sorry."

They sat silently for a time. Then Pete reached over and patted Walter on the shoulder. "You and Ali seem to make quite a team. How do I get to be a member?"

"You only have to ask," Walter smiled. Then added practically, "Though you might well be visiting me in jail. Do you know what's going to happen to me? Do you think there will be any charges – obstructing evidence, something like that?"

"I doubt it," Pete said. "I know a certain investigative journalist in Ottawa who can't wait to meet you."

He felt in his pocket. "Here, take this for safekeeping."

He took out the memory stick, then withheld it from Walter's outstretched hand. "Not so fast. First you have to tell me where you stowed your laptop. I searched that apartment with a fine toothed comb."

Walter grinned, taking years off his face. "I had taken it to a little computer repair shop a couple of days before I fell and told the fellow it needed a going over. I guess it's still there."

Pete handed Walter the memory stick.

"**W**ell here you are," Halstead said to his second in command. "Decided to come back to us for real this time, have you?"

Pete grinned happily. "Yes, there was doubt about other things, but never about coming back to the Island."

"Good. We were worried there for awhile. Jane and I, and even Steph all the way over in Japan. Thought you might have been cracking up."

Pete ducked his head, embarrassed. "I appreciate your concern. Sorry I caused any problems."

"Well you did do that." Halstead settled back in his office chair for the long haul. "And now you're going to tell me all about it."

"Right. But you understand, it's taken awhile for me to sort out the bits and pieces."

It was evening at the Island police station. Jane had gone home a couple of hours ago, Jory had been sent home too and Erich Ritter was spending the night under guard and under sedation in Bonville General. His leg break was messy and complicated and had required emergency surgery.

Halstead waved an invitation, "Chow down, first though." He had brought chicken sandwiches and coffee from the diner.

Pete ate steadily, while marshalling his thoughts. Over coffee, he began, filling the chief in on his conversation with Walter.

Halstead sat quietly, saying nothing till he was through.

"It seems you were in quite a quandary there for awhile," he commented. "to put it mildly. Might have helped if you let me in on the problem. Instead, it seems you play things as close to your chest as your pop."

Pete shrugged. "A family trait?" Then he added more seriously, "I wanted to talk to you, I wanted to talk to Ali. But I had to find out first how deeply Dad was involved. I thought I didn't care, but I did. No matter what issues we had, I couldn't see myself helping to send my own father to jail."

"Just what were you planning to do with him?" Halstead asked curiously.

"At first I didn't know," Pete said. "Then Sandra Arum said she might gain him some clemency for testifying at the ethics committee. I wasn't thinking past that."

Halstead shook his head, marvelling. "And I thought Walter was just uncommunicative. Who would have guessed a number cruncher could be in such a jam? No wonder we never suspected that explosion was set for him. Who would want to blow up an accountant?"

He grimaced. "Well we found the answer to that. Erich Ritter, the nutbar inventor. Sounds like a character from an old horror movie."

Pete nodded. "A smart guy though. I was reading the brochure at GL Solar about the new technology Ritter has been working on. He may not have had it perfect, but the next man will, and they'll be using Ritter's notes."

Halstead demurred. "If he'd been really smart, he'd have shopped around till he found someone less crooked than Lucknow to develop his idea."

"He was smart enough to track Walter down to the Island," Pete pointed out.

"Through the hospital?" Halstead asked.

"Actually, that was more my doing," Pete said. "I left a forwarding address for Walter with Jay Gupta, the apartment manager. Ritter probably just phoned one day and asked for it."

"And Gupta never mentioned this to you?"

"He probably didn't think anything of it. Ritter could just have said he was from the utilities company, or the phone, or whatever."

"So he comes to the Island," Halstead said, "finds the Taylors' Lodge and on the spur of the moment, decides to set off a gas explosion? Because GL Solar might lose a big contract, is that a reason to kill a bunch of innocent people. What kind of a freak is he?"

Pete was remembering what Angela Burke had told him. "You didn't see the photo in the office," he said. "It's a picture of the day GL Solar got the government contract. Erich Ritter was a hero that day, on top of the world. All the company workmen were gathered in the parking lot. Gary Lucknow was handing hin the keys to the Porsche."

"And then four months later, the whole bubble burst," Halstead said.

"Yep. It seems that Ritter took it harder than Lucknow. Lucknow is a businessman, he's likely weathered more than a few financial crises. He's bound to have an off-shore bank account waiting for him somewhere and wasn't going to kill anybody over a business set-back. But Ritter is an industrial designer. More temperamental I guess, like an artist. The new solar panel design was his baby and he took the possible cancelling of the contract personally."

Halstead nodded. "I doubt he was the most well-balanced person to begin with. I bet we'll find that he was booked into that rest home more than once, for a mental break."

"You could be right. Anyway, the upcoming ethics committee review tipped him over the edge."

"You mean he wasn't going to let Walter Jakes drag GL Solar down."

"Exactly"

"Do you think he pushed Walter on the stairs?"

Pete shrugged. "It's possible. Though Dad genuinely doesn't seem to know. The doctor says that sometimes the brain can stop recording during a traumatic incident."

"Hmmm." Halstead said. "So, say Ritter gave Walter the push. That didn't work, so then he gets Walter's address from young Gupta and makes a quick visit to the Island. Sets up an explosion, finds out that didn't work either. Next, he tries to run you down in Ottawa."

Pete nodded. Matt Braden had tracked down the car Ritter had used. A rental charged to the GL Solar company.

"And why did he pull that little stunt?" Halstead asked. "Just for the fun of it?"

Pete shook his head. "I'm pretty sure he also followed me from the GL Solar plant one day. I think he was starting to see me as a threat too. The closer the date for the hearings, the more irrational he got."

Halstead took a cookie from the stash in his desk and bit into the frosted centre appreciatively. "So Ritter makes a second trip to the Island. He's full-blown loco by now. Miranda's lucky he didn't pull a gun on her."

"Lots to be thankful for," Pete said.

"Amen to that. And we know the Retreat part of the story. Which finished with a happy ending too, thanks to young Stutke."

"What will happen to Ritter?"

"An arsonist and a pre-meditating killer? He'll be locked up somewhere. Hopefully prison, though if he gets a good shrink, it will likely be the happy farm."

Halstead shut the cookie drawer and pushed back his chair. "It's been a long day, lad. Let's go home." He smiled wearily, "Though I've got one pleasant duty to perform on the way. I'm going to stop in at the Sordas and give them the good news that Zak is no longer under suspicion.""

"Say hello to them for me."

NEWS FROM THE HILL
PARLIAMENTARY ETHICS COMMITTEE
HEARINGS ENTER SECOND WEEK.
CRIMINAL CHARGES FOR LARIVIERE COULD BE NEXT

Halstead clicked the remote mute button and commented, "If Mr.Lariviere had been smart, he'd have left the country for his Italian residence long before this."

Steph shrugged, "He may leave yet. I'm sure he's got a nice little nest egg stowed away somewhere." She rose from the couch and pulled a sweater round her red silk pyjamas.

"Come, let's go outside for a bit," she said, "we can light the fire."

He looked pained. "Not if I have to wear this kimona thing."

She laughed, and made a playful grab for the silk belt of the gaudily patterned robe. "It's just us and the loons, silly. Nobody s going to see."

"O.K. but the trousers are staying on. It's chilly out there."

They carried their drinks out to the patio. Early October had indeed brought cooler weather, but Halstead had fetched the outside ceramic fireplace from the shed. He lit it now and as the kindling caught, the flames glowed warmly in the dusk.

"Umm that s nice," Steph said, warming her hands.

She pulled two lounge chairs close to each other and they sat happily not talking for a time, listening to the crackle and pop of the burning wood.

"I missed this," Halstead said eventually. "I hope you don't plan to go away again for awhile."

"You'll just have to come with me next time." She sighed, "Hopefully not all the way to Japan."

It was the only flaw in her homecoming.

"Livy's only twenty," Halstead soothed. "You said there are young people from all over the world working at that school."

"She s nearly twenty-one," Steph said. Then added direly. "The age I was when I first got married."

Halstead patted her hand. "There are airplanes, Steph. We ll buy tickets."

"And you'll come with me."

"You bet."

He kept hold of her hand. Down at the darkened shore, the waves lapped softly against the reeds. He felt a deep contentment. Traffic was running smoothly on the completed causeway, and the Island folks were happy for the moment. Of course they d be nattering again soon enough. There was a tax hike coming, he'd heard the notices were in the mail. But that was Vern Byer's department, nothing to bother Bud Halstead, a simple country chief of police.

"There s the loon," Steph said. "How good to be home."

*   *   *

The patio lights strung along the Sordas' deck were in the shape of various coloured butterflies.

Zak rolled his eyes, "Mom's idea. She thinks they're cute."

"They're nice," Gayle approved.

And in fact, the lights were an appropriate touch for this little celebratory gathering. Zak had invited Jory and Gayle over for pizza. The senior Sordas had already departed for a well-deserved extended vacation to see relatives in Portugal.

"Mom's still pretty fragile," Zak said. "So Dad closed the chip truck early this year. They'll be back before Christmas though."

He put some plates and napkins on the table, then looked directly at Jory.

"Dad found something interesting when he was cleaning out the shelves at the chip truck. It was an envelope with two hundred dollars cash. Somebody must have left it during the day. There was no return address or name written on the envelope, nothing except 'Mr. Sorda" written on the front."

"No kidding," Jory said.

"I wondered if you knew anything about it."

Jory shrugged. "Not me. But I hope your Dad kept the money." He grinned, thinking, *Some things do work out.*

Over slices of pizza and a few beers, they talked as young people do, of plans.

"I'm going out west," Zak said. "My course is over in February and I've applied for a job as a sous chef at a ski resort in Banff."

The others didn't need to ask why. He was still raw from having experienced the doubt of his friends and neighbours and wouldn't be in any hurry to go back to working on the Island.

"Good for you!" Gayle said. "It's supposed to be great out there."

"What about you, Jory?" Zak asked. "Going off to the city after your tour of duty here?"

Jory was aware of Gayle's gaze.

He grinned and said lazily. "Oh I don't know. If Chief Halstead can stand having me around some more, I might just stay here on the Island for awhile."

She punched him on the shoulder.

Meanwhile, down at the Island Grill, the customers cheered as Gus switched the television set from *News on the Hill* to the Jays first game of the playoffs.

And in a hospital room across the causeway, a nurse removes bandages from a young man's face. Hesitantly he opens his eyes for the first time in a month – and sees his parents.

At the nursing station in the corridor, several staff members are in tears. In an adjoining room, there is a television set airing *News from the Hill* but nobody is watching.

45

"Grandpa, do you like Kedi? Isn't he pretty?"

"Yes, he's a very handsome cat," Walter said.

"He's not handsome," Nevra corrected, with a three-year old's insistence on accuracy. "He's pretty. Look how he chases the string."

Ali chuckled as the big orange cat ambled lazily across the lawn after the scampering little girl. In the bright October sunshine, playing in the drifts of swirling leaves, they made a sweet tableau. An attractive mix of her parents' colouring, Nevra wore striped leggings and a bright blue hoodie that framed her taffy coloured hair. Worthy of a Renoir, Ali thought fondly.

"I think Kedi's kind of bored with the string game," she laughed. "But he's smart enough to know that Nevra was his ticket into the family and figures he'd better play his part."

Walter watched the scene a little pensively. "I could have taken a lesson from that cat." He smiled. "At least I'm playing my part now."

Ali patted his hand. "And doing very well, Grandpa Jakes."

Walter looked well too, she thought happily. In just a week's residence with his family, he'd gained a bit of weight back and the relief from stress had taken years from his face. He was even wearing some colour, a warm red plaid jacket that Pete had got him at the co-op store.

"We've enjoyed so much having you here, Walter," she said. "It's been wonderful getting to know you."

He nodded. "I'll be back soon. I've got a lot of catching up to do with you and my granddaughter. But I do have some affairs to tend to in the city."

"I'm sure it will all go well," Ali said confidently. "Pete says this Sandra Arum is a very smart lady."

Still, the next morning as she and Nevra waved them away, she was crossing her fingers behind her back.

∗   ∗   ∗

"How did it go?" she asked when Pete came home. Before he had even taken off his coat.

"It was good," he smiled and tossed his travelling bag on a chair. "We talked to Sandra Arum and she thinks Dad's going to come out O.K. He didn't really suppress evidence, she says. He was threatened and then incapacitated for several weeks. And of course his testimony is going to be valuable to the members of the ethics committee. It implicates both Gary Lucknow, plus Lariviere, the really big fish."

"I'm so glad," she said. "And did you get him settled back in the apartment?"

"Settled?" He laughed and stopped to rub his cold cheek against her kitchen warm one. "I should say so. Jay Gupta had let the cleaner in as we arranged, and the neighbour Helen Verga had brought a big bunch of flowers."

She wriggled away. "Cold! Is that the lady with the little dog?"

"Yep, his name is Pepper. And I have a feeling that Dad is going to be seeing a lot more of that pooch. Ms. Verga has already invited him to supper some night."

"No kidding!" Ali clapped her hands in delight.

Pete moved towards the coffee pot, "I talked to Matt Braden too, before I left. He's hoping we'll come up and visit them some time. Nevra could play with their boys. We could pick up Dad too, and do some fishing.'

He said it so casually, Ali thought, dizzy with gratitude that things had turned out so well.

That night they sat squashed happily together on the couch. Pete and Ali, Nevra and Kedi. Re-reading for the umpteenth time, the Johnny Townmouse story.

Nevra smelled like baby shampoo and strawberry flavoured toothpaste.

"Are you going away again Daddy?" she asked.

"Not for awhile," Pete said. "This country mouse has had enough of the city and he's staying home."

Ali batted her eyes over the little girl's head. "You're not going to be missing the chats with the attractive prize-winning journalist?"

"Not when I've got an attractive prize winning teacher at home."

"What prize is that?" she asked.

He grinned. "Two smart people like us, I'm sure we can think of something."

EPILOGUE

In the city, the webcam site shows only a few dried twigs left scattered on the concrete ledge. Soon even these will be blown away and the ledge drifted in with snow.

The fierce, winged ones have left, beginning their journey south. The parents and the young, leaving the city with no regrets.

They have no cameras, no photos, no records, no books. Will they carry memories with them, of warm summer days, of family life?

Of long days in the sky. Of those first, awkward, dizzying drops from the ledge.

Will they recall the excitement of those first successful hunts? Of parents teaching and patient and always there.

Yes.

It's in their miraculous feather-light bones. It's in the ancient river of their blood. And the memories will bring them back.

Printed in the United States
By Bookmasters